LEE NICHOLS

Wednesday Night Witches

RED
DRESS
INK
™

WEDNESDAY NIGHT WITCHES

A Red Dress Ink novel

ISBN-13: 978-0-373-89554-0
ISBN-10:   0-373-89554-2

www.RedDressInk.com

Printed in U.S.A.

ACKNOWLEDGMENTS

I couldn't have done it without Nancy Coffey,
Selina McLemore, Margaret O'Neill Marbury,
Sandy Stark and Louanne Bridges.

✳ 1 ✳

People often stalk me in my line of work, and today was one of those days. I'd felt them behind me for three blocks, but when I checked my back, trotting into the subway station, they were gone—must've lost them on Broadway.

Past the turnstile, the platform was suffocating in the August heat, yet I shivered with relief. Then the fluorescent lights flickered, and I marked a tall man with long blond hair, wearing thigh-high boots and a red mesh shirt, and a feral-looking woman in studded leather pants and a matching bra.

My God. I was being hunted by Mötley Crüe.

The train came in and the doors closed behind me—but not soon enough. Through the morning commuter crowd, I saw them approaching from the next car, a hard, unearthly light in their eyes. The subway lurched forward, and I back-pedaled, a line of sweat trickling down the small of my back. I ran until there was nowhere left to go. They cornered me in the last car, their feral lips curled in anticipation.

I slipped behind a stocky businessman, reaching for my obsidian dagger, and the businessman said, "Hey!"

"Hmm?" I blinked and the Crüe disappeared. *Oh, no.*

The businessman looked at his arm. The arm I was clenching. "I'm using that," he said.

"Oh! I'm so sorry—"

"Leave her alone," said a kid in a baseball cap. "Can't you see she's Amish?"

The stocky businessman eyed me warily. "Do you need help?" he asked.

I stared with mute mortification that my daydream had gotten so out of control. Yes, I daydreamed too much, but I usually stopped short of grabbing strange men on the subway.

"You have to ask like this," the kid informed him. "Doth thee require assistance?"

The subway squealed to a halt and I scurried outside. Not my stop, but I didn't care—anything to get away. In truth, I wasn't Amish, despite being dressed in a long black skirt, beige blouse and brown sweater-vest. I wasn't a vampire slayer, either.

I was a kindergarten teacher.

So why was I dressed like this on a stifling August 30 in NYC? Because today was Open House, the day before school officially began, the most important in a kindergarten teacher's year. And while most teachers would wear seasonably correct linen skirts and blouses, not me. Not Eve Crenshaw. Not with Mrs. Dale as my head teacher.

I waited for the next train, keeping a tight rein on my fantasies, and still got to school twenty minutes early. My boy-friend, Gregory, wasn't his best in the morning, before drink-ing his coffee, reading his newspaper and checking the marginal rates on his foreign investment tax portfolio. It was easier to leave the apartment before he woke and remem-bered I'd moved in three months ago—otherwise, his first look of disappointed surprise could really blow my day.

"Much better," Mrs. Dale said, eyeing me as I entered the classroom. "That is an appropriate outfit."

I pulled paper towels from the dispenser next to the minia-ture kindergarten sinks and wiped the sweat from my neck. "You look good, too."

"Do you like this?" she asked, tugging at her shirt. "It's linen."

"Perfect for this weather," I said. "Maybe I should've worn—"

"Oh, not *you,* Eve! Remember what happened at last year's Open House? You looked like you were trying out for an episode of *Buddies.*"

"Friends," I muttered, tossing the damp paper towels into the trash.

Buddies was Mrs. Dale's catchphrase for anything she found remotely inappropriate. "That's the way they might teach on *Buddies,*" she'd say if I suggested an alternative lesson plan. Or, "One of the girls on *Buddies* is pregnant with her brother's twins," if I mentioned Gregory—a cor-relation I found baffling. She watched the reruns relig-iously, yet had no idea the show was called *Friends*—or that spending the night with my boyfriend didn't mean I was carrying my brother's children. I didn't even have a brother.

Sadly, Mrs. Dale was tight with my principal—hence my Puritan costume. I didn't want to give her any reason to refer to *Buddies* in her evaluation.

After we organized the room, Mrs. Dale said, "Oh! I almost forgot. I have a present for you!"

"Is it one of those hats with the little fans built in?" I made a propeller motion over my sweaty face.

"No."

"Lemonade?"

She handed me the letter *A,* cut out of red construction paper. "Pin this to your chest."

"What? Why?" I didn't want a letter pinned to my chest. "We didn't do this last year."

"You're always saying we should shake things up around here."

"I am, that's true, but…" I stared at the offending red *A.* "Wouldn't you rather wear the *A?* You're the head teacher, after all."

Mrs. Dale pinned a green *B* to her chest as if it were a corsage. "This one matches my shirt."

"Yes, but, um, a scarlet letter?"

"*A* is for apple," she explained.

"Or *adultery.* The way I'm dressed—" I gestured to my homespun magnificence. "I'll look like Hester Prynne."

"Oh, don't be ridiculous. You look very nice."

Before I could answer, a little blond girl skipped into the room, dressed entirely in pink, with her mother following close behind in a matching outfit.

"Quick," Mrs. Dale said, "here they come. Pin it on!"

"But…"

Mrs. Dale's eyes flashed. *"Eve."*

So I pinned the scarlet letter to my chest and prepared myself to be poised and professional when addressing the new parents. And ready with an *A is for Apple* quip, if necessary.

The parents and students poured in, filled miniature Dixie cups with apple juice, and sat in a circle. Mrs. Dale gave the welcoming speech and I refilled the juice, and toward the end the pink mother raised her hand and said, "I have a question for Miss Crenshaw."

I smiled. "Yes?"

"Will they be reading Hawthorne this year?"

"No, that's a little advanced for—"

"Then why are you dressed like that?"

I could've asked her why she was dressed like a five-year-old, but I said, "They *will* learn to read, though, and some classics as well. Beatrix Potter and Maurice Sendak, for example—"

"Will you be dressing like a character from a novel every month?" another mother asked.

"No."

"Yes," Mrs. Dale cut in. "Eve will be reenacting a character from each of our books. That's a wonderful idea."

"If you're not reading Hawthorne," Pink Mom said, "why are you dressed like Hester Prynne?"

"I'm not, I—"

"You're wearing the scarlet letter."

"*A is for Apple!*" I explained, and ripped the letter from my chest, sending a hail of pins to the floor.

"She should dress like Moaning Myrtle," another mother said. "You know, from *Harry Potter.* Will you be teaching *Harry Potter* this year?"

"Well, we—"

"What about the real classics?" a third mother asked. "Like *Tom Sawyer?*"

"Or *Lady Chatterley.*" One of the fathers leered at me, before his wife elbowed him. "What?" he said. "That's a classic."

"How about *Mary Poppins?*" a mother suggested. "Or *Heidi?*"

"Barbie!" one of the girls yelled. "Schoolteacher Barbie!" Pink Mom cleared her throat and pointed to the floor. "Those pins are a choking hazard."

Everyone clasped their *kinder* tightly as I dropped to my knees and searched for pins. Mrs. Dale finished her talk and ushered everyone out. She smoothed her hair in the mirror that allowed us to monitor the toilets from any angle in the classroom, and said, "Principal Lane and I have reservations downtown for dinner. She's being considered for associate superintendent. There's an opening, you know, and she's got a good chance."

"Oh, congratulate her for me."

"She hasn't been hired yet, Eve."

"No, of course not. I just meant—"

"You don't think she will be?"

"No! I mean yes! I think she will be—so…congratulations?"

Mrs. Dale rolled her eyes at the mirror. Maybe she forgot I could see her. Or maybe not. "What are your plans for the boards?" she asked.

"The what?"

"The boards, Eve. The boards."

"Oh! The bulletin boards." We redecorated every month with a seasonal theme and lesson paraphernalia, and the boards were currently blooming with late-summer flowers and early-reading items. "They're perfect for now, don't you think?"

"I've laid out new materials, shouldn't take long. See you tomorrow!"

After Mrs. Dale left, I cleared the decorations from the boards, stabbing pushpins into a tight circle in the corner. With each tack I got madder. I shouldn't be "help"—*stab*—I should be the co-teacher—*stab*—responsible for half the boards and half the lessons and half the discipline—*stab, stab, stab.* Instead, I got stuck supervising potty time, managing snacks and heading up "telephone" circles. Okay, so I quite liked "telephone," but that wasn't the—*stab*—point!

The point was, I wasn't going to let Mrs. Dale push me around anymore, and I wasn't going to comfort myself by drifting off into daydreams of having my own classroom. Henceforth, I'd be assertive and grounded and not take "no" for an answer. I was finished forever with…with… Where the hell were the new bulletin board materials? I spun circles around the classroom, checked every drawer, every cupboard—no craft materials anywhere. How was I supposed to design a gorgeous seasonal board, a testament to my new resolve, without any supplies?

I sighed and started replacing everything in a messy clutter. Boards weren't my thing, despite all of Natasha's tutelage. Natasha, my best friend from NYU, was the prototypical starving artist and she'd given me pointers on collage and design, outlining the basics of composition. Then she'd said my style was like Jackson Pollock—but not so tidy.

I replaced the last construction-paper dahlia and shook my head. Decoration overwhelmed me, just like Mrs. Dale. Why did I always do what she said, like dress in this ridiculous out-fit? Why couldn't I tell her, "It's *Friends,* dammit! There's no such thing as *Buddies!*"

At least I didn't have to come to work dressed like Phoebe. Yet.

I stepped from the stifling mugginess of the subway into the oppressive heat of the street and staggered the two blocks to Gregory's building. Well, to *my* building, except I still felt like a guest. I know my nervousness annoyed Gregory—I always asked permission to use the phone for long-distance calls or finish the carton of milk or claim one-third of the medicine cabinet as my own. I had a key, obviously, but still felt the need to buzz before going up.

"You're late." Gregory's tinny voice came through the intercom. "I'll come down."

"I need to change," I said.

"No time."

"Gregory, I'm dressed like a pilgrim! It'll only take ten minutes and—"

And I realized he wasn't listening; the intercom was dead.

When I got upstairs, Gregory was stepping into the hall, wearing a dark suit from Barney's and a pale gray silk tie. He was tall and slim, with a no-polish manicure and a weekly Pilates class physique. I was short and curvy—usually not such a bad thing, but in the wrong clothes, like today, I looked squat and porky.

Gregory winced when he saw me.

"I told you," I said.

"What happened to your hair?"

"The subway."

"You rode with your head out the window, like a dog?"

"Let me in. I'll only be ten minutes."

"You're an hour late."

"I'm sorry. Mrs. Dale made me stay to finish the bulletin boards."

"Hurry up." Gregory opened the door in a martyred fashion. "No daydreaming, Eve."

"I won't! I don't. I hardly ever do…"

"I can't be late to our company cocktail party, and I can't go with my girlfriend looking like…that. How you look reflects on how they see me."

I pushed into the apartment, the coolest air I'd felt all day. "I'm sorry. I tried to call." A lie, but he was impossible to reach, so a good one. "It's actually kinda funny. You know, I dressed like this to keep Mrs. Dale happy, then when I got there she gave me this letter cut out of construction paper…."

He stood in the bathroom doorway, tapping his watch, as I stripped off my clothes and washed my face. I told him about looking like Hester Prynne, hoping he'd laugh and tell me I was his favorite little Puritan. But of course he hadn't read Hawthorne—he bragged he'd never read a novel in his life—so I lamely finished with "…and, um, then I had to stay to work a little late."

"It's kindergarten," Gregory said. "I'd hardly call it work."

I laughed at his lame attempt at humor. "Seriously, Gregory, sometimes I feel you don't think my job is important."

"Of course it isn't," he joked.

"I teach children. I shape minds."

"You make $52,000 a year, I make $370,000."

"Yes, but—"

"Do the math." He wasn't joking. "My job is eight times as important."

I eyed him. "That's only seven times my salary."

"You're a glorified camp counselor, Eve—and we're still late."

I yanked my little black dress from the closet, willing myself not to explode. Gregory was a good man: he worked hard, and was good in bed, and he treated me okay and…well, he worked hard.

"Not that again," he said. "That must be four seasons out of date."

"Only three."

"Let me buy you a new wardrobe."

"I don't want to—"

"Consider it a business expense, Eve. I'll never make partner with you looking like that."

"You're there sixteen hours a day! Who cares what I wear?"

"Doesn't matter how many hours I bill if I don't look the part. I can be fat and bald, as long as I have a sexy young thing on my arm. I can't afford you looking like a frumpy mess—that's as bad as buying an office chair from a big box store."

I knotted the grosgrain ribbon at my waist, slipped into my kitten heels, and clopped back into the concrete bathroom. A chair. That's how he saw me, as an office chair—not a status symbol like a Rolex or Porsche. A chair.

I shivered in the cold gray room. Before moving in, I'd loved this austere bathroom with the shower that ran into the floor and the contemporary sculptured sink, but after living here a week, I despised it. I was always freezing, and the exposed lightbulbs gave me a cadaverous pallor. Plus, there wasn't room in my third of the medicine cabinet for my cosmetics, so I had to keep them in a basket next to the plunger behind the toilet.

Gregory looked away from his watch. "All I'm saying is, you're stunning when you try. How come you never try anymore?"

I closed the door on him, tamed my hair with anti-frizz serum and applied too much makeup—just the way he liked. Then I opened the door and told him, "See? Ten minutes."

His peevish expression changed to one of hungry approval. We'd always had good sex...but there was no time now. I found my classic black evening clutch in my quarter of the closet, stuffed my driver's license, Visa, lipstick, cell and a fifty inside and headed for the front door.

"You wouldn't believe the day I've had." Gregory complained about his paralegals all the way to the corner, where we stood to hail a taxi.

"I had a long day, too. The open house—"

"Remember, Eve, most grown-ups don't want to hear about preschool. We don't have nap time. We get jealous."

A taxi pulled to the curb. "It's kindergarten, not preschool."

He snorted. "Like that matters."

"It matters, Gregory." I slipped into the cab. "I matter."

I slammed the door before Gregory could follow, and told the driver, "JFK airport."

I stared straight ahead while Gregory knocked at the window, then turned to watch through the back as he grew very small and presumably very angry, then disappeared.

Like magic.

2

The largest island in Casco Bay, Broome Isle, was also the least known. Unlike Peaks Island, Broome wasn't home to the playhouses where Martin Landau and Jean Stapleton first appeared. The Barrymore family never summered on Broome Isle, and no amusement parks rose along her pretty seaside. Henry Wadsworth Longfellow and Harriet Beecher Stowe visited the nearby Great Diamond Island, but not Broome—no historic fort from the Spanish-American War stood sentry on her cliffs, and the single grand hotel built on Broome, in the nineteenth century, burned to the ground hours after the ribbon-cutting ceremony.

A row of old brick buildings crowded behind the busy working harbor, the town hall and bakery, the hardware store, Laundromat and fish house. The village rose above— tightly knit, inward-looking houses built in the 1800s, with views of their neighbors instead of the sea.

Across the island stood another cluster of buildings—a general store and a grange hall, a heating oil company and real estate office—and beyond that, on a belt of pastureland long ago hacked from the wood, was a ramshackle white farmhouse surrounded by acres of crops. A stone's throw from the house, a large barn bore all the signs of renovation: a half-filled construction Dumpster, scaffolding jerry-rigged from ladders and planks, and scatterings of sawdust on the lawn where a portable table saw had been.

Inside the barn, Natasha Kent stepped away from a canvas, wiping red cinnabar and burnt sienna onto her jeans. She crossed to the coffee table for the Jack Daniel's and Amaretto, sniffed her favorite glass—small and French and etched with bees—decided it was clean enough to use and tinkled three ice cubes inside.

She was so deep in her painter's mind that she lost herself for a long moment in the play of light through the ice. She mixed the Jack and Amaretto until they blended into the right color, took a sip and felt her shoulders relax. She'd painted through last night, then crashed for a few hours and started again. She'd long ago decided sleep was for people with suits and salaries.

Natasha sank into her easy chair, facing away from the painting, and picked at a thick rich yellow dab that had dried into a crust on the fabric. What was that? Cadmium Yellow? Naples Yellow? Oh, no—Poached Egg Yellow, breakfast from two days ago. She wasn't much of a housekeeper. Still, a deep and evocative color. Amniotic Yellow. She ought to add it to the work, but how? Lobster buoys?

Yikes. She sipped her drink. At least she hadn't sunk that low…yet.

Her cat, Puck, jumped into her lap, and she scratched behind his ears and said, "Promise you'll kill me if I ever put a lobster buoy in one of my paintings. A quick claw to the throat."

He rubbed his head against her chin and purred.

"Not that anyone would notice the added kitch," she said.

She considered her work abstract, or at least abstracted—loosely based on the world outside her windows but not at all representational. The heavy rectangle broken by faint tracings wasn't the sky, but the shape of the sky. The veins of color were only veins of color, even if they were inspired by the distant islands, the boats and coastline. She sketched tumbling shapes that didn't quite represent the surf, a flat oceanic weight that wasn't the ocean.

Still, as far as anyone else was concerned, she painted Maine landscapes. Small seascapes, really, which she sold through upscale souvenir shops along the coast. She had to pay for booze somehow.

She took another slug of her drink and finally turned back to the painting. She tilted her head left, then right. This piece was eight feet by six feet, with verticals that read like cliffs and a massive, heaving chiaroscuro shape that wasn't quite sky. There was a gesture toward one little house perched precariously atop the cliffs, as if it were waiting for a strong gust of wind to go crashing down.

Her largest painting in years, and her best. The thing was almost finished but it needed…what? Something. It needed something badly, and yesterday's eggs weren't going to cut it.

She sipped her drink again, and the front door banged open. She splashed Jack Daniel's and Amaretto on her hand, jumping at the noise. "Shit! Marco?"

Sure enough, her brother, Marco, had kicked open the door, carrying baskets of eggplants, summer squash, cherry tomatoes and green beans inside.

"You don't even knock?" Natasha asked.

He set the veggies on the cluttered table. "Why would I?"

"What if I were naked?"

"You're never naked." He eyed her with the practiced scorn of an older brother. "When was the last time you even changed?"

Natasha sniffed her tank top and scratched at the blue cotton boxer shorts she'd been living in. She wrinkled her nose. "A couple days?"

"You're repulsive," Marco said, clearing a space amid the tabletop clutter.

"Look who's talking. You spend all day grubbing in the dirt." She downed her drink. "If you'd put in the tub, I'd bathe more often."

"What's wrong with the shower?"

She stood and poured a Scotch for Marco. "I like baths. I think better in baths."

They'd been remodeling the house since last spring, when their parents deeded them the property and retired to an Arizona condo. At least there were two buildings, the farmhouse for Marco and the soon-to-be-remodeled barn/studio for her; if they lived together, they'd immediately revert to age twelve and bicker over Eggos. Plus, the barn was sound. She had an oak floor—which Marco complained was already splattered with paint—and a loft for sleeping and plenty of room for working. But there was an empty pit where the kitchen should be, and no bathtub.

"Start thinking in the shower," he said. "There's no way you're getting a tub till spring."

He flopped onto the couch, probably the first time he'd sat down all day. Marco grew organic vegetables that he sold to markets and restaurants from Belfast to Portsmouth, and often didn't stop for meals, choosing to graze from the garden all day. Every summer Natasha watched him lose twenty pounds, then pack it on again over the winter. His hair was still short from his biannual buzz, the auburn curls missing for another month—he was such a farmer, even his *hair* was seasonal. She'd always envied his auburn hair and tanned skin—she had hair the color of fire and her skin blistered from an hour in the sun.

"But the growing season's mostly over in October, right?" she asked. "Put the tub in then."

"We have to get the place shingled and insulated before November."

"Shingles are overrated."

"Without insulation, you'll have to move in with me."

She shuddered. "Show me what to do, then. I'll get started."

He paused over his drink. She'd always been good with her hands; she'd helped him build his chicken coops and greenhouse, and she could see him considering the idea. Then he shook his head. "It'd take me longer to show you than do it myself. I promise we'll get it done as soon as things slow down."

She was disappointed but understood. Marco was as passionate about growing vegetables as she was about art. "I can do some of your deliveries, if that'll help."

"Natasha, even if you help I won't have time to put—"

"I'm trying to be nice," she said, only lying a little, "not to get you to work on the house faster. Jeez."

"Sorry." He rubbed his callused hands over his face. "I'm tired."

"You're just bad tempered. You don't know what tired is, farm boy."

He laughed and looked at her painting. "You were up all last night?"

"Slept a few hours this morning. Oh! You delivered to Amelia's today, didn't you?"

He didn't answer, still looking at the large canvas. "That one's good, isn't it?"

"I like to think they're *all* good."

"Liar. You hate your surf 'n' turf."

That's what she called the small seascapes she peddled to summer tourists, surf 'n' turf. "I don't hate them. They're just…pedestrian."

"This one's bigger, too." He cocked his head at the painting. "What's it called?"

"It's called *Natasha's Last Hope at Being a Real Artist*."

"*Lost Hope?* That's kinda grim."

"I didn't say 'lost,' I said 'last,' and—" She stopped, seeing his teasing smile. "Oh, fuck you. So you delivered to Amelia's today?" Amelia's was an upscale restaurant in Portland's Old Port district with exposed brick walls that would be a perfect backdrop for her art. "Did you ask about showing my work?"

Marco suddenly found his Scotch fascinating. "Well, they, um…"

"Did you show them my portfolio?"

"Not really…they kinda like the plain brick, I guess."

"Oh." She shrugged. "Doesn't matter, the surf 'n' turf is

selling pretty well." If only there was half as much interest in her larger pieces, in her *real* art. She'd tried reps, she'd tried galleries in Portland—she even had a show once, and sold precisely two paintings, one to her parents and one to her college roommate, Eve, who'd maxed out her credit card. She just wanted her paintings *seen,* that's why she'd asked Marco to hook her up with one of the restaurants who bought his produce. People would splatter them with spaghetti sauce, but at least they wouldn't be stacked in the corner of her barn.

"I'll ask at Davinci tomorrow," Marco said. "They've got walls."

"Thanks." Natasha crossed to the table, looking at the veggies Marco had arranged in a pretty cornucopia. "God! Everyone's an artist. What's all the kale and chard for?"

Marco's turn to shrug. "I don't know. She'll find some use for them."

She was Kim Gray, Natasha's friend and Marco's ex-wife. "You just brought a massive batch of kale without asking her if she wants it?"

"You know we don't talk."

"You could at least drop these off yourself."

"Yeah, and you could be the next Cindy Sherman. How's *that* going?"

"Not well," she said, "considering she's a photographer. I doubt she can even do watercolors." But his comment that Natasha *still* wasn't famous—irked. And had nothing to do with him dropping off vegetables. "Isn't it your bedtime?"

"Can't I watch?"

"Do I watch you work?"

"You lounge in the Adirondack every afternoon with a beer."

"That's different," she said. "I'm keeping you company."

"Well, I'll be keeping you company."

"No, you won't." She checked the clock on the wall where the kitchen should be. "Go to bed. Dawn's only seven hours away."

Marco finished munching his ice cubes, a habit that had irritated her since childhood, brought in four more baskets, then left.

Natasha sprawled in her bed, a white cast-iron frame, and stared at the exposed ceiling beams. Something was nagging at her. The lack of a kitchen? The lack of a boyfriend? The lack of clean laundry? The lack of success? There was a lot lacking. But none of those things were bothering her. At least not right now.

As Puck cat-footed into bed and chewed her hair, purring himself to sleep, she realized the painting needed to be seen through a translucent film. Not fog, but a fine misty white that read like fog, billowing and cool on the viewer's face.

She rolled out of bed and stood in front of the canvas. *Lost Hope*—Marco had been sort of right. The colors were too vivid, too sharp, she needed something almost other-worldly, where you saw more from the corner of your eyes than when you stared straight on. She lost herself in her imagination for a time, then got to work. She painted in a daze, her heart beating fast, her fatigue forgotten. She was in a dream, flying over the ocean, a harbor filled with sail-boats, a field in need of haying, a muddy pasture overrun with Belted Galloways, until she came to the house on the cliff—a real house on Broome Isle. A cottage perched high on a precipice above the sea. If only she could obscure the square of white while drawing the eye to its absence. Make the house disappear into the mist, a vacancy that demanded attention—

The door banged. Her front door. Someone knocking. Natasha stepped back from the canvas and breathed. She noticed the light streaming in the windows…dawn.

She suddenly ached with exhaustion. "Jesus, Marco," she muttered, before raising her voice. "Just because you're up at dawn, doesn't mean I am! Go away!"

"Um…Natasha?" A woman's voice. "It's me."

She glanced at the clock. "Kim? It's six-thirty! What're you doing?"

"Let me in!"

Natasha flung open the door and stared at the little black cocktail dress, the deep cleavage and the far-flung blond hair, before she recognized the face. "Eve?"

The Portland airport was called a "Jetport," which seemed fantastically futuristic for Maine. Without even carry-on luggage, I was first to the curb and caught a cab to the waterfront, through deserted streets and dark city blocks. I've always hated the inside of large boats, which smell like shrimp and pickled BO, so when the ferry finally boarded, I immediately made my way to the fresh chill air at the front.

The bow? The prow? I'd have to learn nautical terminology during my stay on Broome Island. I shivered and crossed my arms as we pulled away from the dock, and one of the ferry guys offered me a blanket and a lingering look.

I took the blanket. I'd already gotten plenty of looks since I left New York, wearing my evening dress and kitten heels—especially during the hours I'd been waiting for the dawn ferry.

Natasha would have something warmer for me to wear, probably something ratty, but I didn't care. That was my only thought: get to Natasha.

I cocooned myself in the blanket and leaned over the railing to watch the parting water. Couldn't see much, but the rippling waves were mesmerizing.

The thing was, I liked to dream. I'd dreamed about a perfect life in Tribeca, sharing a loft with a sweetly attentive Gregory—dreamed about living together for a year before he took me to Nobu and asked me to marry him. Dreamed about the brownstone in Park Slope, the three kids (two girls and a boy) and the family summers of travel and laughter.

Still, here was the truth: Gregory wasn't that bad, really, but I never came first with him. He came first—his career, and maybe even his toys. I'd fallen for his boyish charm and confidence, without realizing they were bundled with boyish immaturity and selfishness. He was like a quad eyeshadow compact with only two good colors.

On the other hand, Gregory was my first boyfriend who really knew what he was doing in bed. The others either fumbled or followed a sex schedule they must've read in *Maxim*. Three minutes here, four minutes there, sixty-eight percent of women like this, eighty-three percent like that. If her toes curl you win the game.

Gregory was too confident for fumbling and too self-centered for formula—his egotism did the trick. Plus, when one of you works sixteen-hour days, the sex is all you've got time for, anyway. That and the dreams.

But now that I'd left, he'd realize how much he was missing. He'd need to grow up fast to win me back. Like Richard Gere in *Pretty Woman* or the hero in any of those Jane Austen books.

I smiled in anticipation and the ferry rumbled beneath me toward the sun barely cresting the horizon—a brand-new day. I spread my wings, clutching the blanket as if it were a cape, which flew behind me for one brief, shining moment.

Then whipped from my fingers and into the ocean.

"Oh, God!"

The waves sucked at the blanket, dragging it under. Shit. *Shit.* I glanced at the little window where the men piloted the boat. Maybe no one noticed. Right. I'm sure cocktail-clad women flapping capes on a twenty-minute ferry ride happened all the time. Before anyone could yell at me, I slunk into the cabin and hid in the corner behind a couple of canoodling teenagers and a family of four dressed in matching red T-shirts.

Not an auspicious start, but no matter. Back in New York, Gregory was on his way to work, having slept in an empty bed, my absence a constant reproach. By the time we docked on Broome Isle, I was wreathed in fantasies about his heartfelt contrition and gestures of reconciliation. I stepped from the ferry with a pleased smile on my face, hitched a ride with the canoodling teenagers and ten minutes later was knocking on Natasha's door.

Five minutes after that, I was still knocking. I plucked a cherry tomato from the plant growing along the wall and the door swung open and *something* gaped at me, wearing only a stiff, paint-smeared T-shirt and boxers. It had bare feet, arms covered with white freckles and flaming-red hair trying to escape from a dingy John Deere baseball cap.

Natasha scowled, then beamed in recognition. "Eve!"

She moved to hug me and I warded her off. "Paint! Paint! Back!"

"What are you wearing?" she said, stopping.

"Me?"

She laughed and spun to give me the whole view. When she turned back, though, her eyes were grave. "Are you okay? Evie, what's wrong?"

"I guess you didn't get my message?"

"You know I don't listen to my messages."

I pushed into the barn, afraid if I gave her any time, she'd start suggesting bed-and-breakfasts. Yes, we had the intimacy of being former roommates, but Natasha could make hermit crabs look social. "Well, I left."

"Left what? Greg?"

"Gregory. Yeah, among other things. Like my clothes, my job, my life…" I'd called in to work from the airport with a family emergency—technically I was on personal leave. Still, I could kiss my evaluation goodbye, and no way was I getting my own classroom next year.

"But—*when?*"

"Um…last night? I kinda…snapped. We had an open house at the school, and I ended up wearing a scarlet letter, then when I got home Gregory had this work party and—and—"

"If you start crying I'll hug you," Natasha threatened.

I stifled a sniffle. "I didn't know where else to go. God, it's freezing in here."

I grabbed an old cardigan from one of the kitchen

chairs—only there was no kitchen. But the rest of the barn was finished. There was a light-filled room with exposed beams, a bedroom loft and an expansive living area, which Natasha had filled with her paintings, empty bottles and buckets of brushes. The place smelled of paint and patchouli, very Natasha.

"You're cold?" Natasha said, disbelieving.

"You're such a Mainer. Blankets?"

She pointed to the loft and I trotted upstairs and rummaged through her closest until I found a down comforter and a pillow and dragged them downstairs like Linus with his blanket.

"Want some coffee?" Natasha asked.

"I need sleep." I tossed the bedding on the couch. "You don't mind, do you?"

"Of course not, but what are you *doing* here?"

"Remember sophomore year? When Pete broke up with me and I stopped going to classes and gained ten pounds?"

Natasha nodded. "You went from solid Bs to double Ds."

"Well, that's how I feel now. Like nobody loves me and I chose the wrong major." I smacked my butt. "And the ten pounds are back."

"Please. You always look great—that's why I hate you."

"And you made everything okay. You got me to drop Latin American Big House Fiction, and did those caricatures of pencil-dick Pete and stopped letting me hide Twix bars in my underwear drawer." I looked at Natasha and realized I was crying. "I just thought you'd know what to do."

"Draw a picture of goat-balls Gregory?"

"And fax it to his office!" I yawned hugely. "Although, he'd probably just bill you."

"First things first." Natasha swept the clutter from the couch. "Sleep. We'll fix things when we wake up."

I sniffed and nodded, and stepped out of my dress as she made the bed.

"Whoa!" Natasha looked away—I forgot I was wearing my sexy black underwear. "Warn a person, would you?"

I giggled and crawled under the comforter. "You always hated sharing a room, didn't you?"

"Only with you."

She tucked me in on the couch and climbed the stairs to her bedroom, her orange tabby eying me from the steps. The room spun as if I were drunk on sleeplessness and paint fumes. I cuddled into the couch cushions and soon heard Natasha's soft snores, which reminded me of our dorm room at NYU. I smiled at the memory, despite the faint worry nagging at me: Natasha truly didn't like sharing a room—and *hated* having people in her studio. What if it took Gregory more than a few days to come to his senses?

3

Between the old stone fences wandering into the dark center of Broome Isle and the tangled coves guarding the periphery, a pebbled stream rambled through the rich earth, then forked into two. One branch, the larger, grew wider and straighter and was filled with water, to feed the thirsty roots and fill stone wells. The smaller, long ago setting out upon a fruitless path, became shallower and dryer until disappearing into the undergrowth. And long ago, the heart of the island had divided in two in much the same way.

The larger section grew hearty, feeding and comforting the pines and lupine, the foxes and bobolinks and settlers. The smaller, however, hungered and ached. Ached to reshape the course of rivers, to wash away the settled paths in a violent downpouring torrent. The clenched, severed fragment of the island's heart burned with the craving to shed the blood of deer and rend lobster apart; longed to hunt, to kill. And this wasn't the first time, either. This hunger had been roused before, and had been stopped before by human hands. Yet nothing that still hungers rests in peace.

Only the hunger kept me from fading into the ether after all these years in chains, all this weakness and impotent craving. Others, like me, had been lost forever. But the knot of longing and desire drove me, kept me whole, reminded me who I was, what I was meant to do.

My day drew closer. I could sense something shift, almost imperceptibly, a new star appearing in the midnight sky. In my prison, I could do nothing but wait and hunger—for her. She'd finally come, I could almost smell her through the walls of my fathomless cell. The one I'd been waiting for. The third of three.

I woke in a total *schvitz*. I threw the comforter to the floor and stood from the couch, removed the wool cardigan and was still overheated. The house was a sauna. No wonder Natasha gave me that look when I'd dragged her blankets from the closet. At least the heat explained my dream: trapped deep below the surface of the earth in a burning cavern, a faceless beast chasing me across a floor glowing with embers. I heard him growling and snapping, speaking in an ancient language I couldn't decipher. Yet his voice was enticing, too, like a deep rumble of the inevitable, of inescapable fate, that almost made me want to get caught.

I wiped sweat from my forehead and listened for Natasha. I couldn't hear snoring, but I couldn't hear anything else, either, which meant she was still sleeping. She always complained of insomnia, but once she fell asleep she was immobile and comatose, and if you woke her before she was ready, she'd take your head off like a bear interrupted from hibernation.

I tiptoed to the bathroom and tried to make myself presentable without showering, which would wake her. There was an appealing glowy dew about me due to the sweating, but also a lot of frizzy hair. I took a large clip from the medicine cabinet—she had the whole thing to herself—and pinned my hair into a tight twist.

I crossed toward the fridge, hoping I'd find a miniature Starbucks tucked inside, then stopped when I saw the kitchen table. The detritus of Natasha—an empty Jack Daniel's bottle, a heap of clean-ish silverware, four wax-encrusted candlesticks, a few dog-eared art books—had been shoved to the side, to make room for a display of produce that looked like one of the Old Masters still lifes.

There was a mountain of kale and rainbow chard, the leaves a deep green and the stems yellow, red and gold. Perched atop were succulent purple eggplants, odd-colored heirloom tomatoes, lush sprigs of basil and three varieties of squash, from long and knobby to squat and flying-saucer-shaped. There was a separate basket filled with green beans, although half were yellow or purple.

I crunched one of the purple beans, and was relieved to find it was green inside and delicious raw. There was a container of cherry tomatoes and I popped one in my mouth—it tasted like candy. Better than a Twix bar. I ate another, glancing guiltily upstairs—was she going to miss them?—then just one last tomato.

Somehow I finished the carton and decided to go outside and pick more. My feet were still blistered from the kitten heels, so I hunted around for a pair of Natasha's shoes—and found myself face-to-face with a painting.

Larger than I'd ever seen of Natasha's, and almost luminescent, a painting of the island cliffs as seen from the ocean, with the roiling surf below and the endless sky above. Except I forgot the first rule of Natasha's art: never tell her what you saw in it. She hated that. Instead, you could only talk about the colors and the composition.

I flipped through her other paintings, and found one showing a row of dark red rectangles I figured were brick buildings. What passed for "downtown" on Broome Isle. And wait—Natasha had mentioned that one of the buildings in town was a bakery.

I squinted at one of the rectangles until I convinced myself I could see a cappuccino machine through the walls. I found a pair of black flip-flops by the front door and slipped into them. Feeling boho chic, in my cocktail dress and thongs, like an Olsen twin who'd started eating, I headed for town.

My watch said ten o'clock. Snack time back home, opening lunch boxes and setting out browned apple slices and cheddar fish crackers. As I walked, I wondered about the new students. I always loved meeting the kids, guessing who they'd become, watching them unfold into themselves. Who'd need help socializing, who'd have a constant runny nose, who'd raise his hand at every question, even if he didn't know the answer?

And how far away *was* this village, anyway?

I flip-flopped along the seaside road, the chill salt air raising goose bumps on my arms, stopping to watch long-necked black birds dive into the water. A car honked, and I turned to find a gleaming limousine pulling beside me, the purr of the engine barely audible over the roar of the surf.

I gaped, and the sunroof slid open, the faint tinkle of opera floating from inside. Gregory stood through the sunroof, a bottle of champagne in one hand and a little velvet box in the other. His face was a perfect picture of contrition and love. Yes, I'd expected him to ask me to come back, but not like *this!*

He popped the cork of the champagne and said, "Um, you need a ride or something?"

I blinked, and the limousine turned into a station wagon, with one of the canoodling teenagers and his mother inside. He asked again if I needed a ride, then told his mother I was wearing the same dress last night. Huh. Small island. But I took the ride, and when they dropped me at the edge of the village, I felt perfectly lost.

Nobody knew me here, nobody would be missing me at home. Did Gregory even care I was gone? He must be missing me by now. Right? Vowing to change his ways. Maybe? Well, surely he was missing the sex, at least.

My anxiety ebbed slightly at the charm of the village, enfolding the harbor with craggy streets and old colonial houses built snuggly together. Many of the houses had signs that listed the date and first owner, most going back to the early 1800s, and I wondered how many of them were still owned by the original family. More than a few, on Broome Isle.

I passed a narrow white house with red shutters, an English-style garden with a pretty arbor, then a square clapboard house built on pilings jutting over the harbor painted a glossy green so dark it was almost black. Beyond the Barnacle, a local hangout for a beer and lobster—where Natasha knew everyone, like an episode of *Men in Trees*—I finally found the bakery.

A bell jingled on the pane-glass door as I stepped inside. The air smelled yeasty and sweet and blessedly of coffee. Assorted breads, perfect little cookies, croissants and scones were all displayed on the old wooden counter. The floors were pumpkin-colored pine, and the tables and chairs were shabby chic, all filled with happily eating customers.

Now, *this* was more like it, a French patisserie on an island in Maine. Maybe I'd never leave.

I ordered a cappuccino, scones and chocolate cookies to go. The woman behind the counter smiled and asked how long I'd been on the island, and we chatted for a minute, and the people at the counter joined the conversation, and it was like, I don't know: home. Everyone was so friendly, and open, and not at all like I expected from Maine, where, according to Natasha, you were considered to be "from away," and not a real Mainer, until the third generation.

Finally, I waved goodbye and wandered through the village finishing my cappuccino. Past the little town green I came upon the elementary school. An old stone building, built a couple of centuries ago, with a few fairly funky modern extensions that didn't detract from the school's sprawling charm.

A burly middle-aged man was whacking weeds around the lawn, wearing goggles and a radio headset with big earphones, and I sat on the stone fence and ate one of the scones, absently watching him. What if I got a *job* here? I could rent a little house, like that green-black one jutting over the water, and have coffee and scones every morning at the bakery, where all the regulars would know me, then stroll over here to teach in my own classroom at a little schoolhouse in New England. Very *Little House on the Prairie.* Minus the prairie, of course.

The gardener turned off his Weedwacker and wandered over, pushing his goggles onto his forehead. "The villa-age is ovah theah," he said in a drawn-out Maine accent, pointing the way I'd come.

"I know." I showed him my paper bag of goodies. "I've just been to Matilda's."

"Matilda makes a supah scone," he said, still with the accent. I was beginning to think he was deliberately putting it on.

"Would you like one?"

His eyes lit up. "Don't mind if I do-oo."

I handed him one of the scones and nodded toward the school. "Have you worked here long?"

"Ayuh, just about forevah."

"I don't suppose they're hiring?"

"You handy with a Weedwackah?" he asked, grinning around the scone.

I laughed. "I've never actually whacked weeds—I'm from New York. I'm a teacher and just wondered—well, it's such a pretty school."

"What grades do you teach?"

"I'm certified for K through five."

"You serious about moving hea-ah?"

I shrugged, not about to tell him I was waiting for my boyfriend to come to his senses so I could go home. "Maybe."

"Are you any good?"

"As a teacher? I—I think so, yes. I've never had my own classroom, but…when I get the chance, I'll be damn good."

"What makes you say that?"

It must've been the caffeine, because I went into a serial-length saga about how I was thwarted at every turn by Mrs. Dale and had been unable to implement the new teaching strategies I'd learned in grad school. He nodded thoughtfully, then asked a few educated questions about specific lesson plans.

Something in his tone made me wonder. "They're not actually *hiring* right now, are they?"

"I don't believe so," he said.

"Oh. No, of course not." I found myself disappointed.

"Because if you have references, you're hired."

"What?"

He held out his hand. "I'm Mark Epper." Only he said it more like *Mock Eppah*. "The principal here at Broome Isle Elementary."

An unearthly shrieking cut across Natasha's dream, and she opened one eye, her head pounding. Late morning, judging from the light in the windows. She pulled the blanket over her head and pretended she couldn't hear the rattling and banging downstairs.

"You won't believe what just happened," Eve called, stomping upstairs, then stopping abruptly. "Oh, God! Did I wake you?"

Natasha peered out from under the blanket.

"Sorry!" Eve backed slowly toward the stairs. "Sorry, my news can wait."

"Go away," Natasha said.

Eve tossed a small white bag on the bed and flew downstairs.

Natasha put her pillow over head, but it was no use now,

she was awake. She pawed at the bag, and sniffed. Sweet. She devoured the scone and croaked, "Coffee."

"Already brewing!" Eve sang out.

Natasha stretched and scratched herself, and considered changing but smelled the coffee and decided clothes could wait. She stumbled downstairs and downed a cup before facing Eve, who was flushed with excitement. Natasha grunted. Eve was so effortlessly beautiful, her curvy little figure and peaches-and-cream face. With the masses of blond hair, she always looked so…ripe. It made Natasha nervous, sometimes, as if Eve might burst open, unable to contain her sweetness.

"What?" Natasha asked.

"I got a job offer! Here on the island, I mean. To teach first grade, which I've never done before, but I'm sure I can do it and it'd be *so* much better than kindergarten, because I wouldn't be in charge of potty time and I wouldn't have to face going back to the city or hearing Mrs. Dale lecture me about *Buddies* or dressing up as Moaning Myrtle! And Gregory—well, he can visit on weekends. Stay in my little seaside cottage, where we'll sleep in late, go sailing and putter around the village, looking for art at that little gallery—*oh!*"

"Oh?" There was *more* to this fantasy?

"I forgot to tell you, they sell art like yours in the village."

"The place with the big whale out front?"

"Yeah!" Eve gestured to the canvasses against the walls. "Only your stuff is way better."

"That is my stuff."

"Uh-huh, and it's way better than what they have at this gallery. You should talk to them."

"That's my stuff at the gallery. I did talk to them. The stuff that isn't as good as my stuff? *Is* my stuff." Natasha ran her hands over her face. "God. I can't believe I'm selling my art at a place with a big whale out front, and even *you,* with *your* taste in art, can see it's crap."

"Oh. Um. Oh." Eve's lower lip began to tremble. "I'm sorry."

Natasha sighed. It was impossible to stay angry at Eve. "You know what you are? A widgeon."

"Am not."

"You have no idea what a widgeon is, do you?"

"So what does that make you?" she asked. "A cog?"

"Huh? I said *widgeon,* not *widget.* And you're only proving my point."

Before Eve could answer, a truck horn beeped outside and a man's voice called a few indecipherable words.

Natasha glanced at the produce on the table. "Uh-oh— gotta get this stuff to Kim this morning or Marco will kill me."

"Is that Marco?" Eve crossed to the window. "I haven't seen him in years. Since the *last* time we were roommates."

"We're not roommates! Now, help me carry this stuff to my car, or Marco will never install the bathtub." Natasha grabbed a basket and crossed to the door, stopping when she saw the pink girl's bicycle with the banana seat in the door-way. "What's that?"

"From lost and found. Principal Epper let me borrow it to get back."

Natasha stopped and stared. "You really *did* get a job offer?"

"You thought I was making it up?"

"Well, you know how you get."

Eve laughed. "It does sound like something I'd daydream about—but it was *real!*"

Natasha grabbed a basket of veggies, inwardly groaning. What if Eve actually took the job? Natasha would love having her on the island, but there was no way they could be roommates again.

✳ 4 ✳

The key to perfect pickled beets was boiling them in salted water, removing them undercooked and setting them aside to cool. At least that's what Kim Gray's grandmother had taught her—to picture the outer flesh of the beets holding on to the heat, radiating inward. *You let them finish cooking in their own good time,* she'd said, *they know when they're done, you just get outta the way.*

Kim smiled, setting the last beet aside, her dark hair plastered to her forehead by the steam. Her smiled waned as she suddenly thought of Marco. During the few months they'd been married, he'd been fascinated by her cooking. He'd sit and watch her at the cutting board and stove, cracking eggs and simmering sauces, and when she'd ask if he was getting bored, he'd just laugh.

He'd tested her, once. She'd been prepping her *niçoise* quiches for sale at the bakery—sautéing the shallots and eggplant, beating the eggs with cayenne and parsley. Marco tossed a dozen beets in a pot to boil, some the size of radishes, others almost as big as grapefruits. He watched her prep a dozen quiches, then a dozen more, occasionally dipping a slotted spoon into the boiling water to extract a beet and set it aside.

Finally, he'd sliced all the beets in half, and laughed. "They're all perfect. How'd you know when they were done? You weren't even watching them!"

She couldn't explain. She just *knew*. It came with the territory.

"Yeah," he'd said, looking into her eyes. "Sometimes you just know."

Kim took a jug of water and bag of cat food to the back door and filled the bowls she kept just outside the garden for the stray cats. Broom Isle was riddled with feral felines. No one knew who brought the first cat to the island, though some suspected it was Kim's great-grandmother Emily, one of the first settlers. Kim thought they were probably right. There was something otherworldly and noble about the island cats, a countenance she never found in cats she met off the island. Several of the regulars milled about as she filled the bowls. Kim didn't dare name them. Or let them inside. Natasha had done that with Puck and had never gotten rid of him. Kim was too afraid of becoming one of those crazy cat women. But that didn't keep her from running up a substantial bill in feed at the General Store each month.

She stepped back inside and wiped her hair from her forehead as she slipped the skins from the beets while they were still hot. This was her busiest time of year. In addition to the beets, she was making dilly beans and pickling garlic scapes, cucumbers and green tomatoes. She'd spend a week doing nothing but canning tomatoes, and hadn't even started on the blueberry jam, rhubarb chutney or corn relish. Her soaps and salves, the lotions and oils and bath fizzes, would wait until winter.

Natasha called her an "Earth Mama," never realizing the words might hurt. They'd been friends forever, yet Natasha simply seemed to forget that Kim wasn't any sort of "mama" at all, despite wanting nothing more keenly than a child. Still, Natasha knew better than anyone what had happened: Kim and Marco married two months after Kim discovered she was pregnant, and divorced three months later. After she miscarried.

Kim and Marco had fit. Like two flavors that combine to make a remarkable third. But the miscarriage had introduced a sour taste of tears and grief, and soon she could notice nothing else.

Earth Mama. Said so fondly that she knew Natasha meant it with love, teasing herself—with her unnatural hours and inability to cook—as much as Kim. But there was nothing really earthy about Kim, either. She didn't wear tie-dyed T-shirts, peasant skirts or even have long hair. She wore black, always, with her dark hair in a pixie cut and her short fingernails a Bing cherry red.

Of course, some days Kim wished she wore hippie clothes; they were so much more affordable. She owned a string of seasonal cottages along the water (her family at one time had owned a good quarter of the island), which she rented to summer people, but her income still needed supplementing. Selling sauce and jams at the General Store and her baked goods at Matilda's during the summer enabled her to pay the property taxes and still buy the occasional cashmere sweater. If she could content herself with L.L. Bean and Carhartt, she wouldn't need the extra cash—but they didn't do a lot in black.

She cored three early-season Macintoshes and peeled them in spirals. She mixed maple syrup with ground cloves, cinnamon, ginger and oats, then poured melted butter on top and set them to bake. She chopped the beets, her knife cutting smooth and sure, and was dividing them among the jars filled with the cider vinegar brine when there was a knock at the door.

"In the kitchen," she called.

Kim screwed the lids on the jars of beets and carefully dropped them into the canner, heating on the stove. Natasha stepped inside carrying a basket overflowing with kale. Trailing her was Aphrodite's little sister, all cherubic curls and rosy skin, half hidden behind an armful of string beans and heirloom tomatoes.

I've never been to France, but as Natasha pulled into the drive of her former sister-in-law's old farmhouse, I felt transported to Provence. It wasn't the architecture so much, which was in the federal style with creamy yellow clapboards and glossy black shutters, but the garden out front. A white picket fence surrounded the house, barely containing a profusion of roses, lavender and herbs. Stone steps led to French doors, upon which Natasha perfunctorily knocked before opening.

The kitchen smelled of fresh basil, caramelized sugar and browning butter, and bouquets of lavender hung from the rafters. The shelves were heavy with copper-bottom pots and cast-iron skillets and other cooking paraphernalia I'd never seen before, half of which must've been antique. There were racks of spices, herbs in bunches, wooden spoons and sharp knives. The sink was huge and made of slate and there was a massive old cast-iron stove.

"Where *are* we?" I asked Natasha marveling at the Windsor table and chairs, burnished from use, the creamy yellow walls and connecting sunroom filled with over-stuffed furniture.

"Why do you bother?" Natasha asked the woman at the butcher's block who must've been Kim.

"Why do I bother what?"

"Saying you're in the kitchen. You're always in the kitchen. Eve, Kim. Kim, Eve." She lifted the basket in her arms. "Where should we put these?"

"The table, for now." Kim smiled at me. There was a warmness about her that belied her striking looks. She had long skinny legs under a short black skirt, with closely cropped dark hair that highlighted almond eyes and pouty lips. "Welcome. You're Natasha's college roommate—I didn't know you were coming."

"Neither did I," Natasha said wryly.

"You get to live here?" I asked Kim. "Natasha doesn't even *have* a kitchen."

"I have a toaster oven."

"This place is amazing," I said. "It's like stepping into Provence. Not that I've ever been to France, but this is even better. It's like stepping into my dream of Provence. You grew up here?"

Kim nodded. "My family's lived here for more than two hundred years." She made a face at Natasha. "God, I sound so patrician. As if Broome Isle has ever had an aristocracy.

The Grays have lived heah for two hundred yeahs." She mocked herself in a sort of Katharine Hepburn accent. "We've always just been too lazy to move, I guess." She ran her hands over the produce on the table, her fingers long and quick. "You'll stay for dinner. Looks like we're having roasted green beans and I'll do a pasta with eggplant and tomatoes."

Natasha crossed to the wine rack and grabbed a bottle. "And a pinot noir," she said, reading the label.

Kim opened the oven and a sugary apple scent billowed into the room. She put an earthenware dish onto the counter and placed three baked apples on the center of three dessert plates—each plate a different design—and from nowhere produced a garnish of crushed cinnamon sticks to sprinkle on top.

"Are you sure you didn't know we were coming?" I asked. I mean, three baked apples, three of us.

"Natasha never calls ahead," she told me, setting the plates on the table. "These were going to be dessert, but let's just call them appetizers."

Natasha settled at the counter, watching her two friends. She'd always felt she and Kim were opposites. She was hot and Kim was cool, she was contemporary and Kim was traditional. But she also felt the opposite of Eve. She was sharp and Eve was soft, she was night and Eve was day.

So how odd to see Eve and Kim together, bonding so quickly and yet so *different* from each other. Tall, composed, striking Kim and short, bubbly, pretty Eve, wearing one of Kim's aprons, which fell almost to her calves, chatting happily as they cooked. Or as Kim cooked, and Eve did as she was told.

"How long are you staying?" Kim asked.

"Until my boyfriend apologizes."

"Ah. You'll be needing winter clothes, then. And a car."

"What? No, I—I'm sure he'll call. Soon." Eve frowned. "Like tonight."

Natasha groaned over her wineglass. "You sure about the winter clothes?" she asked Kim, then shook her head. "What am I saying? Of course you're sure."

"Wait," Eve said. "How do you know he's not going to apologize?"

"Didn't I tell you?" Natasha said. "Kim's a witch."

"Natasha, be nice."

"She doesn't mean it that way," Kim said. "I *am* a witch."

"Oh, you mean you practice Wicca?"

Kim grinned. "Not really."

"She doesn't need to practice," Natasha said. "Or stir potions in her cauldron—eye of newt and wart of frog."

"Wiccans don't do that," Kim said.

Natasha swirled her wineglass. "Well, dance naked in the woods or whatever they do."

"Okay, I'm confused," Eve said. "You're a witch but not a Wiccan?"

"Exactly," Kim said. "My mother's great-grandmother's great-grandmother—maybe with one more 'great' in there—was the first person to settle on this island. Her name was Emily Gray, and she was hanged as a witch. Runs in the family."

"Not the hanging," Natasha said. "The witchery."

"Like in the Salem witch trials?" Eve asked. "None of those women was actually a witch."

"Emily was."

"Oh, right," Eve said. "So what does that mean, being a

witch? You're good with a broom? And how come you have the same last name if she was on your mother's side?"

"Family tradition—the name 'Gray' is passed down through the females."

Natasha could see Eve wondered if she was being teased, but then she said, "That's kinda cool."

Kim smiled. "And no, it doesn't mean I'm good with a broom. It means I know things."

"Like Gregory isn't going to come to his senses?"

"That's more of an educated guess. Mostly I know things about the island, like when it's going to rain, and how the harvest will be, the night of the first frost, things like that." She shook her head. "Sounds silly when I talk about it, and obviously I don't know everything. I didn't know you were coming to visit."

"But then, neither did I," Eve said, with a shaky laugh.

Natasha couldn't tell whether Eve believed Kim or not. Natasha had grown up with the gossip about the Gray women. They all had, laughing about black magic and white magic and "Gray" magic. It was just part of life on Broome Isle.

"The good news is you can take the job," Natasha told Eve.

"What job?" Kim asked, salting the eggplant slices in the colander, as though they hadn't just discussed the fact that she was a witch.

"First-grade teacher at the elementary school," Natasha said.

"But I'm honestly not staying," Eve said. "Gregory isn't— I mean, I know he's not perfect, but he works hard, and he likes me." She tugged at her hair. "Possibly. At least the sex is good. That's worth something, right?"

"God, I wouldn't know," Kim said. "The last time I had an orgasm—"

Natasha lifted her hand in horror. "Brother! Brother! I don't wanna hear it." She also didn't want to hear it because she'd *never* had an orgasm. Well, at least not when anyone else was in the room.

Kim shot an arch look to Eve. "At least I have my memories. So, how'd you get a job your first day on the island?"

"I met Dr. Epper outside the—"

"Dr. Pepper!" Natasha said.

"God, I forgot we used to call him that," Kim said.

"And leave empty Dr. Pepper cans outside his door. Anyway, he offered Eve a job. You know how hard it is to get teachers to live on the island."

"Yeah, they're all afraid of *The Shining*."

"But I can't take the job," Eve said. "I mean, honestly, I'm sure Gregory will call soon. Still, it'd be kinda great. The village is so charming, and living on an actual island, I don't know, it's exotic…."

And she was off, gushingly enthusiastic and annoying. Natasha finished her wine and refilled her glass, aware that it wasn't really Eve she was annoyed with, but herself. Eve was living her life. She'd shown up on a whim, left everything familiar and flown to Maine in her cocktail dress. But Natasha was supposed to be the spontaneous, artistic, creative one, not Eve, not the schoolteacher. Why did Natasha always feel mired in mud? Painting the same landscapes, surf 'n' turf, to pay the rent. After years of living off bread and butter, you start to lose a taste for it. She was stuck, and Eve's arrival only highlighted how much.

"…and Gregory could commute on weekends," Eve was

saying, a faraway look in her eyes, "and maybe he'd even get a job in Portland, and we'll have two Jack Russels and a little cottage by the water, right in the village, just down the block from the bakery and…"

The scent of the kitchen changed as the light dimmed outside, and the food effortlessly appeared, fragrant and casually inviting, as always with Kim. After her first exclamation of delight at the dinner, Eve nattered on, and like a well-trained therapist, Kim drew her out, gently nudging her toward admitting what she already felt about Gregory. He wasn't the man she wanted him to be.

Natasha glanced at Kim over the candlelit table. How did she do it? She'd love to know what was behind that Cheshire grin and envied her ability to stay unruffled, sane, always the voice of reason. An odd skill, for a witch—or maybe not, maybe it was just part of the same thing, the same intuition or instinct. Natasha wasn't sure she believed there was anything more to the witchery than that, but Kim *was* uncannily knowing about the island. And Evie sat across the table, with her sparkly eyes, her whole body suffused with delight. Natasha yearned to trade places with either of them.

Sometimes she wished she were anyone but herself.

Kim macerated strawberries in a yellow ceramic bowl with a little blueberry syrup, then glanced between Eve and Natasha. "So you'll be rooming together?"

"Well, um…" Eve paused at the sink, where she'd been washing dishes. "I mean…"

"Of course, you can stay as long as you want," Natasha said, clearly unenthusiastic.

"It'll only be a week," Eve said defensively.

Kim let the berries sit while she dished bowls of home-made vanilla ice cream, and carefully didn't say anything.

"I said you can stay, Eve. But the couch isn't comfortable and there's no kitchen…"

"I know, I know. You hate roommates."

"But I love you, Evie. It's just the studio— I can't work with someone else around."

"Maybe I could bunk with Marco," Eve said. "In the front house."

Kim felt herself blush and busied herself with the dessert bowls, pouring the mashed berries over the ice cream. The scent of strawberries rose around her. Scent and memory and taste—they wove together in her mind, and she felt herself in the summer before she and Marco married. Marco had lived in the barn then—Natasha was at college in New York—and the barn had been simply a barn, with an old cast-iron bed he'd hauled into the hayloft. She'd known him forever, but one night she'd gone into the Barnacle and seen him for the first time.

Marco had noticed her staring from the door. He'd stood from his table, his friend gaping, and they'd stepped into the street. She found herself in that old cast-iron bed, waking to the rooster crowing, with hay in her hair and Marco kissing a fresh-picked strawberry into her mouth. Months of bliss, breaking through to something she couldn't even name when she'd realized she was pregnant. Then the marriage, and the divorce.

Kim set the ice cream on the table, avoiding Natasha's eyes. Natasha had been shocked, then thrilled that her best friend was marrying her brother—and she'd soon be an aunt. And after everything fell apart, Natasha never really forgave her—

for what, Kim didn't know. But they'd salvaged their relationship by never discussing what happened.

"Nobody's living in your old room, right?" Eve asked Natasha, apparently unaware of any tension in the room.

Natasha twisted her napkin. "Just stay with me. I can put up with anything for a week, even you."

Kim laughed. "I'll rent you one of my cottages."

"Oh!" Eve brightened. "Does it look anything like this?"

"It's more modern, and has a view of the sea. You'll like it." *And it'll keep you away from Marco.* "Plus, it's insulated."

Natasha dug into her strawberries and ice cream, pleased with Kim's offer. Now she wouldn't have to live with Eve, and more important, neither did Marco. The last thing she needed was another good friend thrown at Marco. She still wasn't over his breakup with Kim.

She finished her ice cream as Kim described the cottage to Eve, telling her about the woodstove and laughing at Eve's suspicion that she was being teased. Eve thought woodstoves had gone out with covered wagons.

It was good to see Kim laughing again. After the divorce, they'd had a hard time being intimate anymore, because if they were, they'd have to discuss the breakup, which was too painful for both of them. But with Eve here, the mood was lightened, and the deep undercurrent of awkwardness was dispelled. That was Evie's gift.

"I'll have to teach you to light the stove," Natasha said. "Kim's an earth mama, but she can't start a fire to save her life."

"At least it doesn't take me twenty minutes to get the twigs stacked in a perfect teepee. Your fires look like they're waiting for an exhibition, not a match."

"They *roar*," Natasha said.

"I am woodstove," Eve said, "hear me roar!"

An empty bottle of pinot, crushed strawberries over homemade ice cream, old friends and new…the three women shone with laughter. And outside the farmhouse, a deer with an eye to Kim's rosebushes went stock still as the light pouring from the kitchen window grew brighter, and whiter, like a dimmer switch turned all the way up.

The scent of glass is smooth and chill, like the feel of an old heavy decanter. There is nothing sharp or cutting about it—until the glass shatters. Shards part flesh easier than a surgeon's scalpel. They slice through to the bone, splashing fresh hot blood to the floor.

Now that is a scent.

But not for me. For me, the scent of glass stood like prison walls. The walls had no flaw, no weakness. The only way I'd ever again breathe midnight stillness, inhale the sticky perfume of flesh, was if the gates were thrown open from the outside and I was invited to step through.

I paused in my interminable pacing, my pacing without feet or form, and cocked the head that no longer existed. A stirring at the gates. A suggestion of motion, of attention of…potential.

Was that a hint of fragrance, in the dead endlessness? The scent of a woman, another woman, and a third.

I gathered what little strength remained.

5

The problem with cell phones was this: I had no excuse to call Gregory and tell him where I could be reached. He had my cell number; he could call me anytime he wanted.

Still, I considered calling him to tell him I was all right, and that I wasn't thinking about him at all. I got as far as dialing the first few numbers when Natasha glowered at me. Not that her glowering was so alarming, she'd been brooding ever since we got home from Kim's.

Drunk and exhausted, I climbed into my borrowed pj's and collapsed on the sofa. But Natasha was just getting her second wind. She sat in her ratty old armchair and stared at the giant canvas she was working on, the one she said wasn't called *Last Hope,* or was it *Lost Hope?* I couldn't quite understand her. Then she banged around in the bathroom, returned with a tarp, brushes and paint, and brooded some more.

Then tossed a paperback at my head and told me to stop snoring.

So I climbed into her bed in the loft and crashed. When I woke, she was still awake downstairs, but working on a completely different painting—one of her surf 'n' turfs. A rocky, wave-battered shore with a lighthouse.

I said, "That's pretty," then paled as I realized what I'd just done. Natasha *hated* it when you called her art "pretty."

But she just said, "Isn't it?" in a scornful sort of voice.

"Um," I said, and went to the not-a-kitchen to start the coffee.

"You like my surf 'n' turf better than my real art, don't you?"

I clattered the coffeepot around and pretended I didn't hear. Of course I liked them better. Everyone liked them better. I brought her a cup of coffee and sat in the corner and checked that my cell battery was still charged and that Gregory hadn't left a message while I was asleep. But really, this whole thing was ridiculous. Was I the kind of girl who waited for the guy to call? Well, yes. But I didn't have to be. So I started dialing, and Natasha glared.

"What?" I said.

"Don't," she snapped.

"But we'll just talk, like rational—"

"You call him, Eve, and you'll *never* get more than a third of the medicine cabinet."

"Fine."

"Good."

"Then I'll stay here *forever!*" I said. And she looked so stricken that I laughed. "Oh, stop worrying. I'll go right now and see Kim's cottage. Where are the car keys?"

★ ★ ★

Kim was right. I loved the cottage.

It was about the size of a large one-bedroom NYC apartment, and painted like the inside of a seashell. A floral print couch, two white wicker chairs, and a coffee table comfortably cluttered the living room, with a formal-looking dining room table and four mismatched chairs visible through an open archway. The walls were decorated with old-fashioned prints of shells and starfish, and there were real shells culled from the beach in front, displayed in bowls on the wicker tables. Yes, that's a lot of seashells, not my first choice in interior design, yet it worked. Because—not sure that I mentioned it—the beach was *right out front.*

I could sit on the porch and touch the sand with my toes, while admiring the craggy cove and the vast open sea. There were three other cottages dotted along the beach, all owned by Kim, but she said this was the cutest, and with the weather about to change, the warmest, too. For some reason, she and Natasha had a good laugh last night over the fact that I was sleeping under a down comforter. They thought I'd be a wimp about the Maine winter, but if I stayed (not saying I was), I'd prove them wrong.

I'd stroll the pebbled beach, snow fluttering to the ground, wrapped in some fabulous deconstructed European black wool coat, fur-lined leather boots and a stylish knit hat, my hair magically transformed into face-framing waves. With no access to Chinese takeout, I'd become a slender reed, looking waifish in my voluminous coat. Like a modern-day Jane Eyre.

Gregory would be my Heathcliff.

Of course, the only Heathcliff that Gregory knew was the

cat. It was embarrassing, how little he knew of literature. He'd never read *Wuthering Heights* or *Jane Eyre,* and… Wait a second. If Heathcliff was in *Wuthering Heights* and Jane Eyre was—obviously—in *Jane Eyre,* then how'd they ever meet?

I set this conundrum aside as the bright day turned suddenly gray, and I scurried back to the seashell, closing the door on the now-uninviting ocean.

I plopped onto the couch and grabbed an old copy of *Portland Life* magazine from the coffee table. There were pictures of Portland society, I guess, but they mostly looked embarrassed that they didn't live in New York. I tossed the magazine and went into the kitchen and ransacked the cupboards. They were filled with plastic plates and bowls, cheap cutlery and some basic food staples like white rice, cheap olive oil and a tin of crabmeat. Who eats canned crab? Maybe a Maine specialty. *Crab. The other white crustacean.*

Kim said she'd bring me proper food tomorrow, anyway. She charged $1,500 a week for the place during the season, but because I was a friend of Natasha's and this was September, my rent was only $500 a month. "Is $125 a week, okay?" I asked Kim, because I wasn't staying a month. She'd returned a mysterious grin and taken the money.

I doubt there's ever been a rent that low in Manhattan, during my lifetime. I wanted to call my mother—just to ask if she remembered ever paying so little—but was afraid she'd actually answer the phone, and I'd have to tell her where I was. We'd been getting along great lately, ever since I hooked up with Gregory. She only wanted the best for me, and to her "the best" meant money. "I just want you to be comfortable," that's what she always told me, and somehow I doubted she'd consider fleeing to a tiny island in Maine "comfortable."

My mother was so Manhattan-centric, she thought they should set a *Survivor* series in Brooklyn. And she wouldn't be happy about the abrupt leave from my job, either.

I was starting to get a sick feeling in my stomach. This had been a bad idea. I should've stayed in New York, I should've worked things out with Gregory. Yes, he was a jackass, but he was a jackass who actually wanted us to live together.

A month ago, I was sitting on a crosstown bus, and the woman in front of me was talking on her cell. She said, "Yeah, he's good, thing's are good. We're going out again on Friday. Yep. A *third date.*" She hung up, and all the women who'd overheard got so excited for her, we basically did the wave. A third date! You never get a third date in New York.

What happens is, you finally decide you're too picky, and you settle for a good-natured shlub, a guy who, while he might not exactly be employed, or charming, or—strictly speaking—hygienic, is still basically a good guy. And you're okay with this. This can work. Maybe you'll buy him some new clothes and explain modern dentistry…or no, you'll just love and accept him exactly as is. Then *he* dumps *you*.

That's dating in New York.

But here was Gregory, handsome and successful, and not just employed, but employed in Biglaw, which meant dinners at Per Se and villas in Tuscany. He could be charming, too, and funny and fun. And okay, sure, he was a selfish prick—I knew that, I'm not stupid—but he was a man. How much better did they get?

Not much. But when you're heading into your late twenties… I know it's a cliché, but the good ones *are* taken. The good ones were taken five years ago, and they stayed taken, because that's what good men do. They stick around, they make it work.

Gregory and I lived together in his chilly, angular apartment. That's a real commitment, especially for a man like him. So no, maybe he hasn't appeared in a limo with chilled champagne and an engagement ring, or even given me half of the medicine cabinet, but it still might work. If only we—

My phone rang in my hand, and I almost fell off the couch. Gregory! But no, the ring tone was wrong. I waited a minute, then listened to the message. It was a friend from grad school describing her first day in her own classroom at a swanky Upper East Side private school. She ended the monologue with, "And you wouldn't believe the cafeteria, they've got arugula!"

The call left me with zero desire to phone my mother. Or Gregory. Or anyone. I went into the bedroom instead, stripped off my clothes and climbed into bed for a nap. The sheet and quilt were a crisp white, the walls the same shell pink—though with the gray light seeping through the windows they looked more like Pepto-Bismol. I tossed and turned in my sheets, anxious and unable to nap. What if he never called? What if—

My phone rang again. This time it was the right ring tone—Right Said Fred's "I'm Too Sexy." The song was about vanity and perfectly suited Gregory. I scrambled back into the living room and breathlessly answered. "Hi! Oh, honey, I was just about to call you!"

"Please hold for Mr. Curtis," Gregory's secretary said.

"Oh."

So I waited, listening to the Muzak version of Elton John's

"Rocket Man." Thank God Gregory had come to his senses, at least. It would've been nice if he had the energy to dial himself, but so what? Now I could cut short my not-quite-a-vacation in Maine and go back to the apartment in Tribeca. And Mrs. Dale isn't really that bad. I'm sure I could get her to call the show *Friends.* That'd be my goal for the year— not my own classroom, just convincing her that saying *Buddies* wasn't cute.

Gregory's voice came on the line. "Get the Dortmunder file," he said.

"What?"

"Over there, on the—*Jesus!* No, the blue one."

"Um, Gregory? Hello?"

"Eve," he said. "Yes? Can this wait?"

"*You* called *me!*"

"Hmm? Oh—what's your address?"

I allowed myself a slow smile of satisfaction. He was going to join me. Just for the weekend, I bet, but still… I rattled off the address Kim gave me. "It's a cottage right on the ocean, I mean *right* on the water, and there's this pretty little village, close enough we can walk there in the morning, with a great little French patisserie, and Portland's just a ferry ride away, and— Oh! The clouds just passed and the sun's shining into the bedroom, and it's like this wonderful, heavenly pink, and there's a big, big comfy bed, and we can laze around—I mean afterward—and really talk, and we'll figure how we can spend more time together and—"

"Eve. Eve!"

"It's okay, Gregory. I know you don't really think being a teacher is a joke."

"The thing about you, Eve, is that you make everyone smile."

I felt myself blush. "That's the sweetest thing you've ever said."

"But I don't care if people are smiling," he continued. "I'm not at that stage in my life where I need to care about people's feelings. I'll have my assistant send you all your stuff from the apartment."

"My stuff? You're breaking up with me?"

"—having compliance issues with Kitchener," a man's scratchy voice said, on our line. "Take the contract to the twenty-second floor and—"

"Gregory?"

"Here. I—where was I?"

"You're breaking up with me."

"Right. Sorry to be doing this on the phone, Eve, but I'm swamped with meetings. I'll have the—"

"—tax-base sharing among municipalities," the scratchy voice said, "to deter job piracy and other tax-base competition—"

And it hit me: "You have me on *speakerphone?*"

"My earpiece is broken," Gregory said. "I'll always think of you as—"

"Someone you broke up with on speakerphone."

"Well, that, too. Anyway, about my key. Could you—"

I told him where I'd stick his key and threw my cell across the room.

The deep thrum of the ferry engine abruptly stopped, leaving a sudden stillness as the boat docked in Portland. Natasha tossed her empty coffee cup into the trash and stood, then grabbed at the tabletop as the ferry swayed underfoot. She went downstairs, wound through the cars jammed together and into Marco's truck, then drove out to the street.

Most of the veggie deliveries were to Old Port, where the best restaurants prided themselves on using local organic ingredients, but there were a few in Greater Portland, too. She did those, first, then drove back. They supported local agriculture, why not local art? And even when they *did* have local art, it was always like her surf 'n' turf—the "fast food" of art. They wanted only the finest tomatoes, but the art on the walls was watery, mealy and insipid.

The truck rattled as she drove onto the cobblestoned road toward Amelia's—the restaurant that Marco said liked their walls bare—and her cell rang. "Yeah?" she answered.

"He dumped me."

"Eve? What? Gregory?"

"He dumped me. On speakerphone. Can you believe that? During a meeting. First his *secretary* called, then he put me on speakerphone to dump me."

Natasha ground the gears at a stoplight. "We're going to have to kill him."

"Yeah, but then what?" Eve's voice suddenly cracked. "What am I going to do?"

The light turned green and the person behind Natasha honked. She sped forward and heard some of the boxes shifting in the back of the truck. She hoped the veggies didn't get bruised. If the restaurants complained to Marco, he'd be riding her for weeks.

"Meet me in Portland for dinner," Natasha said.

"No, I mean about my life. My job, my goals, my…everything."

"Well, this is more of a short-term goal. I'll leave Marco's truck in the garage, we'll get trashed and take the ferry home."

"Oh. Yeah. That works."

"We'll meet at Miri's. On Commercial Street."

"Um, I don't even know how to catch the ferry here, Natasha."

"I'll call Kim. She'll pick you up at your cottage. She never drinks much, she can drive us home."

"He broke up with me on fucking *speakerphone!*" Eve said.

"Wait till tonight," Natasha said. "And remember to bring his office fax number."

That got a giggle from Eve, and Natasha smiled as they hung up. Eve just wasn't constitutionally capable of moping, not for long. Natasha parked in the alley behind Amelia's, next to a white cargo van. She grabbed a crate and started toward the kitchen doors as a man came out of the cargo van carrying a large canvas.

"Coming through!" he said, from behind the canvas. "You mind if I cut in line?"

She held the door open with her foot, eyeing the red-lacquered canvas. "Anything for art."

The man laughed. "I wish more people felt that way."

His face was hidden, but she didn't need to see him to know who he was. Last year, she'd enrolled in a life-drawing class at the Maine College of Art—not for the lessons, but for access to a live model. Painting herself in the mirror only went so far, and Kim was too busy to pose for her—and too skinny, too. She liked models with weight and contour. Most of the other students were hobbyists, but the teacher was serious and professional. Educated at Columbia, and connected to the New York art scene, he was someone with grander dreams than selling watercolors at a craft fair. He and Natasha often stayed after class, talking about their work, their goals, art in general. He'd treated her like some of her college teachers had, as if she was going somewhere—somewhere other than Broome Isle.

Natasha watched him disappear toward the front of the restaurant, then she put the crate on the counter while the burly guy in the chef's hat prodded the veggies until he finally nodded in satisfaction. God, he was worse than Kim.

She took the check and, cursing herself for wearing a paint-splattered tank top and fraying yoga pants, wandered to the front of the restaurant.

The artist—Brett—had just finished hanging the red-lacquered painting when he saw her. "Natasha!"

"Hey, Brett."

"What're you doing here? Was that you with the produce?"

"My brother's a farmer. I'm helping him deliver." She bit her lip while eyeing the painting. "You're showing here?"

He smiled and ran his fingers through his dirty-blond hair. "For six months. We'll see if anything sells...."

So the restaurant that refused her stuff, accepted his. "No, that's great, Brett. Congratulations."

He shrugged, his smile turning abashed. "Eh, it's just a restaurant. Still, I like the paintings to get some fresh air, stretch their legs and see the world."

"Yeah, they should try the tiramisu—I hear it's fantastic."

"So?" he said.

She considered pretending she didn't understand, but that'd never fly so she turned to inspect the painting more closely. Not very good, but striking and inoffensive. Brett was a better teacher than artist. Tall and rangy, dressed in jeans and a gray T-shirt that made his eyes appear bluer than they were—he looked better than the painting.

"It's good. Vibrant. Almost architectural, you know... weighty. I like it."

"Yeah, I can tell by your sneer," Brett said.

"I'm not sneering, I—" She stopped when she saw his grin, and remembered why she'd liked him. "You asshole."

"At least I'm not a terrible liar. Tell me the truth. You think it's weak."

"Well, I think it'll sell..."

"But?"

She shrugged. "Not your best."

"Yeah." He sighed. "I'm just ready for something to sell, you know? And I don't have your talent, I know that."

"Oh, I'm a genius," she said.

"No, I'm serious. Where're you showing these days? New York?"

Natasha's eye began to twitch. She'd forgotten she'd told him she was going to send slides to galleries and reps in New York. Still on her "to do" list. "Close. Broome Isle."

He laughed, then sobered when he saw she was serious. "Really?"

"A gift shop with a big whale out front."

"Wow. So we're both totally pathetic."

"Please. A restaurant would be a step up for me." But she felt better. It was good just talking with someone who understood. She missed her chats with Brett. It'd been a relief to find someone else with artistic dilemmas, to know she wasn't the only one struggling to make it work.

"Pathetic," she repeated. "We must be...artists." Then she noticed the ring on his left hand. "Is that a wedding ring?"

"Oh, yeah! I got married."

Natasha gaped. "Wow. Congratulations."

"You've actually met her. Remember Verena?"

"The *model?* You married the 'Swiss sexpot'?" His words, not hers. Most of the models were average-looking, but Verena looked like a WWII pin-up, with her gorgeous breasts and hips, and Brett and Natasha used to sigh over her, he in lust and she in jealousy, after class.

"How else would I know she was a sexpot?"

"Wow. That's...I mean...y'know."

"We should get together, the three of us, talk about art. Or the four of us, if you're seeing someone?"

"No, I..." For some reason, she blushed, and then hated herself for it. "Not right now."

"Well, give us a ring, we'll—"

The burly guy in the chef's hat poked his head from the kitchen. "Your pickup's blocking the door."

Natasha almost kissed him for giving her an escape route. She apologized to Brett and fled to the safety of the truck. She stopped at the light on Exchange Street and stared at the traffic, then remembered she still had a half-dozen deliveries. But when the light turned, she pulled to the curb and dialed Kim.

"He *married* her," she said, when Kim answered.

"Who? What?"

"I mean, he dumped her. On speakerphone."

"Well, which is it? Did he marry her or dump her?"

Natasha could hear a knife *clop-clopping* in the background. "Dumped her."

"And, um, who are we talking about?"

"Eve," she said firmly. "Gregory dumped her, and we're meeting in Old Port to drink away her sorrows."

"Am I invited?"

Natasha smiled. "I told her you'd pick her up. I'm already here. I'll meet you at Miri's at seven."

"Ooh. Margaritas."

"What's our game plan?" Natasha asked.

"You need pointers on drinking? Oh, about Eve? I hardly know her."

"I know, but do we tell her Gregory's an ass and she's lucky, or just keep handing her the tissues?"

"Mmm. Well, if it were *you*—"

"You'd just tell me he was an asshole."

"No, you, I'd push the tissues. Eve, on the other hand, can have a few margaritas and *then* the 'you're better off' talk."

"What? But I'm way tougher than Eve."

"Uh-huh. Sure you are."

"Hey. You hardly know her!"

Kim laughed. "So we'll see you at seven."

"Yeah. And, um…" She didn't know how to ask, because while she and Kim had basically shared a closet growing up, there had been no outfit pooling since the divorce. "It's just I've been delivering lettuce all afternoon and I'm—"

Of course she didn't have to explain. "I'll bring you something to wear," Kim said.

Natasha smiled. It'd been a while since they were that close. She hadn't realized how much she missed it. "Thanks."

"And then we'll discuss who got married," Kim said, and hung up.

That part, Natasha didn't miss.

★ ★ ★

Kim finished chopping the heirloom tomatoes and added them to the whole garlic cloves, fresh basil and oregano that were already sautéing in olive oil in the big cast-iron pot, the one Marco had called her "cauldron." Kim would let the sauce simmer, then crush the garlic cloves, remove the pan from the heat and allow the sauce to stew overnight. *Give your sauces a night's sleep before canning,* her grandmother had said. *And when you wake 'em in the winter they'll be fresh as the dawn.*

If she had a commercial cooking license, this would no doubt violate it, but this batch wasn't for sale. This was for herself, and the next for Natasha and Mar—er, anyone Natasha cared to share hers with.

Kim stirred the sauce, waiting for it to thicken. She tossed in some sea salt and ground pepper, thinking about tonight. It'd been a long time since she'd had a night out with friends. She took off her apron, washed her hands and went upstairs to find an outfit for Natasha. She rifled through her closet, remembering the clothes they'd shared. The beaded mini-skirt, the leather bomber jacket and the pashmina Natasha spilled ink on. Kim smiled, remembering Natasha showing her how to wear the pashmina so the stain didn't show and insisting it looked better that way. There had also been the hundred dollar Earl Jeans, spent when everyone else was wearing Gap. A hundred dollars for designer denim seemed like a bargain now.

Kim dug in her dresser until she found the Earls in the bottom drawer, smelling like cedar. They were skinny and retro and back in style, and since Natasha was on her "no kitchen" diet, she'd easily slide into them. But what would work on top? Natasha rarely cared about what she was wearing, but tonight was different. *He married her.* Hmm. She flipped through the blouses until she reached the olive-green silk with rushed sleeves and velvet detailing. She'd fallen in love with the dramatic styling, but the color made her look consumptive. Besides, she wore black 365 days a year—at least everyone thought she did. In reality it was more like 300. The blouse would suit Natasha's alabaster skin and flaming-red hair, perfectly, though.

The early September warmth would turn cool in ten or twelve days, but the nights were still pleasant, so she chose a midnight-blue knit dress she'd had no excuse to wear this summer—tight-fitted, with a sheer section across her cleavage. She slipped into it and stood in front of the silvery old mirror. Not bad. She was too tall, and had no hips, and her nose was too big for her little face, and her hair was always cut too short. But still, not bad.

She turned to the side and ran her hand over her belly, then shook her head. *Forget that, for one night.* She put a browny-peach lipstick in her bag for Natasha, and headed out the door.

✴ 6 ✴

I was waiting on the porch when Kim rattled down the drive in an old Subaru wagon, which for some reason surprised me. I guess I was expecting something flashier—at least a Mini Cooper. I couldn't figure her out. She was a crunchy home-cooked witch who dressed in urban chic. But maybe Subaru wagons had a secret side. What did I know about cars? I grew up in New York. When I wanted to get my license, my mom shot me a horrified look and said, "Where would you want to drive to?" I'd shrugged instead of saying *some place where you're not.*

Kim stepped out of the car looking less witchy and more Audrey Hepburn with short hair. Like she lived on the Upper East Side, not the east side of Broome Isle. I self-consciously smoothed my dress over my ridiculous hips, and wished my cleavage wasn't deep enough to echo. I wiggled my toes in Natasha's flip-flops and noticed my pedicure was flaking. Great. Dumped by my boyfriend on speakerphone, and out-styled by a Maine girl.

"I think I'll change my shoes," I said as Kim came onto the porch. "I'd change the dress, but I've got nothing else."

"Are you kidding? I love your dress." She ran a finger along the skirt, feeling the fabric. "Is it Prada, Gucci?"

I smiled. "Ann Taylor. Three years ago."

"No way!"

"Way," I said, feeling slightly better.

"And don't change your shoes. You look perfect."

Hmm. Why couldn't Kim be my boyfriend instead of Gregory? Oh, that's right, he's not.

This time, I didn't play *Titanic* on the ferry, so no blankets were lost.

Instead, Kim and I sat upstairs, at a little table partially protected from the whipping ocean wind. We talked about Natasha mostly, how we'd met her and outrageous things she'd done. In fifteen minutes, I felt as if I'd known Kim forever—until I said something about them being sisters-in-law, or ex-sisters-in-law. She immediately turned silent and motionless.

"Oh," I said. "I'm sorry, I didn't mean—"

"It's not you. The divorce is still a sore spot." She smiled sadly. "Sometimes I have a hard time letting go of the past."

"Not me," I told her. "All I have a hard time letting go of is Twix bars."

She laughed and finished her story about Natasha sneaking into school on a weekend and painting a row of lockers to look like prison bars. "But of course, she'd never do that *now,*" she finished as the ferry jolted beneath us, docking.

"No," I agreed solemnly. "She's far too mature to—"

We caught sight of Natasha on the dock, wearing a ragged white ribbed tank that looked like she cleaned her brushes with it, and black yoga pants with holes in the knees. Black Converse high-tops completed the ensemble. She was talking with two high school skateboard boys who were clearly enraptured with her, and looking at a notebook one of them carried.

We were still laughing when we stepped off the ferry.

"Gotta go," she told the kids, then cocked her head at us. "What?"

"You," I said.

"They're working on a graphic novel. It's not half bad."

"I thought we were meeting at Miri's," Kim said.

Natasha shrugged. "I couldn't—"

"Wait to change clothes?" Kim said, handing her a pair of dark-washed jeans and an olive-green top.

"That's not like you," I said. Natasha never cared about what she was wearing.

"I'll be two minutes." She raced into the parking garage bathroom.

While we waited, the skateboard kids clattered over the stairs—I think they were showing off for us, actually, which was pretty sweet. And Kim may be model-tall and elegant, but *I'm* the one teenage boys ogle!

Then Natasha reappeared. At first I didn't recognize her—she was aglow with glamour. She always wore her hair—her crowning glory—in a ponytail. This was the first time I'd seen it down in years. It was shorter than I imagined, falling just above her shoulders and framing her face in sexy red waves. The blouse set off her fair skin and blue eyes and the dark denims hugged her slim hips. I hadn't had hips like that since…since ever.

She fidgeted when she realized we were staring. "What?"

"When did you cut your hair?" Kim asked, frowning slightly.

"Just now."

I shook my head. "What do you mean, just now?"

"Just now," Natasha said. "In the bathroom."

"You have scissors?" Kim asked, as I gaped.

Natasha pulled a pocket knife from her bag. "I just kinda hacked away. It's not that bad, is it?"

I made her turn around so I could fix the back, but she'd done a remarkably good job. It was the artist in her, I supposed.

"What did you do with the hair?" Kim asked.

"It's in my bag," Natasha said.

"Sure," I said, "that's not creepy at all."

"I might do art with it."

"Even better," I said. "*God,* you look good, though."

"Thanks." Natasha fingered the top. "Where did you find this?" she asked Kim.

"Oh, one of my shopping trips. Keep it. On me, it looks like something that should be worn in an open casket."

"Cool." Natasha flapped her high-tops. "But you forgot shoes."

"Never borrow another woman's shoes. You know that."

"Why?" I asked. "'Cause if you ruin them, she'll hate you forever?"

"Wear another woman's shoes and you risk acting like her. The last thing I want is Natasha acting like me. Besides—" she pointed to the high-tops "—those are perfect."

They were perfect, because they were Natasha.

★ ★ ★

Low velvet banquettes lined the walls at Miri's and the bar in the center was the color of ripe strawberries. The place looked a bit like an over-twenty-one Starbucks that sold alcohol instead of coffee. Sort of Bohemian-franchise. Still, there was something comforting about the warm colors and subdued lighting from the candlelit lanterns, and we settled happily into a corner table.

Natasha ordered three margaritas, telling me it was the only decent drink they made, and asked the waitress to bring the dinner menu. I glanced at Kim—I couldn't imagine her eating anything she hadn't made herself, but she was busily looking around. About half the tables were full, most of them with small groups—only one couple in the whole place, which was a blessing.

The waitress returned with our drinks and said, "Those guys, at the table by the door? They'd like to pay for this round."

We played it very cool by all turning immediately to gape at them. Late twenties, wearing Banana Republic and trying to appear nonchalant.

"Do men still *do* that?" Natasha asked.

"Maybe in Maine," I said.

She frowned. "If we take the drinks do we have to sleep with them?"

"Depends on the drink," I told her. "For a margarita, you just have to dance. But if they buy us mojitos, we're talking a hand job." She looked so stricken, I couldn't keep a straight face. "I'm kidding! When was the last time you dated?"

Natasha blushed as only a redhead can, and for once was at a loss for words.

"We'll get to that," Kim said, and told the waitress to thank the nice gentlemen and bring us the white bean dip to start.

We lifted our glasses, and I said, "I have nothing to toast."

"Me, neither," Natasha said.

"To Wednesday?" Kim suggested.

"But it's Tuesday," Natasha said.

Kim smiled. "And tomorrow will be a better day."

We laughed and clinked drinks. "To Wednesday!" I said.

"To Wednesday," they repeated.

And I guessed someone's alcohol dripped into the lantern on the table, because the candle flame suddenly licked the sides of the votive and spewed out the top. Kim reached for the suddenly blazing flame and yelped as she burned her fingers. I leaned forward to blow out the candle and the fire died at my first puff. My body tingled, as if I'd already downed my margarita, but I hadn't taken a single sip.

"That was weird," Natasha said.

"Yeah," I said, shivering. Could the candle have stored up an electrical charge?

Kim frowned, examining her fingers.

"Is the burn bad?" Natasha asked.

"No. It felt so hot, but…there's nothing. No, wait…" She stared into space a moment. "Someone's coming."

Wow, she really took this witch thing seriously. I know her ancestor was supposed to have been hung and all, but did she really believe she could foretell things?

The waitress appeared. "Here's your dip."

I couldn't help myself. I snickered. "I guess someone *was* coming."

"With freshly cooked food!" Natasha said. She was getting tired of her no-kitchen diet.

We all took big slugs of our margaritas and ordered dinner. Then Natasha grabbed a slice of pita, slathered it with white bean dip, and held it like a pointer. "Now. Eve. Go."

I told them how Gregory and I met in a bar, that I thought it was probably a one-night stand, but he'd called the next day. "I couldn't believe someone so successful was interested in me. I guess that was the problem. He was definitely out of my league."

"The assholes have their own league now?" Natasha said, stuffing herself with white bean dip while doodling on a napkin.

"*Natasha*," Kim said.

"I never liked him," she answered unapologetically.

"You never met him," I said.

"I didn't have to. You told me all I needed to know. Like, didn't he make you get a permission slip before finishing anything in the fridge?"

"What?" Kim asked. "Why?"

"He yelled at me once for eating a piece of sushi that had been sitting in there for days. Said he was saving it. I didn't have to get a permission slip, it just…seemed easier to ask than get yelled at again."

Kim made a disgusted face.

"*And* he dumped you via speakerphone," Natasha said.

"Okay, so he's an asshole," I wailed. I shoved a pita into my mouth, to keep from crying.

"He's obviously not worth crying over," Kim said.

"But you don't understand. Neither of you does. Dating is different in New York. Trying to find a halfway decent man who—"

"Ha!" Natasha said, and tossed her napkin to me. "He's not even *halfway* decent now!"

On the napkin was a rough sketch of a naked man—exactly how I had described Gregory to Natasha—in a fancy office…

"What's he doing?" I asked.

"Humping himself in the mirror," Kim said, looking over my shoulder. "Because that's the only person he really loves."

The waitress appeared with another tray of margaritas. "You'll need a team name," she told us.

"Um—what?"

"A team name, for the contest."

"What contest?" I asked.

"The trivia contest," the waitress said. "Tuesday night is trivia night. I thought you were a team."

Natasha shook her head. "No, we—"

"What kind of trivia?" I asked.

"All kinds. The topics change each week. Last week was, um, Pulp Fiction, the Solar System and the Patriots."

"The Patriots? Like Paul Revere?"

"The New England Patriots. Like football."

"Okay," I said. "No way."

"I suck at trivia." Natasha licked salt from the rim of her glass. "Which is ironic, considering."

"It gets pretty rowdy," the waitress said. "If you're not playing, I doubt you'll want to stay. Want me to cancel your dinner order?"

"We'll play," Kim told her.

"What? No we won't." Natasha looked toward me to back her up. "We'll get slaughtered."

"Yeah, that's all I need today."

"What are the other team names?" Kim asked.

"The Three Amigos, Barking Monkey, the Spitballers…" The waitress looked embarrassed. "The Sperminators."

"Who are they?"

"The guys who bought you drinks."

"Wow," Natasha said. "Classy."

"And you thought I was kidding about the hand jobs."

"So what should we be?" Kim asked.

"The Speakerphones," Natasha said. "The Spinsters."

"How about the Wednesdays?" Kim said.

I glanced at her. "The Witches?"

"The Wednesday Night Witches," she said.

"Um, it's Tuesday," the waitress said.

"Only until midnight," Kim said.

"Whatever." The waitress added our name to the list. "But watch out. These guys are serious."

"We're doomed," Natasha said as the contest began and the first category was announced.

"No way." I laughed, feeling a little less gloomy. "I know this! Although, yes, I probably am doomed in real life."

"What are you going to do?" Kim asked as our food arrived. "Move back to the city?"

"I don't know," I said, half listening to the first trivia question. The category was *Friends* and the first question was What was the title of Phoebe's sister's porn film? "All my friends have moved and I don't have anywhere to live but my *mom's* apartment. And—" I rang the little bell the waitress left on their table, to show that I had the answer. *"Buffy the Vampire Layer,"* I called, before continuing. "I really thought Gregory might work out. I mean, I know he's kind of…self-involved, but—"

"Correct," the emcee said. "One point to the Wednesday Night Witches."

"I don't see what the problem is," Natasha said. "You've got a job here—you can live in Kim's cottage and teach at the elementary school."

"What short-lived comedy did the actress who played Ross's sister star in?" the emcee asked.

"The Single Guy," I called, after ringing the bell. "Really? You think I should just move here?"

"I think you already have," Kim said.

"I don't know. Live in Maine? On an island?" I considered the idea. "Sounds kinda romantic, actually."

"Wait till winter," Natasha said. "But yeah, you should stay."

The emcee called out the next question. "*Friends* first aired in what year?"

Ding. "In 1994," I answered in triumph. "Is it me, or are these getting easier?"

"All right, I'm officially weirded out that you knew all that," Natasha said.

"I have a deep professional interest in the show, that's all."

"That's the end of round one," the emcee said. "Wednesday Night Witches in the lead. The topic of round two… Eighteenth-Century Art."

Natasha laughed, her fiery hair falling across her wild eyes. "We might actually win. This is better than sex," she crowed.

"We-ell…" I shared a smile with Kim. Considering how artistically worldly she was, Natasha could be so naive sometimes. Although, she did know her eighteenth-century art. She didn't have my hinky command of *Friends,* but she ruled the category—so much so, the emcee gave her a nickname. Scarlet Witch.

"Favorite artist of Madame de Pompadour?" the emcee asked, and looked at Natasha. "Scarlet Witch? Any idea?"

"Madame Pompadour," I said. "Was that museum named after her?"

"That's the hairstyle," Kim said. "The museum is the Pompidou."

"Shh," said Natasha, her hand hovering over the bell. "I know this. Who was—oh!" *Ding-ding.* "Boucher!"

"Another point to the Witches," the emcee said.

Kim set down her almost-empty margarita glass and said, "Who got married?"

"Nobody got married," I said. "I got dumped."

"Name the English artist," the emcee said, "who, after serving in the British navy…"

"When she called me, Natasha said, 'He got married,'" Kim explained. "She blurted that out first."

"…became one of William Blake's followers known as the Ancients."

Ding-ding. "I—I—" Natasha was so rattled she forgot the answer. "I don't know."

One of the Sperminators chimed in with "Calvert." Natasha gave them a look of respect, like maybe they weren't that bad after all. Then she turned to Kim, who was clearly waiting for an answer. She stopped focusing on the art questions, and told us about taking the figure-drawing class with Brett. "And…well, we'd stay after class to talk. We agreed on art and on—everything, really. He's a great guy, he's funny and sensitive and smart. You know, we artists can be moody and self-involved and take ourselves too seriously—"

"No!" I said, pretending shock.

Natasha snorted. "But Brett seemed to lack the narcissism.

And we liked the same artists and we were both at the same sorta place, you know? And he seemed to like…me."

"So one night after class…" I said knowingly.

"Yeah."

"And?"

Natasha polished off her drink. "I don't know. I guess I was out of practice."

"The first time with someone new can be awkward," I said. "What about the next time?"

"Um. There wasn't one."

"He never called?" Kim said.

"He called."

"But?"

"I never answered." Natasha paused long enough to shout "Charles Willson Peale," to some question about George Washington's portraits and dentures. "And I was too embarrassed to go back to class."

"So you haven't even spoken with him since you slept together?" Kim asked.

Natasha shook her head. "I missed the last two classes. What a waste of a perfectly good model."

"How bad was the sex, exactly?" I asked. "Did he…want you to wear a Nixon mask or something?"

"No, he was perfectly…ordinary." Natasha sighed. "But shouldn't you like to have sex with guys you like?"

"I think so," Kim said.

"He's just not your type," I said.

"Maybe they're all not my type," Natasha muttered.

"Next category," the emcee called. "'Great Moments in Golf.'"

Natasha turned from Kim to me; both of us looked completely blank. So she ordered another round and made us drink every time we couldn't answer. Soon, I was shouting "Tiger Woods" after every question, and even Kim was giggling helplessly for no real reason.

We only got one question right—"Which golfer demonstrated his skill on the Mike Douglas show as a child?" "Tiger Woods!"—but the Three Amigos and the Sperminators split the rest of the category, so the Wednesday Night Witches won the game. For a prize, we drank for free that night…and we stumbled outside, weightless and glowing, and overflowing with delight.

I lay in bed in my little seashell cottage, staring at the ceiling, unable to close my eyes without the room spinning. Gregory had dumped me, and now Mrs. Dale had left a message saying if I wasn't back at work in two days I was fired.

Looked like I was moving to Maine.

I spread my arms and closed my eyes and pretended I was flying. How did that feel, moving to Maine? Not bad. Not after tonight. Natasha was my best friend, and Kim…we'd really bonded. The three of us had a sort of chemical reaction when we were together. I was becoming more intrigued about Kim's witchy ancestors, too. There was something almost magical about the three of us together. I didn't usually believe in that stuff—psychics, vampires, werewolves, warlocks. Sure, I loved to fantasize about it, but believe in it? Not really. Still, there had been that odd thing with the candle tonight at Miri's. It'd be kind of cool to have some real magical powers, like turning invisible, or always knowing how to order the best thing on the menu.

I got dizzy and opened my eyes. I bet Mrs. Dale couldn't

have answered all those *Buddies* questions. Maybe when I called to quit, I'd tell her to call the damn show by the right name. And that I was going to be a better first-grade teacher than she'd ever be.

Then I'd put a hex on her. Yeah, I'd like being a witch.

Across the island, Natasha stood in front of her parents' vintage stereo, having put on one of their old Van Morrison records. She loved the sound of the needle crackling as the turntable spun.

She danced across the floor, reveling in their trivia contest win. Victory! Natasha had almost forgotten the feeling, it was a rush and a blast. Success, even at a silly trivia game, had felt so damn good.

Thing is, she'd always felt she was missing something, some ingredient that everyone else had. Since she was a kid, she suspected she wasn't like other people, she wasn't meant to fly. She was destined to stay earthbound, rooting around in the mud. She talked to other artists, because if she knew one thing about herself, it was that she was an artist—and yeah, they all felt different, which at first she thought was the answer. But turned out they felt they had an *extra* something, not a *missing* something, which just made her feel worse.

Still, she kept trying, she kept trudging along, even though she sometimes forgot what she was heading for—forgot what success was. So yes, it was a silly game. But they'd kicked ass!

She crossed to her armchair, listening to the melody play on the old stereo, as she eyed her big painting. *Lost Hope. Last Hope.* Which one was it?

People talked about the "aura" of famous and well-loved

paintings, the weight of millions of adoring eyes that somehow adhered to the surface of the paint. The *Mona Lisa,* no
great work of color or composition, somehow *made* great
by centuries of adulation. And this painting of hers…well,
without fame and adoration, without even being finished,
she could feel its aura.

Natasha hadn't decided whether it was *Lost Hope* or *Last
Hope,* because she didn't know whether this painting was her
last hope for success, or a material manifestation that she'd
lost hope in her future as an artist. She hunched in the chair,
and shoved her hands in the pocket of her jeans. She found
the scrunched-up napkin with the sketch of a naked Gregory in his office and tossed it into the wastebasket, shaking
her head. Eve had recovered from her disappointment in
about two hours, while Natasha was still mooning over Brett.
Eve was so resilient. Probably came from being so damned
bouncy.

Bouncy and curvy and…*succulent.* It was ridiculous how the
men in the bar couldn't stop looking at her. Wasn't only her
looks, either—Eve just seemed so ripe for pleasure. Natasha
didn't even know if Eve understood that sex could be awkward and uncomfortable and entirely…nothing. And Kim always smiled her secret little smile when they talked about sex,
probably thinking about Marco, which was even worse.

Did *everyone* like sex more than she did?

Nah—she'd just sublimated all that passion into her art,
that's all. She stood back from the chair, took three paintings
from the rack, propped them against the wall and paced.

Kim lay awake in bed, her head where her feet should be,
rubbing one bare foot against the antique wooden head-

board—the only antique that wasn't a family heirloom. She'd bought the headboard with Marco, during their honeymoon in Vermont, and it was the one thing of his that remained in the house.

Kim had watched Eve tonight, struck by her transparency and exuberance. She was so vulnerable, so open. Even her life was at a turning point, everything new, without encumbrances or the weight of the past. Kim worried for her, not wanting to see that spark start to dim—but also envied her.

Her own life wasn't so open or unencumbered. Even her jobs were as constant as the seasons. She rented cottages in summer, baked and canned in the fall. Winter was for making tinctures (lavender water and such), and spring for planting and preparation. She went to bed at ten o'clock every night and woke at six every morning. She loved her house with a thoughtless devotion, but sometimes she felt she was just the latest incarnation of the same Gray women the house had been extruding for generations.

Except, the others all had children. Kim sometimes worried the line of witches would die out with her.

She needed a spark in her life. The candle at Miri's tonight had been a spark, a sign, somehow, but she didn't know of what. While she knew she liked her routine, perhaps she'd become too rigid about having the same coffee in the same mug ever morning and the same two shortbread cookies every afternoon. She'd been worse since leaving Marco; the sameness had been a way to deal with the grief. But four years had passed, it was time to let go.

Maybe she'd move. Off the island. Away from Marco.

She laughed to herself. Impossible. Well, maybe tomorrow

she'd have chocolate chips in her shortbread. That, she could handle.

She traced one of the carved wooden ornaments on the old honeymoon bed frame with her big toe, over and over, saying with each loop, "I miss him. I miss him. I miss him."

⟡ 7 ⟡

School started in two days; by then my hangover would be gone. Probably. Anyway, I called Dr. Pepper—I mean Epper—and he was serious. I had a job. Not only a job, but my own classroom. Which was a good thing, because I still didn't have much else: like anything to wear except a black cocktail dress and the sweats Natasha lent me. Or a ride that didn't have a banana seat.

Or what I really needed: a highly caffeinated beverage. I closed my cell phone, tamed my hair and stepped onto the porch. Chilly this morning, though I soon warmed up riding to the bakery, down the long bumpy seaside road....

The bell jingled as I stepped inside, taking in the scent of rising bread and fresh-baked molasses cookies. The few customers I'd met there before smiled at me, and the woman who worked there sang out, "Started your latte when I saw you coming!" before I'd even taken a seat at the counter.

"I hear you're the new teacher," the man at the next stool said.

"First grade," I told him, after I took a bite of the raspberry coffee cake the woman set before me. "I start in two days."

"Well, you'll be teaching the twins, then." He grinned at me, and I was suddenly struck by how handsome he was. How come Natasha had never mentioned what cute guys there were around here? "Good luck."

"You—um—have twins?" The "um" was because I'd noticed he wasn't wearing a wedding ring.

"They're my nephews. Have you seen any of the *Chucky* movies? Imagine two of him, egging each other on."

I laughed. "They can't be that bad."

"Just wait," he said, and smiled as he offered his hand. "I'm Frank McKerney."

"*Sheriff* McKerney," the woman at the counter said. "And yes, sole heir to the McKerney fortune."

"The what?" I said.

"I'll tell you over dinner," Frank McKerney said. "If you'll let me fly us down to New York tonight."

I gaped, and found myself still riding down the long bumpy seaside road. Right. Daydream. But what a lovely one. Still, at least the bakery was real.

I propped the banana-seat bicycle against the brick wall of the place and pushed on the front door, painted a rich aubergine. Forget the coffee cake, I'd have a chocolate croissant. But the door didn't budge. And, um, the lights were out.

I read the sign on the front door.

Thanks for another wonderful season!
See you next May. Stay warm this winter!
—The Reed Family—

Closed? It was only September 3! I was stuck on an island with no *pain au chocolate* until May? "No latte!" I squeaked.

My heart clenched and the world swayed. An island in Maine? What was I thinking? There wasn't a single movie theater. Not a single Starbucks (forget one on every other block). Hell, there wasn't a single taxi. I couldn't live here, I was a city girl. Here's what they don't tell you about fish out of water: they die.

When I stopped hyperventilating I remembered the General Store on the other side of the island. I checked my watch. Eight-fifteen. All I had to do today was prepare my classroom for this afternoon's open house at two o'clock—well, that and figure out how I was going to teach my first-grade class without a lesson plan. But I'd handle that a lot better if I had some caffeine in my system. Plus, the General Store was only a mile away, and probably all the regulars who weren't at the bakery were waiting for me there.

I rode past a sprawling old shack, looking for the General Store. Then I headed back the way I'd come. Then I turned around again. And, finally, I stopped at the old shack. I'd heard Natasha and Kim mention the General Store a couple of times, and the fondness in their tone led me to expect something…charming. Not a big shack with a sign reading:

Smelts
Crawlers
Cheese

What were "smelts"? The "crawlers" made me think it had something to do with fishing, but the "cheese" threw me.

And made me wonder, do fish have a sense of smell? I'd have to look it up. Seemed the kind of thing a first-grade teacher should know.

One thing was certain, the store was open. Doubtful they'd have a croissant, but a fresh doughnut would do. Inside, the floors were yellow linoleum, the shelves of canned goods were metal and crammed full. There was a dinette counter in the far corner, barely visible down the narrow rows, where a few geezers sat muttering over breakfast. Behind the counter a skinny middle-aged woman cooked something dubious at an old electric stove, but the place smelled pleasantly of bacon, and against the back wall I saw the Holy Grail: a small espresso machine, the kind sold in Williams-Sonoma catalogs for home use. So a latte wasn't out of the question.

I smiled at the old coots and sat at a vinyl stool that had been ripped and repaired with duct tape, and ripped again. The day's offerings were listed on a chalkboard on the wall, white toast chief among them—available with jam or peanut butter or margarine. There were bright red—I mean *bright* red—hot dogs in a steamer, and a sign reading Clam Baskets, with the words crossed out.

I said, "Good morning!"

One of the old coots said, "Colder than a witch's tit."

"Um," I said.

"It's only September. Use the hay bales for banking the house, like I told you," another said, ignoring me. "That'll keep you warm—you and the mice both."

"Do I order here?" I asked the woman.

She ignored me. So did the men, though they fell silent. Which I supposed wasn't totally ignoring me.

"So, you're all from the island?" I asked cheerily.

None of them answered.

"I'm the new teacher at the elementary school."

Still no answer.

"Um…what do you all do?" I knew they were retired, but figured I'd win them over by pretending they looked younger than prehistoric. They didn't look won over, so I continued, "I mean, what do people do on the island?"

"In the summah," one said meditatively, not looking at me, "we fish and we fuck. And in the wintah, we don't fish much."

I ventured a laugh, then immediately became unsure if that was a joke. Or if I was the butt of it. So I stopped laughing and a sort of glutinous silence fell. The woman served scrambled eggs and bacon to one of the men and turned to me.

"I'll have what they're having," I said, not wanting to make waves. "And a latte."

"That was the end of the bacon."

"Just eggs, then," I said.

"And the eggs, too. What was that last thing?"

"A latte?" I said, nodding toward the espresso machine. "Cappuccino, or if you'd just froth some milk, I'll have a café au lait."

"That thing makes coffee?" one of the men asked through a mouthful of egg.

"Not that I know of," the woman said. "Bought it last year for ten dollars from one of the summer people staying at a cottage at Gray Cove. They didn't want to haul it back to New York."

"Gray Cove?" I asked. "Is that one of Kim's cottages? I know Kim. Kim Gray."

"I knew her grandmother," one of the men said.

"We all did," another coot intoned. "As well as you can know Gray womenfolk, at least."

Oh, boy, they didn't actually believe that witch lore, did they? "Well!" I said. "That's where I'm staying, in one of her cottages. Actually, I'm a college friend of Natasha Kent's."

"The artist," one of the coots snorted. "What a waste of time."

"Yeah," I said. "She oughtta be sitting around on her flabby ass, talking about the weath-ah and shoving cholesterol in her pie-hole." It was one thing for them to turn their noses up at me, but I wouldn't stand for them picking on Natasha.

The woman laughed and told me, "Maybe I do have some of that eggs and bacon left. Here's your coffee."

The desultory conversation continued as I ate, but I felt like I was being ignored in a less pointed fashion, so I decided not to push my luck by asking what smelts were. I finished my eggs, left a tip and went outside into a cold drizzle.

I climbed on my banana seat and set off, squinting against the chilly mist. Halfway along the road I came across an old woman. She was stooped and white-haired and leaned a gnarled hand on a gnarled wood cane as she slowly trudged through the rain. I'd never actually seen a crone before, so I'm afraid I stared a little as I slowly passed.

She turned quickly when she heard me—the bicycle screeched a bit. Her eyes, pale blue from cataracts, bore right into me. "You're the one! He's been calling you. Waiting. Waiting!"

Okay, my first thought: Gregory had been phoning the wrong number and got the old crone, instead of me. My second: this is the island crazy lady. Every island's got to have one, right?

"Um. I'll call him, okay?" I squeaked past her. "Tell him to stop calling you."

"He'll never stop," she cried. "I hear him in my dreams." Water dripped in rivulets down her cheeks. I couldn't tell if it was tears or just the rain. One thing was certain, she was soaked through. I vowed to call the police or whatever passed for law enforcement when I got back to town. What if she collapsed out here?

"I'll have someone come for you," I called out to her as I peddled quickly away.

"It's too late for that," she said, and I thought she might be right.

I was soaked by the time I got to school, but at least I wasn't wearing a scarlet letter. I parked the bicycle in the rack, found a pay phone and called the island emergency number. I told the dispatch about the old woman and she said they'd take care of it.

The door to the school was open, as Dr. Pepper told me he'd leave it, and I found my classroom without trouble. My classroom. A small tidy room, with the desks in orderly rows—it looked just like any other classroom, but this one was *mine*. I found an old towel in the storage cupboard and dried my hair while I inspected the room. Maybe a semi-circle would be better than these rows, giving us room to sit on the floor for stories and music. The reality of having my own classroom suddenly hit me. I felt a little dizzy and sat in the chair behind the teacher's desk. I was trained for this, yes, and experienced—but how was I going to fill every single day by myself?

What's the worst that could happen? I flashed on the image of being tied to my chair with jump ropes as fifteen little heathens set fire to the classroom. No. I knew I could do this. I'd been dreaming of this chance and I was going to make the best of it. Maybe I was stuck on an island without Starbucks or pastry or shopping, but that just meant I'd focus all my attention on the classroom. First task: organize the room. I tied my hair in a knot and got to work.

Natasha and Kim showed up an hour before the open house. Natasha was back in her usual Natasha-wear—yoga pants and an oversize, paint-splattered T-shirt—and carried my freshly laundered black dress, the only thing I had to wear, with a plain blue cardigan, so I wouldn't look like I thought the classroom was a nightclub. She also carried a tall thermos of what I hoped was strong coffee. I was starting to fade, and needed to be peppy and bright when the parents came. Kim wore a black T-shirt and long linen skirt, and carried a plate of cookies which she almost dropped stepping into the room.

"Oh, my God!" Natasha said. "I can't believe they left this mess for you."

"Looks like they've been using it for storage all summer," Kim said, clearly dismayed.

Natasha headed for the door. "I'm talking to Dr. Pepper—they can't leave you with a room like this."

"What?" I said. "What's wrong with it?"

"You've got an open house in an hour—this is unacceptable."

"No, I, uh…" I stopped to look over the room with fresh eyes.

I'd dragged half the chairs into a semicircle before getting distracted by a box of illustrated books. They were scattered in the corner now, where I'd left them after practicing reading aloud in theatrical voices. Then I'd found the storage cupboard with the colored tissue paper, and wasted a dozen sheets before deciding I really *didn't* remember how to make tissue flowers. I'd scavenged farther in the cupboard, looking for inspiration for the bulletin boards, and had come across some old Thanksgiving decorations, which I'd tried to modify to look more generically autumnal. In short, I was left standing in rubble.

"It's my mess," I admitted.

Natasha stared at Eve. It was like a tsunami had hit the place. She knew Eve was messy—they'd lived together, but this… Good God, what had she done to the chalkboard? Natasha was going to have to confiscate the colored chalk and make sure Eve was only left with white.

"I hope you're a better teacher than a decorator," Natasha said.

"Oh, God," Eve said, her face an almost comical picture of dismay. "Me, too!"

"We can fix this," Kim said calmly. "How much time have we got?"

They all glanced at the clock over the classroom door. Fifty-three minutes.

"Oh, *no*," Eve wailed.

"You pick up," Kim told her. "Natasha, do the walls and chalkboards and I'll arrange the furniture."

Natasha started with the wall decorations, figuring if she had time she'd create something spectacular with the chalk, but if not, they could always just erase the atrocity Eve had perpetrated.

"Is this supposed to be stained glass?" she asked Eve, removing shredded tissue-paper clumps from the wall.

"Flowers," Eve mumbled.

"Right. Flowers."

"These books all have missing pages," Eve said, stacking them on a shelf. "Do you think I should toss them?"

"Gimme." Natasha grabbed the box of donated books. None of them was stamped school property. "Now, finish picking up."

"Just who's in charge here?" Eve asked.

Natasha looked at her.

"I'll just pick up, shall I?"

Using scissors and paste, illustrations from the salvaged books and Eve's failed flowers, Natasha started weaving together a collage.

When Kim finished straightening the room, organizing the kids' tables and arranging Eve's desk, she was drawn to the collage Natasha was making. She'd always considered Natasha's art just one of those things—not a hobby exactly, but nothing particularly serious. She hadn't taken a close look at any of Natasha's paintings in years. But in thirty minutes, in a first-grade classroom, Natasha effortlessly created a fairy-tale motif, framing book illustrations with fuzzy colored tissue. The pictures trailed in a jagged line around the room. It was absolutely off-the-cuff and frivolous, yet obviously the work of a rare talent.

Kim looked at Natasha, who was brushing the hair out of her face as she finished the collage.

"What?" Natasha said.

"I'd forgotten how amazing you are," Kim said.

"Yeah?"

"What do you mean, 'yeah'?"

Natasha shrugged. "I'm not getting paid to decorate classrooms."

"I'm sorry," Eve said.

"No. I didn't mean it that way. I'm just stuck with my own work. This was fun."

"Here," Kim said. "We can pay you in shortbread. It's chocolate chip."

They finished the room and the shortbread at the same time. Almost two o'clock. An hour earlier than Kim usually had her shortbread—yeah, she was a rebel, all right. Only she wasn't sure she liked the chocolate chips. Maybe next time she'd try lemon. Oh, boy, it had to get better than this.

"There," Natasha said with a flourish. "Beautiful. Now you can stop pacing, Eve."

"Can't," she said. "Drank all the coffee."

"All of it?" Natasha asked. "I made that coffee." Meaning she'd used twice the amount a normal person would.

"Way better than at the General Store," Eve said, buzzing around the room, looking at Natasha's collage. "I like this part." She pointed randomly. "No, this part. This is my favorite. Oh, no, this one. If I'd seen this first, this definitely would've been my favorite. How do you know you could do this? I never would've thought of it. This shortbread is like mana!"

Natasha snorted. "This is reminding me of school when you used to cram for exams."

Kim examined the collage more closely. "I want to live in a picture book."

"Me, too," Natasha said.

"'The Three Little Witches.'" Eve stopped pacing. "As

long as it had a happy ending." She moved to the window. "Ohmigod! Here they come!"

Natasha and Kim vanished as the first student poked his head in the door. Maybe I was crashing from the coffee high, but my energy seemed to desert me when they left. Which was funny, because I was feeling good—proud and excited. The place now looked amazing and I was standing in the middle of my own classroom, watching *my* students file inside, followed by anxious, smiling parents.

Of course, I had no idea what to say. Still, upon seeing the parents' expressions when they looked over the room, my courage returned, and I smiled reassuringly and introduced myself. Then I leaned against my desk and opened my mouth, and this is what came out: "I'll get to school at least half an hour before the first bell, which rings at eight-oh-five, and the kids can either come into the classroom or stay on the playground until the bell. This is also the time when parents can come speak with me informally—if you need to tell me something about your child, a doctor's appointment or an issue at home, or any questions or concerns about homework. After we get settled, we'll do an opening—going over the seasons, say, doing our calendar, practicing counting by tens, fives and twos. We'll also work on threes, but not so early in the day!"

The parents laughed obligingly. Laughs were always a plus when you weren't particularly funny.

"At about eight-forty, we'll start our English section. We'll have two stories per week, and our activities will center around those—then a snack and recess. After we burn off some energy, we'll come back for writing. We'll work on expository paragraphs, fiction, poetry. Then lunch and math. We have a workbook for that, which I have to admit I haven't seen yet, but we'll put our heads down and plow through…because next is our reward. Art! Now, I'm not what you'd call artistically inclined, but local professional artist Natasha Kent will be joining the class periodically—" even if I had to drag her here by her hair "—and then we'll have science, which is always fun—and often messier than art, to tell the truth—and finally social studies. So that's what a typical day will be. But more important—" I smiled, and the parents smiled back "—I'm here for your children, to teach them and listen to them. This is my job, the job I love, and I'm honored to be part of your children's lives. Now. Any questions?"

Nobody asked me if I'd been teaching *Breakfast at Tiffany's,* even though I was still dressed like Holly Golightly, in my black cocktail dress and kitten heels. In fact, they all just seemed to welcome me, as if they were excited to have me. Dr. Pepper had told me the school had a hard time attracting new teachers to the island, and I was beginning to suspect he'd spread word that I was a fancy, big-city educator who'd have the kids winning the regional spelling bee or something.

So, in my cautious and modest way, I lapped up the attention. Maybe the bakery was already closed, maybe my boyfriend dumped me, maybe the only single men on the island were the old coots at the General Store. But I was exactly where I needed to be. This was going to be the best thing that ever happened to me.

⁜ 8 ⁜

"I'm so boooooored," Eve said, lying in the claw-foot tub in the middle of Natasha's living room, wrapped in a down comforter. "God, it's boring here. I'm bored, bored, bored."

Natasha looked up from her sketchbook. "I thought you loved your class."

"Yeah, but *then* what? I still have seven hours a day to kill."

"You've only been here a week, Eve."

Eve moaned. "A week without pastry."

"Three days ago, you said moving here was the best thing ever."

"Three days ago was before the Ice Age."

They'd been meeting every day after school to sit in the Adirondacks, sipping beers and chatting with Marco in his garden. But yesterday, Eve suddenly declared the weather had turned and insisted they hang out inside. And today, she'd wrapped herself in the comforter and climbed into the claw-foot bathtub Natasha had found at an antique shop up the coast.

If only Marco would install it. Natasha sighed. They'd started on the insulation last week, and the kitchen was next—at this rate the tub would still be there next summer. At least there was a silver lining. Seeing Eve lying in the tub, all but her head submerged in the white comforter, had given Natasha an idea for a painting. She sat behind Eve, sketching her—and Puck after he jumped in—making sympathetic noises as she worked.

"It's not that I don't like it here…." Eve said, her hand groping out of the tub for her wineglass on the floor. "It's just the old junker I bought cost too much, and there's no way I have enough sweaters for winter, and…" She sipped. "This is good. Pinot?"

"Cabernet," Natasha said. "On sale at the General Store."

"It's just *that!* There's no other place to buy wine but the General Store. And why doesn't it have a name?"

"What?" Natasha glanced at the label on the wine bottle. "It does. Avilia. Santa Barbara County."

"No, the store. Why can't it be called Marie's, after the owner, or I don't know…the Smelts Shop?"

"The Smelts Shop is a pretty weird name for a general store."

"They sell 'em," Eve said.

"Yeah, but…" Natasha shook her head. "I don't know how to argue with that."

"I can't believe the bakery closed for the season."

"Hmm." Natasha was so used to it, it didn't occur to her to miss it. That was like missing the fall foliage in the winter, or the snow in the summer. Seasons changed, that's what seasons did.

"Or that I'd get sick of the food at the Barnacle," Eve said.

"In a *week?*"

"I'm fickle."

"I never get tired of the clam chowder."

"But don't you ever crave Chinese, or Thai or Indian? Or pizza?"

"You can get all that in Portland," Natasha said, exasperated. She knew what was wrong with the island, she'd lived here practically her whole life. She didn't need Eve to tell her what was wrong.

"But you have to plan it. You can't just call and have it appear at your door in thirty minutes. And you can't just pop out to a movie anytime you want."

"Evie, this isn't New York—it's not even Portland. Surely you noticed. This is Broome Isle. You just have to learn to appreciate what it offers."

Eve drained her wine. "Like what?"

Natasha glanced around the room at her paintings propped up against the walls. They were all painted on Broome Isle, they were all part of Broome Isle. She loved this place. The fields, the sea, the village, the lobstermen. The fresh salt air, the rust-orange and bright yellow creeping across the green trees in the fall, the crunch of snow underfoot, the rocky coastline, the deep cool woods. Yes, the island could feel impossibly remote and crushingly slow in the winter, but it was also warm inside the houses, and Kim would dish up a perfect caramel banana cream pie, and you'd get a hot toddy at the Barnacle, and you could walk the frozen streams winding through the woods, making paths to places you couldn't reach in the summer.

Natasha wasn't sure city-bred Eve could relate to any of that, so she'd have to think of things Eve did love. "Stop wiggling and I'll tell you."

"I'm not wiggling," I said. "I'm just cold. I'm always cold."

"But who cares about the cold when you have your own classroom? And you're free of Mrs. Dale. And you live right on the beach."

Those were good things, but not enough. "Why don't the guys at the Smelts Shop like me?"

"What? They don't like anyone. Why can't you make coffee at home?"

"Because I work with kids all day. I like a little adult inter-action to get my morning going."

"Those aren't adults, Eve. Those are grouchy old trolls."

"Yeah, but they should still like me. God, and that coffee's gonna kill me. Maybe I should just quit and go back to New York."

"Because of bad coffee?"

"Because I'm not cut out for this…aloneness! I stayed late at school last night, and Natasha, Dr. Pepper's starting to look good to me."

She laughed. "So what—you'll go back and live with your mother?"

"People are always looking for roommates." The thought filled me with dread: sharing an apartment with some single woman with *tchotchkes* everywhere, a smelly cat and a shower full of hair and soap scum.

"Eve, you've barely given it a chance. You always wanted

to teach. You told me you were going to be a teacher your first day at NYU. Someone told me the first year teaching on your own is the hardest, until you get into the swing of things."

"I told you that," I grumbled.

"Well, it's probably true, anyway. All you need is a break. We'll go to Portland—all three of us, the Wednesday Night Witches."

"But trivia night is right now. It's Tuesday. And I'm not leaving this tub."

"So we'll be literalists and go tomorrow. You got your clothes, right?"

"Yeah." Gregory's assistant had misaddressed the boxes and they hadn't arrived until this morning. One can only be so creative with a black cocktail dress, kitten heels and Natasha's meager wardrobe. "That's not a bad idea." I scratched my nose, planning what I'd wear. Going out would give me a chance to dress up.

"Stop wiggling!"

"So, um…what are the logistics of hooking up with a guy?"

"In my experience? First you meet him in art class, then you never return his calls."

"I mean, do you go to his place? You can't make him take the ferry out here, can you?"

"Okay," she said, nodding.

"What?"

"Huh?" She looked up from her sketch. "Oh—this sketch. It's not bad. I might do a painting."

I pressed, but she showed a total lack of interest in sleepovers. So I switched to discussing my outfit for tomorrow.

She wasn't interested in clothes, either, but I had no problem keeping that conversation going single-handedly.

The next morning, I arrived at school at seven-thirty. Two of the kids—Conner and Sarah—came a few minutes later, and to my horror chose to play outside in the frigid arctic wind. Then one of the fathers dropped off his daughter dressed in shorts and a T-shirt. I made a joke about how cold it was, and he looked at me funny. This winter was going to be very, very long.

At eight-oh-five the bell rang, and we all got to work. We'd already fallen into a comfortable routine, and I reluctantly had to admit that laboring in the educational salt mines under the cruel lash of Mrs. Dale had been pretty good preparation. I knew how to handle a class. Sure, I'd learned all the theory and content in college, but lacked the confidence and discipline until now. Everything seemed to just come together. Maybe the kids were easy, or their teacher last year had been particularly good, but I was having a lot of fun.

I usually ate lunch in the teachers' lounge while the kids were in the cafeteria. I'd run out of all the food Kim cooked for me as a housewarming gift, so was back to "cooking" for myself, which today meant peanut butter and jelly. Dr. Pepper pretended I'd stolen one of the students' lunches, and hilarity ensued. He was the Noel Coward of the Broome Isle intelligentsia. Actually, it was fairly pleasant, sitting there with my fellow teachers. They were a bit distant, because they figured I was only here for one semester, but they were polite and helpful, and I think a little impressed by my early success.

I finished the day with some photocopying and lesson

plans, and shivered in my junker—a 1976 Volvo with 289,000 miles—until, ten seconds from home, the heat finally seeped through the vents. I set fire to the newspaper in the woodstove, then dug through the boxes Gregory had filled with all my clothes and sundries. There wasn't much. You'd think a young career woman of twenty-six would have accumulated more worldly possessions. Still, there was enough to make myself presentable. I only changed clothes twice, and was waiting at the window when Kim and Natasha drove up.

I stumbled back inside four hours later, my hair wild from the ferry and my lipstick smudged from kissing some guy. At least, I think that's what happened. It was all a blur as Natasha dragged us to five different places where we danced, drank and flirted. I sank into bed, feeling better about Maine. Sure, this wasn't New York. But hey, even *New York* wasn't New York, sometimes. And a night out with friends every week was the perfect antidote to the help-I'm-trapped-on-a-backwoods-island blues I'd been feeling.

The next day started with a man in my bedroom.

"You look like hell," he said.

"Marco," I moaned. "Water."

He brought me a glass. "Natasha told me to stop by, make sure you got to school today."

"What time is it?"

"Seven."

Half an hour to claw from my freshly dug grave and get to school. "Coffee!" I gasped.

"In the thermos. And I put some apple cinnamon scones in the kitchen. Fresh-baked."

"From Kim?"

He grunted and left, and I struggled from the blanket. God, you couldn't even mention her name around him. Or his around her. They so needed to just sleep together again. I should've told him about all the men eyeing her last night. Though, in truth, more of them were eyeing Natasha and me. Kim came across as sort of standoffish. And sober, she didn't really like to drink—unlike Natasha and apparently me.

School went well, despite my headache, and I'd finally pressed Natasha into service on my "autumn leaves" art project. She gave me simple-enough instructions that I figured I was okay with the art curriculum for a month.

Friday night, we met at Kim's kitchen and watched her cook dinner. This was a spiritual and meditative act. Think aromatherapy, crossed with low-impact culinarobics (chopping and slicing and mixing and dicing), crossed with nutritional perfection. Oh, and red wine.

Kim took me on a hike the next day through her property, which extended endlessly into the middle of the island. Then when Natasha woke in the afternoon, she and I went gallery-hopping in Portland and saw a photography exhibit at the School of Art. There were these pictures of people's forearms that fascinated her, so I left her there and went to Starbucks. There are two in downtown Portland, and I went to both.

The next week was a bit warmer, and I'll admit to a glow of self-satisfaction at how well I was settling in. I'd landed on my feet and nothing could possibly go wrong.

So far, Kim had made classic Italian spaghetti sauce, spicy vegetable soup, both hot and mild salsas, tomato chutney, tomato-ginger soup and green tomato relish. She stepped away from the stove, drying her hands on her apron. *Tomatoes.*

She saw them when she closed her eyes, dreamed of them at night and woke in the morning thinking of canning recipes. Every year she never wanted to see another tomato in her life, but knew she'd only be off them for a month and thrilled to see them again in November. At least she was coming to the end, only one flat left.

She'd make roasted tomatoes. There was nothing easier, they'd keep for months in oil and in February would taste better than heaven. Kim sliced the tomatoes in half, scooped out the seeds and lay them on the baking sheet. She minced garlic—an entire bud—into a bowl of olive oil, and drizzled the combination over the tomatoes. She added a little salt and pepper and set them in the oven to bake for two hours at a low heat.

It was Wednesday morning, and the Witches were heading to Portland this evening, on what was becoming their weekly outing. Funny, after years of being the only resident witch on the island, it felt good to have some company—even if it was in name only. Kim turned around twice in the kitchen and felt the storm coming. A bad one. They might get into Portland on the ferry, but never back. So they were staying here tonight.

But what to cook for dinner? Nothing with tomatoes, that was clear. Marco had spent the past week harvesting and Natasha had dropped off baskets full of winter squash and root vegetables. She'd roast them with mushrooms and rosemary and serve them with tossed spinach salad and homemade bread. Hmm. Biscuits would be quicker and even better with the roasted vegetables. And for dessert? The Cadbury chocolate bars she kept hidden from herself in the pantry. The biscuits would be enough work.

Kim tidied the kitchen and stepped into the herb garden, just outside the French doors, for the rosemary. The sky was windy and clear, but damp. She inhaled the scent of fallen leaves. She loved this place, and was as rooted here as the old oaks, but since the miscarriage and the divorce, her love of the island had been tinged with melancholy. It was evident from her nights out with the Witches that she was incapable of even the slightest flirtation—she'd been living half a life and mourning too long. A quarter of all pregnancies ended in miscarriages, and other women seemed to move on. Why couldn't she?

She knelt in the garden she'd been nurturing all summer. She'd started the herbs in the spring from seeds in little pots in the kitchen window. When they grew too big, she transplanted them to the garden, but not before the end of May— before then a frost was likely to kill them.

The phone rang inside. It would be Natasha, saying she'd heard a storm was forecast on the radio. Kim smiled as the message began, snipping the rosemary to its woody roots, then collecting the end of the basil and oregano and lavender. None of the herbs would survive the storm. She'd tie them with twine and hang them from the rafters in the kitchen. Marco had insisted it was better to dry them flat on screens, but she loved how they looked hanging from the ceiling—and they reminded her of drying roses from a first love. She'd kept every flower Marco ever gave her, including the tiny violets that grew in the grass. Especially the violets, wild and fragile.

Let me just say that silk-screening is a hellish activity, and should be forever banned. I told the kids to keep their paint shirts on, but that we were starting another project, so I called Natasha.

"Tell me again which colors combine?"

The cell reception was terrible on the island, but I still heard the sigh. "Red, yellow and blue are the primary colors."

I repeated this to the class, and told them they'd better remember because I never could.

"Yellow and blue make green. Red and blue make purple. Red and yellow make orange."

I parroted this information, and Conner—an adorable kid, if far too curious—asked, "What makes red, yellow and blue?"

"They're the primary colors," I told him, whatever that meant.

"There's gonna be a big storm tonight," Natasha told me. "I heard on the radio. Do you mind going to Kim's instead of Portland?"

Would there be men at Kim's house? "It's only a little snow," I said. "What kind of Mainers are you? Chloe! Keep your paint shirt on!"

"The kind who stay close to home when the weather's bad."

"Is Kim going to cook?"

"She mentioned homemade biscuits."

"Biscuits are better than men," I said. "Of course, so are paper cuts. I'll swing by the General Store for snacks and a few bottles of wine. Two of the guys there are almost *acknowledging* me now! Oops—gotta go."

"Good luck," Natasha said, and I didn't know what she meant until I got to the General Store at five-thirty and found it closed.

"Ugh," I cried. "It's not even snowing yet!" They were supposed to be open until seven on weeknights.

"Storm's coming," a woman's voice said from nowhere.

I shrieked and spun and saw the old crone sitting on the rickety wooden bench in front of the store. So she'd made it through the rain. "Oh! Yes, I heard," I said, recovering. "Can you believe the store's closed? How bad a storm can it be, anyway? It's only October."

"A storm's coming," she said, again.

"Yes, so you said. What's your name, dear? I'm Eve. I teach at the elementary school. Do you need a ride home?"

"And the winds will whip into a fury," she whispered, her wrinkled face intent. "And the oceans will boil, and the Muses shall sing and dance and sip from the cup, and the beast shall tear free from his cage."

"Is that Revelations? I'm not very good with Bible quotes. Here, it's getting cold—why don't you let me drive you home?"

"Do not drink the sweet wine of youth." Her eyes, pale from cataracts, focused somewhere in the distance. "Do not undo what has been done. One the first time, two the second, now three together will…will…"

There was a sudden gust of wind and, for the first time that day, I felt what everyone was talking about. Sure enough, a storm was coming.

"Um…" This woman was officially creepy, but the schoolteacher in me wouldn't let me leave her here. "Do you need help home? Are you here with someone?"

She abruptly stood from the bench, straight and dignified, banged her stick on the porch a few times and scurried away into the gloom.

Well. That was weird.

"The storm!" the old lady yelled, from nowhere I could see. "Take shelter from the storm!"

And getting weirder. I'd have to ask Kim and Natasha if they knew who she was.

9

I flopped into the kitchen chair. "No wine. The General Store closed early."

"Yeah, we know," Natasha said. "We live here."

Kim set a bottle down on the table. "Cizer." Another bottle. "Mead."

"What's cizer?" I asked. "Are these homemade? 'Cause if so, you're really starting to put Martha Stewart to shame."

"Cizer is like apple mead. To make mead, you start with a gallon of honey, and—"

"Kim," Natasha said. "Does this *look* like the Food Channel?"

Actually, it kinda did. But she was right, I didn't want to know how she made the stuff, I wanted to know when we'd start drinking it. "No regular wine?"

Kim put a third bottle on the table. "Witch's Brew. Last

bottle. I had to dig around to find it, but I thought with our team name…"

"What is it?'"

"Beer." She poured pints and handed them around. "A porter, actually."

I looked at the label, a poorly drawn picture of a witch with a wart on her bulbous nose, a broom in her right hand and a huge mushroom in her left.

"Why is she holding a mushroom?" I asked, sniffing my glass suspiciously. "Is this *mushroom* beer?"

"It's not a mushroom. It's a frothy pint of ale."

"You should have had Natasha draw the labels."

"I asked, but she said the alcohol content wasn't high enough to justify the effort." She raised her glass. "To witches!"

We toasted and I took a swig. "Tasty."

"Like two percent alcohol," Natasha said.

I pushed my glass away. "Not worth the calories, then."

Natasha downed her pint and grabbed mine. "I'll take it."

I eyed her with envy. Something about her shorter hair made her appear even skinnier and more striking. "You can afford it," I said, tugging at my waistband so my stomach wouldn't bulge so much. I traced my finger over the witch on the beer label. "Tell me about your ancestor again. The one who got hanged. Why'd they think she was a witch, because she predicted when storms were coming?"

"That, and she banished a nature demon when she got here."

"A demon?"

Kim shrugged. "Some sort of evil spirit. That's what they say."

"You believe them? That's bigger than knowing about the harvest."

"My aunt Hazel says the first Gray woman released the demon by stepping foot on the island. That contact with Emily Gray somehow...gave the thing physical being."

"Right," I said. "And what exactly does a demon do?"

"It feeds," Natasha said. "Eats the animals, feasts on human desires, sacrifices things to itself. You know, your average demonic day job."

"Well, why'd they hang her for banishing it?"

"They hanged her for summoning it in the first place," Kim said. "Although the story's kinda fuzzy about that. According to Aunt Hazel, the demon itself killed Emily Gray, his last act before being banished."

"And how'd she banish it?"

"Magic?" Kim said. "Actually, I've no idea."

"They named the island after her," Natasha said.

"After they killed her," Kim said.

"That was unfortunate," Natasha said.

"Like ye olde broome?" I asked.

"No, like Nathanial Broome," she said. "That was her husband's last name."

"Yeah," Natasha said. "And you know Ash Street, in town?"

"Sure," I said.

"How do you think it got its name?"

"From the ash trees lining the road?"

"After the ashes of Emily Gray," Natasha intoned.

For a moment, I believed her—then I laughed.

"I knew she wouldn't go for that," Kim said.

Natasha sighed. "Nobody has since seventh grade."

"Is this an act you two have?" I asked. "You ought to get together with Dr. Pepper and go on tour."

Natasha grinned around her glass. "I used to bring ashes from the woodstove and spread them around Ash Street. I told kids that no matter how many times they swept the street, the ashes kept coming back."

"The demon came back," Kim said.

"And I can guess why," I said. "To haunt the sixth-grade classroom."

"No, when Aunt Hazel was a girl, the demon returned. She says it took two of them, she and my grandmother, to release him the second time. Actually, she's not really my aunt, she was my grandmother's best friend. Anyway, they somehow managed to cast him out again."

I coughed. "And you guys believe all this?"

Kim and Natasha exchanged a look. "I don't know," Kim said. "Aunt Hazel's sort of odd, but Emily Gray definitely was hanged, you can check the archives in the Historical Society. Most of this is from Hazel, though, and—"

"She's a few toadstools short of a potion," Natasha said.

"Wait, what does she look like?" I told them about the old woman at the General Store.

"That's her."

"You island people are weird."

Natasha burped after finishing her beer. "Is there any more of that?"

"That's the last jug. Have some cizer."

The wind started howling outside. The trees were creaking and the house rattled as the storm grew fierce, but we were cozily enfolded in the toasty kitchen, wrapped in the scent of roasted vegetables and baking biscuits.

★ ★ ★

The cizer and mead were, strictly speaking, gross. All that work for nothing, Kim thought. Even Natasha wouldn't drink it.

"Okay, so I don't know how to make mead," Kim said. But she did unearth a three-quarters-empty bottle of Stoli. It was buried beneath a mountain of plastic bags full of blueberries in the garage freezer.

"I don't have any tonic," she said, back in the kitchen. "What else can we mix vodka with?"

"Orange juice," Natasha said. "Or cranberry."

"I've got apple cider."

"Um, yuck," Natasha said. "But straight up is good."

Kim grabbed clean glasses from the cupboard. She liked a few drinks when out with friends, and was surprised by how much fun she'd had barhopping with Natasha and Eve last Wednesday night—but still, she never really enjoyed drinking for its own sake.

"We can use the blueberries," Eve said, grabbing the vodka bottle.

"Very Maine," Natasha said. "What would you call that? A blueberry Seabreeze. A Seaberry."

"A Bluebreeze?" Eve said.

Kim pulled the biscuits from the oven, along with the parchment-wrapped roasted vegetables, and set them aside to cool. She took the salad she'd left chilling in the fridge, squeezed the juice of a lemon into a bowl and whisked in some Dijon mustard and red wine vinegar. After adding olive oil, she had an easy lemon-mustard vinaigrette.

"What?" she said, noticing Natasha and Eve staring.

"Cooking show, again," Eve said.

"Yeah," Natasha said. "But in a good way. At least she doesn't narrate herself." She grabbed plates and silverware and started setting the dining room table.

Kim smiled, watching Natasha move the candles from the wooden hutch in the kitchen to the table. Kim would've been happy eating in the kitchen, but Natasha loved that dining room. It had been painted in the trompe l'oeil fashion sometime in the early 1900s. One of her relatives had evidently been a Seurat fan, because it was heavily reminiscent of *Sunday Afternoon on the Island of Grande Jatte,* only it was the Island of Grande Broome. The ceiling was like a cloudy sky.

Natasha found matches in the hutch drawer and was lighting the candles when Kim set the plates on the place mats. Eve followed—bearing vodka glasses with what looked like little turds floating in them—and gasped when she saw the room.

"When I die," she said, "I'm going to live here."

"Oh, no!" Natasha said, staring at Eve's dreamy face. "What have you *done?*"

"What? I didn't mean I wanted to die anytime *soon,* Natasha."

"Forget dying. The drinks!" Natasha eyed the vodka glasses, horrified. What was floating in them? How could Eve ruin a perfectly good shot of vodka? Didn't she understand rations were low? "What *is* that?"

"I call it Smelts on the Beach," she said.

"You put smelts in there?"

Eve laughed. "They're frozen blueberries. I thought they'd be pretty, but they're all stuck in clusters. They look a little like bird droppings."

"More like rabbit pellets," Kim said.

"Deer poop," Natasha said, raising her glass. "Here's to us. We're the..." She eyed her glass again. "Shit, I guess."

They snickered and sipped, chomping frozen blueberries as they took their seats around the table.

"Weird how something so cold goes down so warm," Natasha said, feeling the heat of the vodka spread in her chest.

Kim shuddered. "Yech. At least the aftereffects are good." She dished the salad, then turned to Eve. "Why Smelts on the Beach?"

"Like Sex on the Beach, without the sex. Because none of us is having any." She sighed. "God, it's been forever."

"You've gone, like, three weeks," Natasha said.

"I *know!*" Eve said sadly.

"But why smelts?" Kim asked.

"Because they sell them at the Smelts Store, and I have no idea what they are."

"At the what?"

"She means the General Store," Natasha said.

Kim laughed. "You're going to be so disappointed, Eve. They're just little fish used for bait."

Eve frowned. "So they're not some Maine delicacy?"

"We've got lobster," Kim said. "You want more than that?"

Eve bit into her biscuit. "Mmm. Who needs anything, when you've got biscuits like this?" She licked butter from her lips and mewled, which made Natasha uncomfortable. Everything Eve did always made her look on the verge of an orgasm. Not that Natasha really knew what that looked like.

She shoveled her own biscuit into her mouth, hoping for the same reaction. Hmm. She tried more butter. Nope. "I need another drink."

She grabbed the glasses and went into the kitchen. Eve had left the frozen blueberries on the cabinet and they were starting to pool in their own juices, so Natasha—feeling very Kim-like—tossed them into a cup and mashed them with sugar into a syrup. She strained them into lowball glasses and added the end of the vodka.

Back in the dining room, Eve was saying, "Then what's a grain hall? Like a silo?"

"It's a *Grange* Hall," Kim said.

"Home on the Grange." Natasha handed each of them a drink. "They're places farmers used to gather, like community centers."

"They have weddings there now," Kim said. "The one here on the island, at least."

"Don't forget the line dancing," Natasha said.

"Oh," Eve said. "That sounds charming."

Natasha noticed the far-off look in Eve's eye. "It's not like *Pride and Prejudice.*"

"There's no Mr. Darcy," Kim added.

"There's a Mr. Dawson," Natasha said.

"He's seventy-five."

"But frisky!"

"Speaking of *Pride and Prejudice,*" Eve said, "did you read who Keira Knightley is dating?"

"He totally doesn't seem like her type," Kim said.

Natasha drained her drink while they discussed Hollywood gossip. Who the heck was Keira Knightley? She didn't understand how they knew all this stuff. Were they actually reading *Star* magazine? She finished her biscuit and roasted vegetables and admired the trompe l'oeil. No matter how many times she sat in this room, she never grew tired of it.

The scene was of the village commons in the twenties, with everyone in the village present, sitting with picnic baskets or promenading to the sea. One woman stood in the center of the wall, her dark hair long and loose, unlike the other women in the painting. She wore a sleeveless knee-length dress of steel-blue, with coral beads wrapped twice around her neck and a headband holding her hair in place. She was the only figure dressed in evening wear, which Natasha always found curious.

"What do you think, Natasha?" Kim asked.

"Hmm?"

"Gaucho pants, in or out?" Eve asked. "You're the deciding vote."

"What?"

"Kim says they're in. I say out."

"They're flattering," Kim said. "I love them with knee-high boots."

"On you, with your mile-long legs and slim hips," Eve said. "Try wearing them when you're dumpling-shaped."

Natasha blinked at them. "Gaucho pants? Are they western wear?"

For some reason Kim and Eve found this hilarious, but Natasha ignored them and said, "Who's that woman?" She pointed to the woman facing her from the wall.

"I always thought she was the artist," Kim said. "But I don't know."

"She's the only one facing outward," Eve said. "I wonder why she was painted like that."

"Because she wants out," Natasha said.

"Yes," Kim agreed.

"Out of where?" Eve asked. "The painting?"

"The life she's made," Natasha answered.

Kim nodded. "The places she's stuck, the—"

The wind rose into a shriek—tree branches scratched at the clapboards outside and the lights flickered and died.

"Oh!" Eve said, her flushed face lit by the fluttering candles. "The lights!"

"Power's out," Kim said, glancing toward the kitchen.

"I love a blackout!" Eve said. "Always reminds me of snow days and haunted houses. The house isn't haunted, is it? Is there dessert? More vodka? We should start a fire."

Natasha shook her head in the dark. Never let it be said that Eve didn't make her feelings known. "That was the end of the vodka," she said.

"We can start a fire, though," Kim said, standing. "And I'll get more candles."

"There's nothing at all left in the house to drink?" Eve asked.

Kim paused. "Well, there's probably a few bottles in the old cellar. Elderberry wine or something."

"Oh, no," Natasha said. "No way."

"Why not?" Eve asked. "I've never had elderberry wine. I didn't actually know it existed."

"Well, it doesn't," Natasha said firmly. "We'll just crack open the cooking sherry."

"You don't like elderberry wine?" Eve asked. "The alcohol content is too low?"

"There are two basements in this house, Eve. The 'good' cellar and 'old' cellar. No way I'm going back in the old cellar. Not even for booze."

The summer Kim and Natasha turned twelve, Marco locked them in the old cellar. It was a rainy afternoon and the three of them were alone in the house, engaged in a marathon game of hide-and-go-seek. There were intricate rules that neither Natasha nor Kim could recall, but the afternoon culminated in Marco luring them down the rickety wooden steps into the cold, dank, horrible basement. To be fair, it was girls against boy, so they'd conspired against him all afternoon—but he'd won his revenge and more.

The house was over two hundred years old. The basement floor was dirt, and the old cellar had a row of shallow depressions that looked terrifyingly like graves. Plus, they both knew—because they'd told each other so many times—that in the old days, before backhoes, families stored the dead in the bottom of the house if they died during winter. The bodies stayed cool and preserved until the spring thaw.

As Kim and Natasha banged at the latched wooden door, with the splintery planks under peeling paint, they started thinking some of the bodies had been forgotten. Scratching noises sounded in the dark behind them, the smell of fresh-dug earth grew overwhelming. There were no windows in the old cellar, the ceiling was low and crossed with beams, knobbed with old nails and covered with cobwebs. *Things* crunched underfoot, dried husks of insects and horrible…*things*. A single bare bulb hung from the ceiling, with a broken chain—and burned out a minute after they lit it.

Then the screaming started.

"Which one of you screamed first?" I asked.
Kim and Natasha looked at each other.

"We didn't," Natasha said.

"At least, not at first," Kim added.

I giggled. "You guys are still scared!"

"I haven't been down there since it happened," Kim said. "My mother was forced to move the laundry to the down-stairs bathroom, because I refused to even open the cellar door."

"She never forgave Marco," Natasha said. "He deserved it, leaving us down there for two hours. With that... *thing.*"

Wow, this was serious. Natasha never slammed Marco to others. To his face, sure. "What thing?" I asked.

Natasha shrugged. "I don't know, whatever screamed."

"It wasn't two hours," Kim said. "It was like ten minutes."

"What do you mean, whatever screamed?" I asked.

"Something screamed."

"Was it the *demon?*" I asked in my spookiest voice.

"It was probably the foundation settling," Kim said primly. "Or—I don't know, some animal got in."

"Or the boiler in the other room," Natasha scoffed. "Like your mother said. Sure."

"This is crazy!" I said. "What else would it be?"

They both looked uncomfortable.

"Oh, my God," I laughed. "You guys *do* think it was the demon!"

Neither of them laughed back. I stood and grabbed them each by a hand. "C'mon! Let's go—this city girl will show you there's nothing to be afraid of."

They looked at each other and Natasha started to soften, no doubt craving elderberry wine. "Well, it has been fifteen years."

"Pre-Buffy years," I said. "All the cool girls are demon-slayers now."

"I don't know…." Kim said.

So I told her the story of my daydream on the subway, and she laughed—and when I grabbed a candle, they both did, too. They begrudgingly led me past the kitchen to the sewing room—the very existence of which alarmed me. Kim had an actual "sewing room"? But they were both so silly about this cellar that I stepped passed the old foot-pedal sewing machine without teasing her. The moon was full outside the window, and snow had started to collect on the shrubs in the yard and was speckling the glass. And the door to the "old cellar" looked like…a door. With a cast-iron latch. Nothing special. I tugged at the doorknob, but it was stuck.

"That was the night I got my first period," Kim said, almost to herself.

"Me, too!" Natasha said.

"You're not going to creep me out," I told them, and wrenched the door open.

A cool, earthy upwelling of air brushed my face. Inside, wooden stairs led down into darkness, and there was an old broom and dustpan just inside, and a few rolls of what looked like shelving paper.

I couldn't help myself, I howled like a ghost.

"Hey," Natasha said.

"Yeah," Kim said. "There'll be none of that."

I giggled. "Then let's lay these demons to rest."

What they heard, all those years ago, hadn't been a scream. I have no mouth—I cannot scream, or speak…or feed. I can merely wait, and brood and want. No noise had frightened the girls, the redhead who burned with a cleansing fire, and the brunette whose bloodscent I knew so well. A cry of wordless desire had issued from me. Should have been impossible for such as them to notice, but they had.

The force of my craving was strong enough to be felt. They'd fled from my power, but I'd not mourned their passing. Not then.

Because then, they'd been incomplete. Not simply for being children, but because the third of them had not yet arrived.

Now she was here. They all were.

I felt them approach. Even through the glass of my prison, I smelled them: damp and warm, honeyed musk. Thrilled and afraid. Yet they were still not ready.

The brunette, the granddaughter and great-granddaughter, was replete, full of inchoate knowingness, yet untrained and unfulfilled. She needed filling of a different sort.

The redhead, also rooted in my land, my island, was born with the gift and burden of sight. Yet she could not explain her visions, or cast her gaze upon herself. She saw, but didn't understand.

And the blonde. A confection. I salivated at the scent of her, at the plump succulent presence—she knew nothing. But she felt. And I felt her feeling.

The fear tasted like the first wine of the season, a thin promise of what was to come. Kim. Natasha. And they named the blonde "Eve," how fitting. The dreamer. She imagined herself venturing into a crypt, her torch held high, stepping through a secret door into a chamber dazzling with treasures, with rubies and silk and gold.

With the little strength I'd gathered…I loosed something, some small part of myself. And a jewel beckoned my Eve, and she bowed her head….

★ ★ ★

"You two are ridiculous," I said from the landing.

"Go all the way down," Natasha said, still waiting by the door. "Then say that again."

So I went all the way into the cellar. And sure it was creepy, but *all* basements are creepy—especially in remote Maine farmhouses in the middle of a storm with only candlelight. But my motto was WWBD: What Would Buffy Do?

I squared my shoulders. "You guys would never make it in the city. The subways are way worse than this."

I looked at the old shelves and dark corners, and the shadows seemed to flicker at me, and I gasped. Calm, Eve. Be strong. What if I were…a tomb raider? I crept through an ancient labyrinth, my .45 at my hip and my torch burning in my hand. There! A breeze touched my face, coming from a blank stone wall, and I found the secret door at last. Soon, the treasure of— "Ow!"

"What? Eve? Are you okay?" They two of them huddled at the top of the stairs. "What happened?"

"Stubbed my toe." I looked down. "Oh! On a bottle."

"That's not where my grandmother kept the elderberry wine," Kim said.

"Maybe your grandfather got into it," I told her. "Looks like a wine bottle to me."

"What's that smell?" Natasha said, wrinkling her nose.

"Rats?" Kim said. "Or rotten eggs—probably an old bird's nest or—"

Her candle blew out. Then Natasha's went black. And something moaned.

I charged upstairs.

★ ★ ★

Kim turned round and round in the sewing room, feeling her heart pound and the hair raised on the back of her neck. She grabbed the sewing scissors and faced the cellar stairs.

But Eve slammed the cellar door closed and slumped against it, her shoulders shaking with laughter. "The wind! For fifteen years, you two have been scared of the wind!"

"Didn't sound like wind to me," Natasha said, her eyes wide.

"Through that little vent," Eve said, still giggling. "Or coal-chute door, or whatever that is. I felt the breeze, and I saw the cobwebs blowing—it was totally the wind."

"Yeah, that's why you flattened me, running upstairs," Natasha said.

"I almost peed my pants!" Eve said, wiping her eyes. "That was like the best haunted house, *ever.* You two have been on this island way too long."

"Well, I know one thing," Natasha said. "Now I really need a drink."

Eve raised the bottle she'd taken from the cellar over her head and stepped back toward the kitchen, with Natasha following. Kim hesitated in the sewing room for a moment, unsure about…something. Unsure even about what she was unsure about. Then Eve's merry voice floated back to her. "What we need is a Ouija board!"

And Kim couldn't help smiling. She went into the kitchen, where Eve and Natasha were eyeing the bottle. Not a wine bottle—at least not a mass-produced one, this was older, with smooth ripples and little air bubbles trapped in the glass. Red twine looped around the neck, and a gold tag hung down.

Eve turned the tag over. "It's blank."

"Doesn't look like elderberry wine."

Natasha picked up the bottle and tapped the glass. "I love it. They don't make glass like this anymore." She fiddled with the tag. "Probably a label, it must've faded. If it's not elderberry wine, what is it?"

"Vodka?" Kim said. "Half our land used to be given over to growing potatoes."

"Only one way to find out." Eve uncorked the bottle, and a sudden scent suffused the room. "Hmm. Smells like…"

"Baby powder," Kim said.

"Turpentine," Natasha said. "Good turpentine smells almost sweet."

"Roses," Eve finished.

Natasha took three glasses from the cabinet. "I say we drink it."

"Sure, nothing's smoother than a shot of paint thinner," Kim said.

"*Baby powder?*" Natasha said.

Eve poured the slow, clouded liquor into the glasses and handed them around. "Here's to—*oh!*"

Kim followed her gaze to the window. Outside the snow had turned to rain and was freezing on fluttering leaves and bare branches. The ice-sheathed landscape glimmered in the moonlight. Kim walked to the window, Eve and Natasha beside her. The moon was huge in the sky, below the clouds and pure white, the light almost harsh, caught and reflected by ten thousand frozen droplets.

"We should make wishes," Eve said softly.

"It's nobody's birthday," Natasha said.

"Who needs a birthday to make a wish?" Eve said.

"Then we have to tell one another," Natasha said.

"Deal."

They lifted their glasses in the light of the moon, the flames in the old kitchen fireplace casting shadows on their faces—and touched the rims together.

"I wish…for my art," Natasha said. "I wish I could get the art out, get what I see onto the canvas. And I wish people liked it. I want to finish one great painting."

Eve flushed, as if she were embarrassed by her wish. "I wish—I wish I wanted to wish for being the best teacher ever, or…or to climb Mount Everest or something. But my real wish is just to fall crazy in love. With someone who falls crazy in love with me."

Kim raised her glass, watching the liquor undulate slowly. I want Marco. I want Marco. I want Marco. But she couldn't say that, not in front of Natasha. Instead, she allowed herself another truth: "I want a baby."

They clinked glasses, and drank.

10

I woke with a start, from a dream of being spun by a massive spider into an icy cocoon. I gasped for breath, sat up and found myself in a bathtub. Cold and smooth—that explained the dream, at least. I expected Natasha's claw-foot bathtub, sitting forlornly in the middle of her living room, but this bathtub was in an actual bathroom. Pretty shower curtains, and colored bottles of homemade potions, lotion and soaps. Could only be Kim's house.

Yikes. Long night. I lay back in the tub and checked my watch. Ten of eight! I was late for school. I stood up too fast, slipped on the porcelain, grabbed for the shower curtain and whacked my head on the tile wall. Ow. I Almost passed out, but stood there swaying, instead. Finally I stepped out of the tub and over to the sink, and turned the cold water on full. I drank and drank and drank.

I once had a summer job as a ticket seller at a movie

theater. It was one of those old-time theaters with the little freestanding booth out front. I'd work six hours straight, with no break and no air-conditioning. After the first day, with no one coming to relieve me or my bladder, I'd made it a policy to never drink anything before starting my shift. Each day, when I was through, I'd down a gigantic bucket of diet cola. That thirst was a like a mildly dry tongue compared to this.

I held my wrist up so I could check the time again while still slurping the best water I'd ever tasted. Kim seemed to have her own spring water running through the taps. Due in front of twenty first-graders in ten minutes. I was never going to make it. Especially if I didn't stop drinking. Kim could bottle this stuff and make a fortune. Why was I so thirsty? I couldn't remember anything from last night. How much did we drink?

I had to force my right hand to shut off the faucet, or I'd have been there all day. I licked the last wayward drop from the spigot and straightened to examine myself in the mirror, wincing preemptively against what I'd find. But...*hmm*. I didn't look that bad. In fact, I looked kinda good. Glowy and fresh-faced and rested. Odd, after partying like we must've. I usually looked like the "before" picture in a plastic surgery ad.

I washed my face and found an elastic in a drawer under the sink and used it to tie my hair back. Sure, I was wearing the same clothes to school as I did yesterday, but my hair was different. I'd fool everyone.

I tiptoed from the bathroom, not wanting to wake Natasha and Kim if they were still asleep. On my way to the kitchen I found Natasha crashed on the couch. Why did she get the couch and I got the bathtub? And there had to be extra beds upstairs—why weren't we sleeping in them? I was tempted to wake Natasha and ask her what had happened, but I was so late and knew better than to rouse the bear.

I stopped for another gallon of water from the kitchen tap before slipping into my boots and coat. My car was parked outside—I only hoped it would start. If I hadn't been in such a hurry, I might have paused at the front door to admire the way the storm left a coating of ice along the branches and leaves of the maple trees and evergreens. How the morning sunlight sparkled on the telephone wires. How little rows of miniature icicles lined the eaves, dripping down.

How the driveway had become an ice rink overnight.

I took my first step and gravity reversed. My foot flew skyward, and I clutched the door frame with both hands, yelping in surprise. I caught my balance and tried again, skittering and shuffling across the ice, never quite falling on my butt, and finally made it to the car. I steadied myself against the door, breathing a sigh of relief. Ha! Is that all you've got, Maine winter?

I grabbed the door handle and yanked and—

I checked my watch again, the dial backlit by the trees and morning sun. One minute after eight.

Yup, officially late. And wedged feet-first under my Volvo.

I'd accidentally used the door handle as leverage for swinging my body under the car, my feet slipping on the sheet of ice. This is what comes from being city-bred and refusing to leave the car unlocked. I was like the Wicked Witch of the East, only with my head sticking out instead of my feet.

I stared at the cold blue sky. Okay. Maine 1, Eve 0.

I twisted and shoved, further lodging myself under the car. This was fast becoming not so funny. I couldn't budge. My back was freezing, my hair was sticking to the ice, and I was getting close to tears. Embarrassment be damned: I screamed for Natasha and Kim to help me. But they were lying in drunken dazes inside, and nobody came. I tried rolling onto my side, then gave up.

What a way to go. I could already see my obituary: "Eve Crenshaw died like she lived: trapped under a used Volvo." God, this was ridiculous. "Okay, Maine winter," I told the sky. "You may think you've won, but I—"

Two large boots appeared at eye level. Thick, fur-lined boots that laced up to midcalf and had those plastic crampons for ice wrapped around the soles that I'd seen on sale at the Smelts Store.

"What are you doing?" the boots asked in a deep, amused voice. A nice voice, the kind of voice you always wished would whisper in your ear when out barhopping.

Not while wedged like a dead witch under a Volvo.

"What could I possibly be doing?" I said. "I'm *stuck*."

"Well, you could've been changing your oil."

"Yeah, I find my bare toes are perfect for loosening the icy oil cap."

"So, I guess you need help?"

"No. I'm good."

"Okay," the boots said. "See ya."

"Hey! Wait!"

"Yes?"

"I'm late for school."

"School's canceled, because of the ice storm."

"Ice?" I said. "Is there ice somewhere?"

The boots laughed, and a pair of leather-gloved hands grabbed me under my arms. "Okay. One, two—" He slid me out from under the car, straight onto my feet. There was a dizzy moment of warmth as I was cradled against him, my back to his front. The world was right-side-up, and I was warm and grounded and secure. His mouth was close to my ear and I could feel his breath as he said, "Are you all right?"

I didn't want to turn around, this moment was too perfect. Okay, his discovering me jammed under my car didn't exactly fit into any previous fantasies. But having a warm male body to snuggle against in the cold felt pretty right, and…well, I liked his voice. What if I turned around and he had a waist-length ponytail? Or a tattooed neck? Or a wedding ring?

"Just a little shaken up," I said, not turning.

After a slight pause, he seemed to realize that he was cradling a perfect stranger in his arms, and stepped back a bit. "Oh, well…um. Good."

"You're wondering why I'm still facing this way, aren't you?"

"A little, yeah."

"Maybe I'm disfigured," I told him.

"Right. Are you?"

"Don't be ridiculous." I tapped a fingernail against the roof of my car. "Do you have a ponytail?"

He laughed. "You're a little odd, aren't you?"

So I turned. He was average height, average build and had average features. His hair was somewhere between brown and browner, his eyes were the same, and he was wearing jeans and a parka. I'd be hard-pressed to pick him out of a lineup. He was Mr. Average.

"See?" he said. "No ponytail."

I said, "Is your name Joe?"

"No." He smiled. "It's Jack."

I lost myself in that smile.

When Kim woke, her bedroom was pitch black. She lay still in the down comforter, with a pounding in her head— and at the front door. Now? In the middle of the night?

She turned on the bedside lamp and saw that the thick brocade curtains were closed—she never closed those. She staggered from the bed and pulled a curtain back, and daylight shone inside. It wasn't midnight. Wasn't even early morning anymore. She stumbled downstairs, past Natasha, who was asleep on the couch, and into the kitchen. She pulled a quart mason jar from the shelf and filled it with tap water. Downed it, filled it again and gulped that. Her head stopped pounding, but the door hadn't.

Kim checked herself in the mirror by the front door, and was surprised to see she looked okay, considering last night. After they'd drunk that elderberry wine—or whatever— and...huh. What exactly *had* happened last night? She smoothed her hair, trying to remember, but came up blank.

The knocking started again. She opened the front door, an apology on her lips for taking so long, but stopped when she saw him. For an instant, neither spoke, and she felt the same moment of clarity she'd had only once before in her life: years ago stepping into the Barnacle.

He finally said, "Mrs. Kim Gray?"

"*Ms.* Kim Gray," she said. "I'm divorced."

A glint appeared in the man's eyes. "I've always had a thing for divorcées. Even the word, *divorcée*. Extremely hot."

Kim laughed. "Well," she said. "I've got a thing for strangers."

"I can do that," the man said. "I can be anyone you want."

"I want *you,*" she said, and took his hand.

Kim couldn't remember what happened last night, but this morning she knew she was different. Finally ready to break out of her shell, to drop her mourning, to live again. Forget jazzing up her shortbread. What she wanted was sex. She'd always liked sex, in the same way she'd always liked fresh-baked pie, but she'd never felt so…hungry before. And here was a man ready and willing, because weren't they all?

She led him to her bedroom. Ice glistened along the branches of the tree that filled the bedroom window. The room was warm and welcoming, and they fell into the honeymoon bed.

Natasha opened one bleary eye and surveyed the living room. What happened last night? Wasn't like her not to remember. That couldn't be a good sign.

She croaked, "Kim? Eve?" No one answered, though she thought she heard voices upstairs. "Water? Bring water."

Still no answer, so she sighed and roused herself from the couch. She found a flower vase in the kitchen, filled it with water, drank the whole thing and put it under the tap again. She checked her reflection in the window over the kitchen sink. Weird. She looked better than usual. Natasha wasn't vain, and as an artist she saw the flaws in her face. If she were to draw herself, she knew where she'd erase and start again. But today she looked different. Must be the light, the sun reflecting through ice.

She drank another vase of water, which was finally enough

to slake her thirst, and tried to recall last night. She remembered the trip to the cellar, toasting with the bottle Eve had found…but what happened after that? She looked for the bottle, but it wasn't in the kitchen on the dining room table or the living room.

God. She'd blacked out. She hoped she hadn't made a scene in front of Kim and Eve. She knew Kim thought she drank too much—and apparently she did. Maybe Kim had hidden the bottle from Natasha. They were probably upstairs, planning an intervention.

But how come she didn't feel hungover? Was that one of the signs? She halfheartedly called out to Kim again, but was glad when there was no answer. She wrapped herself in her old black wool coat and the ink-stained pashmina Kim had finally given her, because she thought it was out of style. Natasha didn't know what she was talking about. It was still a gorgeous shade of jade and really toasty, especially when you wrapped it right. She pulled on her fleece-lined boots and left by the kitchen door.

Natasha smiled at the ice-encased driveway and skated toward her truck. Performed a spin and slid into the driver's seat. Funny, but she felt different today. Excited for the first time in too long. She drove slowly to her house, parked in Marco's spot, and found Puck waiting outside the front door.

"Sorry, baby." She hadn't planned on spending the night at Kim's, so had left the cat outside. But knowing Puck, he had yowled at Marco until he let him into the house, so she doubted he was left out in the cold. "You must be hungry."

She opened the door, glancing toward Marco's garden. He was probably out making deliveries. Hell, he'd probably been up at dawn, assessing the damage, complaining the frost came too early (which he said every year), and fretting over how much heat he was losing from the new green-house.

Well, he wasn't the only industrious one in the family. She fed Puck and stood at the storage racks of paintings, chewing her lower lip. She'd promised a batch of surf 'n' turf to a gallery in Camden, which was gearing up for the leaf-peepers, tourists who came to Maine to see the leaves change. They probably went to Nebraska to watch the corn grow, too. But they could be counted on to buy a few pieces of Natasha's second-rate work, which would keep her checkbook balance more positive than her outlook, at least.

She listened to Puck messily eat and flipped through a few old canvases, looking for the ones that to the untutored eye might look like foliage. She often wondered who took them home, if they hung them in the living room or bathroom. How often they really looked at them, and if they still liked them years later.

Perversely, Natasha usually offered the few galleries that took her stuff her worst work. That way, if nobody bought them, it was because they weren't her best. But today, she was pulled again and again to her favorites. The village scene that looked closed and mournful, autumn in Marco's garden, with plump pumpkins sitting among withered vines, the apple tree on a hill of snow, still hung with desiccated fruit. She stacked them together and laid them in the back of her truck on a soft cloth, with another on top to protect them from weather. It was time to take a few risks.

She usually dreaded the delivery work—it took all day to

ferry into Portland and drive up the coast and back. She'd rather be painting, especially on a day like today, with the crisp cold light. But she was proud of delivering this work, even if it wasn't her true art—even if some New Yorker just decided to hang it over their toilet. At least it was out there.

She grabbed a granola bar and pulled a plastic water bottle out of the recycle bin to fill it from the tap. She drove toward the ferry in a happy haze, through the ice-sheathed trees and rocks. She'd always loved an ice storm; it transformed everything into a sort of fairy wonderland, and never failed to spark ideas for art. And always in the back of her mind was the large canvas, her *Last Hope,* the one she'd never been able to finish.

She was getting closer, though.

Maybe if she made the cottage on the cliffside brighter, more prominent, and added a figure? Perilously close to realism, but perhaps that's what this painting needed. A marriage of the abstract and the real. But a man? A woman? The painting was good, some of her strongest work, but hadn't come alive yet.

She buzzed past the General Store, and a guy jogged into the street directly in front of her.

She slammed the brakes, felt the truck lurch and slide. She pumped the brake pedal, skidding sideways on the icy road, then stopped with a *thunk*.

She'd hit him! Oh, God. Oh, God.

She climbed out and ran to the side of the truck and the man was nowhere. "Fuck. Fuck!" She ran around the truck. "Hey! Hey, hello? Oh, God. Are you okay?"

She followed her skid marks back toward the General Store, and heard voices from a shallow ditch on the side of the road. She looked down and found a man sprawled in a patch of ice, with another man standing over him.

"C'mon, Johnny," the standing man said. "Stop lying around."

"Oh, God!" Natasha said. "Is he okay? Are you okay?"

"He's fine." The man shook his head. He was tall and skeletal and hunched, like she'd always imagined Ichabod Crane, and wearing a suit with the jacket open to reveal a vest with gold buttons. "He's just pissing me off."

"Well, I *did* run over him," she said, scrambling into the ditch.

The tall man shuddered. "Never admit that! Don't you know anything? At the scene of an accident, the last thing you should do is—"

She stepped around him, and saw that the man she'd hit, Johnny, was holding one of her paintings. Must've flipped out of the truck when she'd slammed the brakes. "I'm so sorry," she said. "Are you okay? Should I call 911?"

He stood, ignoring her and scowling at the painting. "Where did you get this?"

"What?"

"The painting," he said. "Where'd you get it?"

"Um—I just—" Natasha gestured back to the road. "Are you sure you're okay?" She looked at the tall man. "Is he okay?"

"Johnny's like a Rolex."

"You mean a Timex?"

"And tenacious. You'd better tell him where you got that, or he'll never stop asking."

"I painted it," she said.

Johnny finally looked away from the painting, and his intensity seemed to fade as his smile grew. "Well, you paint better than you drive. This is good. This is damn good."

I paused, shivering on the steps to the Smelts Shop. The only available man on the island—and one whose smile turned my knees to jelly—and I'd fumbled. Sometimes I wished I was cool and mysterious like Kim, or sharp and edgy like Natasha. Instead, I was just overenthusiastic and bumbling and totally transparent, like me.

I cursed myself and pushed inside and found something really unexpected. Two days ago I was getting the cold shoulder from the old coots. This morning I walked in and was Norm on *Cheers*.

"Eve!" The oldest of the coots, Eldon, touched one of his liver spots in greeting. "Fine morning."

I turned to see if there was some other Eve behind me, one who warranted a cheery salutation. There appeared not to be, so I returned a timid wave.

"School closed?" another asked. "In my day—"

Two more of the coots hooted him down before he could continue. "In my day," one of them said, in a faux querulous voice, "we lived in squirrel nests and ate venison raw. And we went to school in five feet of snow—"

"—naked!" the other finished.

"Come and sit, Eve," the eldest said, guffawing.

I resisted the temptation to look behind myself again. I didn't even know they knew my name. Maybe I'd introduced myself the first two or three times I'd come in. Okay, every time. It had become a perversion, waiting to see if anyone would respond. No one ever had, but apparently I'd penetrated their granite exteriors.

"Over here, hon," Marie, the owner, called, setting a place for me beside the other regulars. "I've got some nice bacon cooking. Chester here just slaughtered his prize pig."

I sat and Chester told me about Princess, who—he claimed—won every prize in every fair in Maine that year. I drank my coffee, listening contentedly, my anxiety over dropping the ball with Jack fading as I settled in. Between the hum of the generator out back and all the people helping themselves to coffee and doughnuts—and Kim's preserves, she'd be pleased—the Smelts Store was jumping.

"You slaughtered *Princess?*" I finally said.

"That's what a pig is for."

"But…why'd you name her Princess, if you were going to—"

"I was gonna name her Pork Chop," he said wistfully. "But you shoulda seen her. She had that royal…" He looked down the bar. "What's that she had?"

"Royal bearing," one of the other coots reminded him.

"Royal bearing," he repeated. "She was the Cleopatra of pigs."

"Well, I'm not sure I could eat a pig whose name I've known."

"She's good eatin', Eve. Don't let her die in vain."

"Of course not. Marie? I'd like some of that bacon."

"Coming right up."

Oh my God, I was loving this! Wait until I told the folks back home about eating some old-time Mainer's prize pig. Of course, who was I going to tell? Gregory wouldn't have the remotest idea why I found it charming and my frenemy from graduate school would tell me how fattening it was or that they were serving prosciutto in her private school cafeteria.

I finished my coffee, and Marie appeared with a refill. Well, I'd won over the denizens of the Smelts Shop. If only I'd had as much luck with Jack this morning. Like I said, I'd gotten lost in his smile. Sadly, it had taken a while to get found again. This is what happened:

"I'm Jack," he'd said, and smiled.

Then I'd gaped like an idiot.

And he'd finally said, "So. You come here often?"

"What?" I shook my head. "I'm sorry, I haven't had my coffee yet."

He looked at the house. "Do you live here?"

"No, I rent a cottage on the beach, actually. It looks like a seashell." Shut up, Eve. Shut up now, please. "I mean on the inside. It's sort of pinky and satiny and—like a seashell." Oh, boy. "See? No coffee. Would you like to get some? At the Smelts Store?"

"The where?"

"The General Store. Like I said." Then I realized what a terrible idea that was. So just as he was about to say "Sure" or "Surely not"—who's to say?—I cut him off. "You know, I actually have to be somewhere." I opened the car door, this time without catastrophe. "Right now."

"I thought you had a snow day."

"Hey, do I criticize *your* lies?"

He did that smiling thing again. "Listen, I'm new on the island and I—"

"See you around, then!" I said, closing the car door and pulling away.

I went directly to the Smelts Store, of course, driving

about five miles an hour to keep from sliding off the road, where Marie was now setting down my plate of Princess— I mean, bacon—and I took a bite.

"She's delicious," I told Chester.

But he'd suddenly reverted to granite as a man sat down next to me at the counter. It was Jack. He told Marie he'd have a coffee, and didn't seem to notice the coots, or care they were ignoring him.

He was too busy looking at me. "I almost didn't recognize you without your car."

"It's my signature piece," I said. "Some women wear Hermès scarves, I wear a Volvo."

He laughed like I'd surprised him, then held out his hand. "Jack," he said.

"I remember."

"And what should I call you? Volvo Girl?"

Was it just me, or did that sound like *Vulva Girl?* "No, I don't think any woman wants to be named for a...big boxy car."

"But they're so safe. They look like tanks."

"Oh, better and better," I said, before I realized he was teasing. I finished my first piece of bacon and turned toward the coots. "Excellent bacon, Chester. I can tell she was an aristocrat of pigs."

"A pearl among swine," he told me.

"You're local?" Jack said. "I thought you said you rented a cottage."

"I just moved here a few weeks ago," I said.

"You make friends quickly."

"And you?"

"No," he said. "I make a terrible first impression."

He hadn't on me. "I mean, when did you arrive? How long are you staying?"

"I'm not sure yet. My plans are fluid. A little hiking, a little fishing, a lot of relaxing. I figured on a week, but…" He shrugged.

"You're not due back at the office?"

"No, I'm a consultant. You know what they say."

I didn't, but I nodded, anyway.

"How about you?" he asked. "A schoolteacher. Principal? Wait, no—drama teacher!"

"Drama teacher?" I said, unable to keep myself from returning his smile. "I'm not sure that says anything good about me. No, I teach first grade."

"Funny, you don't look like a teacher."

"What do I look like?"

"Hmm." He tilted his head. "More like…"

The girl next door? A vanilla éclair? A blond dumpling?

My phone rang. *I'm too sexy for my…* I sighed and answered, "This is me."

"Eve, I need a favor. A huge favor, and I know we—"

"I'm sorry, who's calling?"

A pause. "Gregory."

"Greg!" I said brightly. "Good to hear from you! You need a favor?"

"Um. Yes. Please, Eve. I know I—"

"What's the magic word?"

"Please? I already said *please.*"

"Try again." I hung up and turned brightly to Jack. "Scarlett Johansson?"

"What?"

"You were telling me who I looked like. I was helping."

His smile glowed bright. "No, not Scarlett Johansson. Maybe—"

My phone rang again. I apologized to Jack before answering. "Still me."

"Sorry?" Gregory said. "Is that the magic word."

"It's a start."

"Listen, Eve, this is crazy, but…when I woke up this morning I was, um, in my office. And, er, I was naked. And suddenly everyone else came in."

"Wait. Is this really Gregory? Because even I couldn't come up with a fantasy this good."

"This is real, Eve. I don't remember anything. Oh, shit! They're coming back. Listen, I told them you were getting back at me for breaking up with you. You came to the office for…well, you know. And then you took my clothes and left me naked."

"You told them I came begging for one last bang?" My eyes swiveled to Jack, who was listening with keen interest. I shook my head no, telling him I went nowhere for one last bang.

"Eve, they think I just got naked and passed out…and that's creepy."

"But you did."

"Well—"

"And you *are* creepy."

"You've gotta help me. If I put you on speakerphone, will you play along?"

"Of course not."

"This could finish me. You know how I feel about my career. How hard I've worked. Please, *please*. I'm sorry."

Oh, man. I was loving this! "Hmm. Let me think, am I at

a stage in my life where I need to care about other people's feelings?" I turned back to Jack, nodding yes, I did care.

Gregory didn't answer. Instead there was a click on his side of the line, and the shuffle of people stepping into his office, trying to be stealthy.

"Well, Eve," he said, back in his normal blustery tones, "I admit, you got me. But taking my clothes after one last fling on the office couch…that was low."

I looked around the Smelts Store, from the old coots to the shelves of dusty staples to Jack, who watched with open curiosity. Gregory seemed so distant, like the memory of a life lived by someone else. Would it kill me to help him out? "You deserved it," I said.

"Some of the people here—" His voice got lower; clearly he was looking at someone in particular. "Some of the back-stabbing bastards here are pretending I just did that to myself."

"There's only one thing I regret, Gregory. Having sex with you one last time. When you sweat, it's like steak juice. All clammy and gross and—"

Someone laughed, and Gregory's phone went dead. I hung up with a triumphant flourish.

"Steak juice?" Jack asked.

"Oh, that was just a favor for a friend."

"Remind me not to ask for any favors."

I gave him my coy look. "Were you going to?"

"You've got a little bacon, right there." He touched the side of his mouth. So much for coy. "And as a matter of fact—" A horn honked outside, and he looked toward the door. "Damn, that's for me."

"Fishing guide?"

"No, a meeting. It's a sort of working vacation." He took a last sip of coffee and pulled his wallet from the back pocket of his jeans.

"I'll get it," I said, as the honking continued. "The least I can do for rescuing me this morning."

"That was my pleasure." He shrugged into his parka, turned to go, then stopped. "Tell me your real name, Volvo Girl."

"Eve."

He nodded. "Yeah. That's exactly who you look like."

"That's crap," Natasha told the man in the ditch. "One step above craft fair watercolors."

"The subject is derivative, but the composition and— look at the brushstrokes!"

"I, um—" Natasha felt herself blush. "It's just surf 'n' turf."

"No," he said, climbing out of the ditch. "The right answer is 'thank you.' And what's surf 'n' turf, anyway? Like bread and butter, for Mainers?"

"Yeah. Are you sure you're okay?"

"You didn't hit me. I'm fine."

"I told you," the tall man said. "C'mon, Johnny, let's go."

Johnny gave the painting to Natasha. "Who reps you?"

"I don't have a rep. I don't even show my good stuff. If you want, I mean—I don't live far, and I feel bad for running you off the road. I could make us some tea or something. I've got gunpowder."

"Gunpowder?" The tall guy said. "Next you're gonna shoot him?"

"It's a kind of tea, Simon," Johnny said.

"We've got a meeting," he said. "Remember?"

"You can handle that," Johnny said. "I'll catch up with you tonight."

For a moment, Natasha worried about inviting a strange man to her house, but then the two men started bickering like an old married couple and the brief anxiety vanished. Finally, Johnny quelled Simon with a look, and he stalked off, his leather-soled dress shoes slipping on the ice.

"He works for you?" she asked.

"We're old friends. He's a lawyer—even on vacation he worries."

"Well, he seems really…" She paused, thinking. "Tall."

Johnny laughed. "He doesn't like the cold."

"Ah." She smiled awkwardly. "So…do you want to ride with me?" What was she doing? What was he going to think? What was he going to *do?* He was good-looking—athletic build, nice voice and fine features that would grow on you. No wedding ring, either. Still, inviting a stranger home was maybe not her smartest move. "My brother and his hunting buddies might be there, I don't know if they're back yet. I mean, it's not hunting season yet, but they're all bow hunters."

"Right. I'll follow you, if that's okay."

"Great," she said. At least she wouldn't have to make small talk in the cramped cabin of her little truck.

The minute they were inside her house, she regretted her impulse. The house was its usual mess and Puck for some reason hissed at Johnny before scampering upstairs.

"Vicious cat?" Johnny asked, grinning. "Worse than your brother, I bet."

"I really do have a brother."

"Is he a bow hunter?"

"Well, he's deadly with a spading fork."

"That's almost—" He stopped, seeing the canvases against the wall. "Whoa."

"Well, that one's not done, and those aren't my best, but—"

"Right, I get it." He held up his hand, a polite way of getting her to shut up while he wandered the perimeter of the room as if it were a gallery, which the old barn resembled because of its size. Although, in a gallery Natasha's pictures would've been hung, which she was always too lazy to do. Instead they loitered against the walls like teenagers at a school dance. Johnny walked around the room twice, stopping in front of each painting, stepping close, scowling and muttering sometimes, shaking his head sometimes.

She wanted to think he was a pretentious jackass, trying to get into her pants by showing her his etchings. But these were *her* etchings. And, though he was definitely attractive, she wasn't sure she wanted in his pants. At least, not yet.

She finally could take no more, and actually made tea, which wasn't exactly an everyday occurrence. When she gave him his mug, he was staring at *Lost Hope*. "You're just about there, aren't you?" he said.

For a moment, she was tempted to laugh that off to say, "You can't get the-ah from hea-ah," in her thickest Maine accent, but for some reason she couldn't. "I hope so. I think so."

"It'll be monumental," he said.

"Who *are* you?" she said. "And what are you doing to my ego?"

He laughed. "You seem pretty grounded."

"Let me tell you, Johnny—" She started, then stopped. "Is it John or Johnny?"

"Well, that's what Simon calls me, but only when he's pissed."

"I like it. 'Johnny.'" She covered her wince by taking a sip of tea. Was that flirting? Sharing a pet name with the Tall Guy? God, she was pathetic.

"Your stuff reminds me of…Ruth Rosen, but less pared down." He moved to the next painting, talking mostly to himself. "And Sara Sue, too, a little. There's something almost sculptural here. Architectural, I mean. But Rosen and Sue, they're nothing alike."

"They *are,*" Natasha said. "I mean, their stuff isn't—you'd never confuse them—but it's the intelligence behind the work that—wait—you *know* who Ruth Rosen and Sara Sue are?"

"A good friend spent the past ten years trying to educate me. I think she'd like your work."

"Well, if you like Rosen—"

"Her name is Mandy Michaels," he said.

Natasha stared at him. "Amanda Michaels? The gallery?"

"I think of her more as a human," he said, smiling. "But yeah, that's the one."

"Okay. Okay." She looked around the room. Could there be a hidden camera? Maybe he'd *jumped* in front of her truck. Sure. A camera crew landed on Broome Isle to make Natasha Kent look like an ass. "Okay."

"I think she'd be interested in seeing your paintings." He pulled his cell phone from his parka pocket. "I'll call her, shall I?"

"Okay." Natasha said.

★ ★ ★

All around Kim, the world stretched and purred in lazy pleasure. The comforter snuggled her loosely, keeping her warm and sleepy. He'd left hours ago, and after one last kiss she'd fallen into a deep slumber and dreamed of pleasure.

Rosy light filtered through the windows when she opened her eyes—and he was back, standing beside the bed, watching her.

"Hi," she said, suddenly shy. "I thought…this morning…I thought it was a one-time thing." Because she could handle a one-morning stand: more that that—well, she wasn't sure she was ready.

"I'm not into one-time things," he said, his voice rough.

Okay, so maybe she *was* ready. "You're so greedy." She crawled to the end of the bed and pressed herself to him, her warm, naked skin against his cool, rough thermal shirt and jeans.

He kissed her. "I want it all." He ran his fingers through her hair, down her neck to the tip of one breast. "Is this… Are you okay with this?"

For an answer, she pulled him backward onto the bed and wrapped her legs around his waist. It went against Kim's nature not to worry: about the fallout and the future. But at the moment, she wanted exactly one thing. And she wanted it now.

11

I wasted half my snow day at the Smelts Store, waiting for Jack to reappear and drinking gallons of coffee. Finally, my stomach could take no more and I'd retreated home. Spent my unanticipated free time settling in, shifting the furniture, tossing the knickknacks around, and going through my freshly filled bureau and closet and sighing at my lack of anything appropriate for Maine.

Which is the only reason I overdressed for school the next day. It had nothing to do with the fact that Jack knew where I worked and knew my name, and was stuck on the same island, and could hardly fail to stop by for a flirtatious visit.

Yet somehow, he failed. And I went through an entire day of school wearing a tight sweater, high-heeled boots and black miniskirt, looking delicious for nobody but Dr. Pepper and the other male teachers—all of them married. But that was fine. You know how you meet someone, and you can tell he likes you, and sparks fly and then…nothing? Happens all the time. There's nothing you can do. Maybe the sparks weren't as sparky as I'd thought. Maybe he just wasn't that into me.

On Friday, I decided I was past that sort of juvenile daydream. I mean, I was in Maine now, making a life in the rugged north, forging through snowbanks on the way to the one-room schoolhouse and catching salmon with my bare hands and all that. In fact, *that* daydream kept me going through my morning cup of coffee at the Smelts Store—where the old coots were "grizzled trappers" and my Volvo was a dogsled—and through a schoolday inspired by *Little House on the Prairie*.

I had yard duty after school, which entailed making sure all the kids got on the bus. I'd been warned to keep an eye out for the few possible troublemakers—the "spirited" kids—and reined them in early. I was feeling pretty pleased with myself, until the driver came to me complaining she was missing one of the first-graders.

"One of *my* kids?" I said.

"Yeah. Conner," she said.

"Conner Davis?" I asked, as if there were a dozen Conners in my class.

I was surprised, because of all my boys he was the easiest. And the most engaging. And charming and bright. And, well, my favorite in every way. In fact, this morning he'd been about the only kid interested in my unit on pioneers, log cabins, butter churning and cooking with acorn flour. He was the least likely kid to go missing.

The driver grunted. She was a middle-aged woman with a man's gut and a smoker's voice, and she told me if Conner didn't show in two minutes, she was gone.

I raced into the classroom and the playground, circled the school building and finally spotted him across the street, in the front yard of a stately bed-and-breakfast. I yelled for the driver to wait and ran to get Conner, who was scurrying around the yard.

"Conner!" I said.

"Hi, Miss Crenshaw."

"What are you *doing?*" I asked him.

"Collecting acorns," Jack said from the B and B steps, holding a BlackBerry with the earpiece in his ear. He was dressed in jeans and Timberlands, and since the weather had turned warmish again, an Adidas track jacket instead of a parka. "His teacher told him you can make muffins out of them."

"You can!" Conner and I both insisted. Then I remembered myself and said, "I mean, Conner, the bus is waiting."

His mouth opened in an O of surprise. "I'm sorry!"

I held out my hand. "Let's go."

"Wait," Jack said, removing his earpiece and stuffing his BlackBerry in his jacket pocket. "Have dinner with me."

"I'll have to ask Mom first," Conner said.

I grinned. "I think he means me. I'll have to ask my mom first, too."

The bus driver honked and I shepherded Conner across the street.

"He's cute," the driver said.

"He's a good kid," I said from the bottom of the bus stairs. "Most of the time."

"No, I mean the guy." She nodded toward Jack, still watching from across the street. "What's his story?"

I peeked at him around the bus. "I'm not sure. But I think I'm about to find out."

"Let me know if he's single."

Was she serious? She looked like his mother. "Absolutely," I said. "Although…" I winked at her. "I saw him first."

She shot me a dismissive look and shut the door. What, I wasn't even competition to middle-aged bus drivers with beer bellies now? I turned back to Jack as the bus exhaust wafted romantically around me.

"What did your mom say?" he called.

"She said 'maybe.'"

"I've been waiting for two days to ask you. Look, I even brought a gift." He pulled a Granny Smith from his jacket pocket. "An apple for the teacher."

"That's so cheesy!"

"Yeah," he said. "But I figure if I embarrass myself before dinner, I won't spill the soup. So how about tonight?"

"Tonight? Where?"

"That place on the water. The Barnacle?"

I've read all the books, right? Don't accept the first date. Say you're busy, maybe some other time. Make it clear he'll be lucky if you *ever* say "yes."

"See you there at seven!" I called.

Back home, I frantically dialed Natasha, hoping she'd come help me decide what to wear. She had no interest in fashion, but could always be counted on to tell me what *didn't* look good. She wasn't home, so I called Kim, thinking maybe she'd loan me something fabulous, even if it was all black. Again, no answer.

I changed twice, trying to find the right balance between attractive and casual, then was forced to imagine Natasha sitting in the corner of my bedroom, and Kim lying on the bed, both of them critiquing everything I put on. There were a lot of nasty comments until the imaginary Natasha said, "Stick with the black and the red. It's chromatic." Whatever that meant.

So I arrived at the Barnacle in what I'd worn to school, red cords and a black fitted cashmere sweater. At least I'd switched my Dansko clogs—aka teacher's shoes—for high-heeled suede boots, changed my earrings and added my fitted black peacoat, which made me feel more like a city girl. Too busy to do anything but change my accessories.

I stepped inside and told the hostess I was meeting someone, and Jack appeared and said, "Okay, the apple was cheesy, I know. And this, well…I got you these."

A bouquet of yellow daises, bright and cheerful. "They look like little sunshines," I said.

"I was going to bring roses but…these reminded me of you."

The hostess motioned to us, and gave me a "he brought you flowers!" look as she led us to our table. I sat across from Jack, beside a window facing the harbor in the fading light.

"You look great," Jack said.

"Thanks." I noticed he'd changed into a brown long-sleeved polo that made his eyes look a little green. "You look nice, too."

"I do what I can." He set his menu aside. "We're not going to have a really stilted conversation, are we?"

"Well, we *could*," I said. "If you want."

"Maybe we should. It's a sort of rite of passage."

"So…what? I ask you what you do?"

"Yeah, that works. Then I say I'm a consultant. You ask what kind… God, I'm already boring myself."

I laughed. "We can just look out the window, instead. Go straight to the comfortable silences."

"They would be comfortable, too, wouldn't they?"

He looked at me with such sudden fondness that I turned away, blushing, and looked out the window where lobster boats and water taxis bobbed in the harbor. Across the bay were the lights of Portland, lit up enticingly. This wasn't like one of my daydreams of being swept off my feet in a limousine or with a diamond ring the size of my head. Jack was…normal. Bringing an apple for teacher—how corny was that? But he *knew* it was corny, and he still did it, just to what? Break the ice? Make me smile? This was something special.

"We could've taken the ferry to Portland," Jack said. "I've heard Fore Street is good."

I glanced around at the scarred wooden tables and directors chairs covered in royal blue canvas, the walls decorated with old fishing gear and seaside menus from long-faded restaurants. I liked it. It was all so *Maine*.

"But I like this," he continued. "It's so…Maine. Maybe we'll do Fore Street next time."

"Next time? We haven't even gotten our drinks yet." I attempted to shoot him a quelling look. "I can't tell if that's confidence or arrogance."

"Neither, it's…" He shook his head, a slow smile spreading across his face. "Well, maybe both."

"Are you arrogant?"

"Not really—at least I don't think so."

"What are you like, then?"

"I don't know. I'm a good guy? A good friend, I like to laugh, I like to learn, I like to—" he was going to say *love,* I thought, but he shrugged instead "—have fun."

"'A good guy'?"

He grinned. "What's better than a good, ordinary guy?"

I laughed. "You sound like a single woman."

"You haven't been single long, have you? I mean, judging from your conversation with Steak Juice."

"Steak Juice," I smiled. "That's the perfect name for him."

The waitress came while I was still laughing and asked if we wanted wine. I agreed to white and Jack ordered a chardonnay and the steamers.

"It's not like New York, is it?" he said, when she left.

"How'd you know I'm from the city?"

"You talk way too fast."

"That's what my students say. I should try talking like a Mainer, and add three syllables of 'ah' after every word."

"Is that what they do?"

"Yeah-ah-ah. Pa-ah-ahk the ca-ah-ah in the do-ah ya-ahd."

He almost choked on his water. "That's terrible!"

"Oh, I suppose you could do better?"

"I know better than to try. What's a doo-wah ya-ad?"

"The door yard!"

"What's a door yard, then?"

"I don't know," I admitted. "It's something my friends tell me Mainers say, but I've never heard anyone say it."

"Not even your friends at the General Store?"

"Not yet," I told him, "but give me time. I did eat one of their prize pigs. Princess. And I've overheard them arguing about fiddleheads, so there's that."

The waitress returned and we ordered dinner, and ate, and talked, and somehow circled back to Gregory. I guess that conversation Jack had overhead was pretty odd. So I told him the whole story—more than I should have, probably. But he knew how to listen, and it already felt like we were old friends. But not *just* old friends, more like old friends with a high wire of sexual tension running between us.

Then he said, "And what about you? What are *you* like?"

"I'm like…" I considered, swirling my wine in my glass. "I'm like what you see is what you get."

"God," he said, his voice suddenly raspy. "I hope so."

And for a moment we were alone. Just him and me, nobody else. No waitress, no diners. No restaurant. Nothing but him and me. I felt a heat creep from my neck to my face. It wasn't a blush or embarrassment. It was something else entirely.

Then the world slid back into place, and I was afraid he could actually see through me, so I blurted the first thing that came to mind. "Are you staying at the bed-and-breakfast across from the school?"

"Hmm? What? Oh, Simon and I have a suite there for—"

"Wait," I said. And when he stopped, I didn't know what else to say.

But he waited.

"Okay," I finally said. The truth was, this was the stupidest thing to do on a first date. I knew that. I knew that like Kim knew canning and Natasha knew paint. But I didn't care. If I was wrong, I'd be horrified and rejected. But I'd also know if I was wrong. I wanted, more than anything, to know. So I said, "Is it just me? This. What I'm feeling, right now. Is it just me?"

"It's not just you."

"It's all going a little fast."

"I know. For me, too. It's like we've known each other longer than this, like we've…I'm freaking you out, aren't I?"

"No," I said, half surprised. "You're not."

"A little?"

I laughed. "A little. Not you, just…*this.*"

"Well, freaking out a little is good, right?"

"Um…is it?"

"Just agree with me on that one."

"Oh—then yes, it's totally good."

He nodded. "Good. Now. What do we do?"

"How about dessert?"

His smile never failed to warm me. "Dessert, of course."

We sat in one of those comfortable silences we'd mentioned earlier, until the waitress came with the dessert menus. We ordered a chocolate-hazelnut torte and two decaf coffees.

When the waitress left I toyed with a crumb on the tablecloth. Then, without looking up, I said, "Whatever this is… between us—I like it."

He said, "Me, too."

✳ 12 ✳

That was Friday night. Jack and I had kissed goodbye outside the Barnacle—which was more romantic than it sounded—and I'd driven the Volvo home without quite touching the road, as if it were a boxy Swedish Hovercraft. Then I'd floated into my bedroom and flopped on the bed and beamed at the ceiling.

Saturday morning, I called Natasha. Way too early—before noon—but I didn't care. I wanted to gloat—I mean, to share my happiness. Of course, I expected her to just grunt into the phone, but I didn't need much more than the occasional indication that she was still alive.

Instead, a man answered her phone.

A man! In her house, in the morning, sounding entirely at home. Well, Natasha was beautiful and sexy and smart and talented, so it shouldn't be such a surprise. We hadn't spoken since Wednesday. I guess there was plenty of time for her to have met someone. Well, of course there was—look at me. Still, an overnight guest? She didn't usually move so fast.

"Oh!" I said, in my smooth way. "Hi. Hello. Hello, there. Good morning."

"Don't get excited, Eve," he said. "It's me, Marco."

"Well, that's anticlimactic."

He chuckled. "What every man wants to hear."

"Is she there?"

"Painting. She's in a manic frenzy, she's been painting for two days straight, I think."

"Oh. Hmm."

"Yeah, forget about Natasha for another two days, that's my advice."

"What are you doing there?"

"Tossing raw meat into her cage. You know she forgets to eat when she gets like this. Well, and working on the house, actually. Do you want to talk to her?"

"Not when she's like that, no. Just tell her I called."

"She knows it's you. She's mouthing 'no' to me, and drawing a finger across her throat. Except it's not a finger, it's a paintbrush and she—" His voice got softer. "Jesus, Natasha! You're such a child, would you—"

I found myself laughing at the dial tone and decided to try Kim. I should've started with her, anyway. While Natasha would keep me grounded, by pointing out the negatives, Kim would do the same, yet somehow leave me feeling encouraged.

"Eve!" she said, when I reached her. "I was just thinking about you. God, is this the most beautiful morning *ever*? Sometimes I roll out of bed and I can't believe how blessed we are, living here, surrounded by beauty, the woods and the sea, and friends and—oh! My muffins."

I recognized the sound of her oven opening and wondered aloud what kind they were.

"They're cranberry. Cranberry muffins." Her voice was softer and syrupy. "There's the boy! There you are! You hungry, mangy little lug."

"Uh? You're not talking to me, right?" I may have been a lug, but was certain I wasn't mangy.

"I didn't tell you about the dog that's been hanging around?"

"I thought you only had cats." Natasha had told me Kim fed any stray that came around.

"Well, now I have a puppy. A little black Lab with his ribs showing, all mangy and afraid. He won't come inside and can hardly stand. I've been cooking for him and leaving scraps on the porch."

"A puppy?"

"Well, more of a gangly adolescent. His ribs stick out and I think he must've been beaten he's so hand-shy." She babbled baby talk, apparently out her kitchen window, for a moment, then said, "How was *your* week? I keep hearing what a wonderful teacher you are."

"From whom?"

"Well, you know what a small island it is, everyone talks about everyone. And Jeanine—you know, Jeanine Davis?— her son's in your class, Conner. I can't believe she has a kid in first grade. We're the same age, almost exactly, and look at her! I, on the other hand—"

"Kim!" I said. "Wait! Do me a favor."

"Of course. What?"

"Look at your feet."

"Um. Okay. There they are."

"Are you wearing my shoes?"

She laughed. "I just feel *good* today. Happy and full of… Oh! It's simmering. I need to add the eggs—gotta go!"

"Wait, Kim—" But she'd already hung up. Not exactly the grounding presence I'd expected.

I showered and dressed and, inspired by Kim's muffins, made pancakes. Then I threw the uninspired pancakes in the trash and had cereal for breakfast. I considered calling my mother, but that was always a bad way to start the weekend, so I washed my dishes instead, and the phone rang.

"Eve," Jack said, and I could hear the smile in his voice. "Did you sleep well?"

"Actually, I've been leafing through my copy of *He's Not That Into You* and—"

"But what if he *is* that into you?"

"Would you stop that?" I said. Because I couldn't take all of this hope. Plus, my mouth was starting to ache from smiling.

"Sorry. I'll slow down. My wife says I—"

"Your *what?*"

"Kidding! That was me slowing down."

"Not *that* slow, Jack. That's stopped. In fact, it's Reverse."

"Well, I prefer Drive," he said. "Even if it's ten miles an hour. Are you free Monday night?"

"You can give it more gas than that," I said. It was only Saturday morning. I was, at least, hoping for a lunch date on Sunday.

"Believe me, if it were my choice, pedal to the metal, but I've got meetings all weekend. Monday, though, there's a Bean Supper at the Grange Hall."

"Ohmigod, really?"

"I thought you'd like that."

"The Grange Hall! That's like the inner sanctum of Mainers."

"Maybe some of your Smelts Shack buddies will be there."

"I have the *perfect* outfit to wear, too."

"To a bean supper? I don't think you're supposed to dress up."

"Oh, I'm dressing up. I do not take a bean supper lightly."

"Well, then I'm looking forward to seeing you and what you're wearing."

Which left my heart revving.

A snuffling sounded outside the bathroom window, and Kim turned from the mirror. "Stay!" she called to the dog she knew was skulking around the house. "Stay, boy, you stay there."

She set a bowl of food outside the French doors and stepped back into the kitchen. In a moment, a glistening black nose poked around the corner, twitching wildly. Then the skinny black Lab skidded to a halt at the bowl, inhaled all the food and scooted away. She shook her head at his coltish, uncoordinated movement.

Kim watched the pup skitter away and crossed to her office to do the bookkeeping for the cottages. She finished, put everything back in the rolltop desk and went to the kitchen, running her hands along the soapstone countertop.

She felt like making something honeyed and delicious. Baklava or crème brûlée. Or pumpkin pie. Not just *any* pumpkin pie. Her grandmother's pie, a recipe that was almost sinful. She started with the crust, sifting the flour and sugar with a pinch of salt and cinnamon. She cut in the butter, and heard the front door open.

She didn't bother turning from the counter. She'd known he was coming. Why else would she have made the pie? She worked the butter into the flour, and felt a wash of heat, a tingle of anticipation. The butter melted in her hands and turned the flour into crumbs. She knew his eyes were on her, hungry and hot, but she kept her back to him, kneading the dough, parting her legs slightly, her black skirt falling to her knees.

The first thing was his breath on the back of her neck, then his lips. She moaned and tilted her head, and he pressed himself against her, stroking her sides then moving his hands to her breasts.

She whispered, "Now, here—don't wait."

He made a noise deep in his throat. Grabbed her skirt and lifted it to her waist.

Mandy Michaels. The Amanda Michaels Gallery. During the first day, Natasha had thought of nothing else. Her mantra was *Mandy Michaels. The Amanda Michaels Gallery.* Then, sometime around midnight, her mind went dark and she thought of nothing at all.

She moved, though, and painted. As if a spark flowed from the canvas, to the brush, through her body and back to the canvas. Johnny had stopped by the other day, but she'd hardly said two words to him. She was working—she didn't have two words to say. He'd stayed, anyway, for more than an hour, somehow effacing himself so effectively that she hadn't even cared he was there—or noticed when he'd gone.

Except for what he'd left behind. Not candy, not flowers, not a bottle of wine. A little sheet of stickers. Red dots. Like galleries used, to show which paintings were sold.

She'd smiled, set the coffeepot on the burner, and returned to her painting.

The Grange Hall looked like a sleepy old farmhouse, though the parking lot was full and the "Bean Supper" sign beckoned me forward. It was down the lane, past the Smelt Shack, with a tidy lawn and wide, empty porch.

I'd arranged to meet Jack here, but I was shy of entering by myself. This was such a tight-knit community, and they were sure to think I was an outsider—mostly on account of me actually being one. I was maybe a little overdressed, too. But if I stayed on the island, this would be my social life and I was determined to embrace it.

I parked in the lot and weaved between the other cars toward the entrance, a side door lit up by two lamps casting a welcoming glow. I'd almost reached the door when Jack stepped into the light, watching me approach in my dove-gray satin cocktail dress and red heels.

He was wearing a dark Hugo Boss–ish suit, a gray shirt and matching tie, and I loved that he'd been waiting for me. I stopped and stared—enjoying the sight of him in something other than jeans and a T-shirt. He'd done it for me. Then he said "nice," and I said "nice" back, and we smiled at each other some more.

Then we went inside and he paid the $11.00—$5.50 each. This wasn't the regular monthly bean supper, this was a special fund-raising bean supper to help Louanne Bernson's "little niece, Emma" with some scary-yet-undefined dental problem. A woman gave us a ticket and told us to get our pie first—pick out one slice, and be seated. So we did. We went to the pie table, chose slices of apple and sat at the long communal tables, pie by our sides, before even getting any beans. Don't ask me. I don't know why these Mainers do anything.

We were just ridiculously overdressed, I mean laughably so. Across the table Chester laughed, and so did Marie—and a few others whom I didn't even know. But they laughed *with* us, and I think maybe they were a little pleased, too, that the outsiders didn't come to the Grange Hall to slum or pretend they were natives. They dressed up and enjoyed themselves.

There were a lot of beans. "Bean supper" is not meant as a metaphor, like say, "lemon law." There were yellow-eyed beans, Jacob's Cattle beans, kidney beans and navy beans all baked to perfection. When Jack asked if I wanted some brown bread, I said yes, expecting…brown bread. But no. In Maine, *this* is brown bread: molasses, brown sugar, buttermilk and flour, all baked together in a can. I kid you not.

He may be a New Yorker, but Jack looked at home in the Grange Hall—completely comfortable with himself, yet curious and polite. He wasn't condescending, sitting there in his nine-hundred-dollar suit, and he wasn't treated like an interloper. Mainers might eat some strange stuff, but they aren't stupid, and they weren't gonna let some stranger patronize them. And they could give the cold shoulder like nobody else. But they didn't. Maybe because I knew some of them from the Smelts Shack and others as parents of my students. Maybe because Jack was so unassumingly charming. And maybe because they liked basking in the warm glow of me and Jack falling in love.

★ ★ ★

Wednesday night I met Natasha and Kim at the ferry dock to Portland, for our now-traditional night on the town. The weather had been strange all day. Cold, for the most part, but then suddenly a warm breeze would hit and you felt like you were in Florida. The minute you stripped down to your T-shirt, the warmth passed and you were left shivering in the forty-degree air.

I could tell Kim and Natasha had been feeling the same thing, because they were fiddling with their coats when I got to the dock, trying to decide whether to keep them on or not. Well that, and Natasha said, "The weather's weird."

I nodded and shrugged out of my peacoat. "Where's this hot air coming from? It's October."

"Global warming." Kim unbuttoned her black wool jacket. "We're all for it in Maine, but this is ridiculous."

"Yeah. Time enough for hot flashes later," Natasha said.

"You're already kinda menopausal," I teased. "Mood swings, insomnia—"

"Hey! I'm two months younger than you."

I was about to respond when something wet and cold rubbed the back of my hand. I looked down and saw that a skinny black Lab had appeared beside me. Glossy black fur, bright pleading eyes, a nose twitching with curiosity.

"Hello, cutie," I said as I bent down to pat him. "Is this is your new pup, Kim?"

She scratched him behind the ear. "He must've followed me. And just a few days ago, he could barely stand. Look at him, isn't he a handsome beast?"

I looked. Despite being a mangy, near-skeletal mess, he *was* handsome. Big square head, white teeth and long pink tongue, and his black eyes were alight with interest under his wrinkled brow.

"You got a dog?" Natasha asked Kim.

"He just showed up."

"Who does he belong to?"

She shrugged. "How should I know?"

"Because you keep dog biscuits in your purse, and know every dog on this island and whether they prefer peanut butter or chicken snacks."

Kim grinned sheepishly. "True. But I don't know this one. He must've been left by some tourists." She unzipped her black leather bag. "And he likes beef—turns his nose up at peanut butter." She gave a biscuit to the dog and said in a puppy-talk voice, "Are you my little carnivore?"

I smiled at Natasha, who rolled her eyes at me. "What're you calling him?" I asked.

"Nothing, yet. He won't come into my house, and first I have to make sure nobody's looking for him. I'll put a poster up at the General Store."

The dog wetly gobbled the biscuit, then lunged at Natasha, who tried warding him off. "Down! Down, I'm a cat person. Speaking of which, what do your cats think of him?"

Kim looked guilty. "I don't have any cats. You mean the strays?"

"Kim, everyone knows those cats belong to you," Natasha said. "They're strays in name only. They would've been rounded up long ago by pest control, if everyone didn't know you were feeding them."

She sighed. "Actually, they've been kind of scarce lately. I think it *is* the dog."

"He's probably eating them," Natasha said.

The dog turned and—I swear—smiled at me and Kim, then barked as the ferry arrived. He tried to follow us onto the ramp, but Kim stopped him, and when the ferry pulled away, he sat whining on the dock.

The three of us stood on the deck and watched the island fade into the distance.

"I hope he's all right," I said.

"He'll find his way back to my house," Kim said. "Or maybe he'll go back to his real home."

"Anyone else notice the size of his—"

"*Natasha!*" Kim said.

"I'm an artist. I notice these things. He must be part horse."

Before I could recommend that Kim name him "Black Stallion," we hit a cold front. "Oh, my God," I said, shoving my arms into my coat and scurrying into the cabin. "It's freezing!"

Since they didn't get to Portland last week, Natasha figured they could afford to splurge on Fiora, an expensive restaurant in Old Port. She gave her name to the hostess and led Kim and Eve to the Victorian velvet couches near the bar and—knowing Eve was feeling homesick—ordered Manhattans.

The overstuffed cushions cradled her, and she felt herself relax. She'd been working nonstop since Johnny gave her exactly the motivation she needed, but she was about to collapse. She needed tonight, needed friends and food and conversation to recharge. She sighed and looked from Kim to Eve—then back to Kim.

"What?" she asked.

"Hmm?" Kim said.

"I know that expression. If you were a cat, there'd be cream on your whiskers."

"I'm happy we're here," Kim said.

"Yeah," Natasha said. "And?"

"And look at Eve."

Natasha did, and Eve was shining with eagerness, flushed and bright-eyed. "Yes, Eve?"

"Well, I—" She stopped when the bartender laid the drinks out. "We need to toast."

"Toast what, Evie?"

"I met someone."

"A man? On the island? Oh, God—not Dr. Pepper?"

Laughter at the lame joke bubbled out of Eve.

"To Eve's someone," Kim said, raising her glass. "Tell us everything."

They clinked glasses, and Eve said, "Remember last week when we all crashed at Kim's house? God, what *happened* that night? Anyway, when I went outside in the morning, there was ice everywhere, and I kinda slipped and slid to my car, and yanked on the door, and somehow levered myself underneath and—"

"Underneath your car?" Natasha asked.

"Yeah, and—" Eve paused to wait for the laughter to die down. "Yeah. I was the Wicked Witch of the East."

"Not exactly the best way to meet a guy," Kim said.

Eve smiled. "I don't know, maybe it was."

Natasha swirled her drink, waiting for Eve to reveal the details. She could tell by the color it wasn't how she would've mixed it, but she wasn't sure where the bartender had gone wrong. Maybe a little too much sweet vermouth?

"Anyway, I was so embarrassed, I just drove away," Eve said. "But then he found me later at the Smelts Shack and we had coffee and—"

"It's a shack now?" Natasha said.

"When wasn't it? The old coots are totally warming up to me, though. And I ate Princess."

"I'm not gonna touch that," Natasha said.

"Princess the pig, Chester's prize pig."

"Ah," Kim chided. "You knew her name and still ate her?" Kim was basically vegetarian.

"Sorry," Eve said, then turned to Natasha. "It was so good, though. She tasted like victory."

Natasha found herself unable to keep from smiling. She knew how happy Eve was that the locals were opening up to her. "So you had breakfast with him, and then what?"

"The whole encounter lasted like five minutes. Four of them ruined by a phone call from Gregory. He heard me telling Gregory he sweats steak juice when we have sex."

"He does *what?*"

"It was a total lie—he had me on speakerphone again." And Eve told some odd, convoluted story about Gregory waking up naked in his office, and needing her to accept the blame. "Or, I guess, the credit," she finished.

Kim furrowed her brow. "That's odd."

"I should've let them fire him," Eve said. "But he's so pathetic, all he has is that job. I felt sorry for him."

"Don't you remember that scribble Natasha drew, with Gregory naked in his office?" Kim asked. "And then he actually *was.*"

Natasha shrugged. "Yeah, that's weird, Eve dated a perv. Who would've guessed?"

"Hey! I don't date pervs. Much. Anyway, then two days later, I ran into this other guy outside of school."

"He lurks outside the elementary school?" Natasha asked. "Oh, no, that's not a perv."

"He's staying at the B and B across the street! *Sheesh*. And he asked me to dinner. And I said yes. And we had dinner, and…you know all those dating games you play?"

Natasha said, "You mean like with mojitos and—"

"Not *that* kind, Natasha. I mean when you try to be brighter than you really are, and more interesting, and you're thinking, 'Well, do I kiss him? Do I sleep with him? Is he really this guy he's pretending to be, or is he just another jerk? Who does he want *me* to be?'"

Kim nodded. "Dating. Sure."

"You never pretend, Kim." Natasha said. "You wouldn't know how to pretend. You're always just you."

"Once, with Marco, I pretended to be a harem girl."

"Aaaaagh!" Natasha said, covering her ears. "My brother, remember? Would you stop that?"

"I'm just saying—"

"Well, stop saying! Now, Eve…all those dating games, yes?"

Eve stopped giggling. "Things are different with him. We don't really play by those rules. We play *with* those rules. I mean, we both know them, but it's all out there in the open. We're honest, I guess." She fiddled with one of her curls. "I don't know. I've only known him a week, but there's something about him. He feels right, like we've known each other forever. And I know he's thinking the same. Have you ever felt like that with someone?"

Natasha hadn't, but sensed that Kim and Marco had been like that. She glanced at Kim, who was staring down into her drink, stirring the ice with her forefinger.

"Yeah," Kim said quietly.

Natasha wanted to ask more—what had gone wrong?— but couldn't. She and Kim had been getting along so well, she didn't want to rehash all those old feelings. She hadn't realized how much she'd missed hanging out with Kim until Eve had come and somehow diffused the tension between them.

"What's he do?" Natasha asked Eve, to change the subject.

"He's a consultant—some kind of environmental studies. He's measuring the impact tourism has on the island's environment."

"So basically he's Greenpeace fabulous," Kim said.

Eve smiled. "Exactly!"

"And?" Natasha asked.

"And what?"

"And how's the sex?" Natasha asked, because that was always Eve's final test with a new guy. He could be selfish and vain, but if the sex was okay, Eve would overlook other shortcomings. Witness the catastrophe that was Gregory. The way she was raving about this guy, the sex must be phenomenal.

Eve gulped her drink. "I don't know."

"You mean he's great, but the sex is only so-so?" Kim asked. "Maybe that'll get better."

"I mean I have no idea how the sex is, because we haven't had any."

Natasha stared, gape-mouthed.

"I've only known him a week," Eve said, slightly defensively. "It's not like I hook up with anyone I like in under a week."

"Do you not recall college?" Natasha said.

"This is different."

"Because you're not sure of him?" Kim asked.

Eve was quiet for a moment. Then she said, "Because I *am* sure. I'm scary sure."

All this talk of romance worried Kim. What if they asked about *her* love life? She wasn't ready to reveal anything about her little affair—she'd told him they should keep the whole thing to themselves for now. Not from embarrassment; she just wanted to protect this fragile beautiful thing, plant the seed in a warm, sheltered spot and let nature take its course. He'd agreed, but he didn't have inquisitive girlfriends to pry his secrets from him.

Natasha and Eve probably didn't know anything was going on. Okay, that look Natasha gave her when Eve asked about a "feel like you've known him forever" relationship had thrown Kim, but Natasha would hardly keep quiet if she knew anything.

The hostess led them to their table. She was wearing a tomato-red sweater Kim recognized from the J. Crew outlet in Freeport. She'd loved it in the store, but it didn't come in black—yet suddenly the ripe red color appealed to her.

She decided she'd make the trip to Freeport next weekend. The journey took almost an hour, including the ferry ride, and was far better if you had company. But Natasha hated going, even though it was as good as outlet shopping got. Quaint old brick buildings lined the Main Street. Ralph Lauren was in the old bank, Banana Republic in the old town hall, and Abercrombie & Fitch in the old library, which Natasha claimed was ironic: "An institution of knowledge replaced with mindless consumerism." "Sure," Kim had said. "But you know you like their tank tops," which Natasha hadn't been able to argue with.

They sat down at a large table in the back room, set with Provencal-looking napkins and blue water glasses. One wall was made of windows, the other obscured with racks of wine.

Kim turned to Eve. "You wanna go to Freeport this weekend?"

"What's in Freeport?" Eve asked.

Natasha rolled her eyes. "Outlet shopping."

"There are *outlets?*" Eve asked, excited. "Which ones?"

Kim ran down the list. "And Patagonia and Cole Haan and—"

"Are you kidding?" Eve said. "Hell, yeah." She turned to Natasha. "You coming?"

Natasha snorted. "Do I look like I outlet shop?" She was wearing the olive-green silk-and-velvet top Kim had given her.

"You look like you wear fabulous castoffs after *Kim* shops."

"Exactly. But I'll meet you for coffee, I've got a delivery up in Camden, and Freeport's on the way."

"I thought you were doing that last week," Kim said.

"I was. But, uh…"

"I *knew* you had news," Kim said.

"Well." Natasha looked abashed, then finished her drink. "I ran into a guy."

"Really?" Kim gave Natasha's hand a squeeze. She knew how much Natasha wanted to meet someone—even if

Natasha wouldn't admit it to herself—and how difficult she found dating. "I'm so happy for you. Who is—"

"Calm down, Kim," Natasha said. "When I said I ran into him, I mean I ran into him. I hit him with my truck."

Eve laughed loudly enough that heads turned at the next table. "Well, that's a new way to meet men."

"Is he okay?" Kim asked.

"I wasn't trying to meet him," Natasha said, indignantly. "I didn't even see him. And I only nudged him into a ditch. It was the day after the storm."

Kim watched Natasha. There was more. Natasha was as excited as she'd ever seen her. "And…? I know there's something else."

"He likes my art."

"Keep talking."

Natasha toyed with her fork. "He offered to introduce me to Amanda Michaels. He calls her Mandy."

"Oh," Eve said, brightly, "so they're close." She frowned. "Who is she?"

"An art dealer in New York who has her own gallery. She's huge. She discovered Kyle Jacobs! She's like the hottest young person in art. I mean, she's always on those lists of the most influential people in the New York art scene."

"And this guy you hit with your truck knows her?"

"Yeah, really well, I guess. I couldn't believe he offered to phone her for me. In fact, I *really* didn't believe him. I thought maybe he'd just called his home number and pretended to talk."

"So what'd you do?"

"I called her office in New York."

"And…"

"Her assistant said they're expecting my slides, and Mandy can't wait to see them."

"Oh, my God!" Eve squealed. "That's so exciting!"

Kim smiled, tears almost coming to eyes. "I'm so proud of you, Natasha."

"Well, nothing's happened yet." She took a big breath. "But yeah, it's awesome. I mean, I'm finally getting a break. I have a real shot, here."

"And what about the guy?" Kim asked.

Natasha smiled almost secretively. "Are you kidding? He knows Amanda Michaels—I'm in love."

"But you're not," Kim said.

"Yet," Natasha said. "I've been working like crazy all week, painting and taking slides, and—well, we'll see, now that I have a little time. He knows artists, he's smart and good-looking. Hell, I don't even mind him in my studio when I work."

"Hey," Eve said. "You never let *me* stay."

"He doesn't squirrel around and paint his toenails."

"I don't squirrel."

"And he actually knows something about art. I mean, he claims he's just a fan, but…it's great having someone around to talk art with."

"We'll talk art with you," Eve said.

"Yeah, but he doesn't just talk, he also understands—like when I mention 'axis' and 'balance.'"

"We understand," Eve said. "Axis of evil. Do these pants make our axis look big?"

Kim grabbed the salt off the table. "And watch me balance this salt on my hand."

"Exactly my point." Natasha grabbed the salt from Kim and tossed the few grains that spilled over both their shoulders.

They quizzed Natasha about the New York gallery, the "run 'em down" school of dating, and the work she'd been doing through the appetizers. Then Eve said, "Enough about Natasha. What's your story, Kim?"

"Me? I don't have a story."

"No, of course not," Natasha said.

"Silly me," Eve said.

They believed her! Well, that was easy. She bit into her pasta before glancing up at their wicked grins. "What?"

"Remember when I stopped by on Saturday?" Natasha asked.

"What?" Kim said. "Tell me you didn't stop by."

"And I didn't bother knocking, either."

Our dinners came just as the conversation was getting juicy. Natasha's comment had surprised me— I can't believe she didn't call to tell me what she'd overheard. But then again, unlike me, she wasn't really a gossip. I'd only known romance was in the air because of the love bite just below Kim's left ear. You couldn't hide those with short hair.

Kim ordered a bottle of California pinot noir, clearly trying to delay the inevitable—but the waitress immediately pulled the bottle from one of the racks along the wall. Natasha was the official tester, and when she was satisfied and the glasses were poured, we both looked expectantly at Kim.

"Well," she said. "Good wine?"

"I *heard* you," Natasha said. "Half the island heard you. The shutters were banging off the walls of your house."

"We weren't that loud!"

"Well," I said, "anyone who missed the racket would've noticed your hickey."

"Right below the ear," Natasha said. "So we know he's a traditionalist."

"Very primal," I said.

Kim clutched her neck and groaned. "Okay, yes. I'm seeing someone."

"Who?" Natasha asked.

"A man."

"Yes, I figured that much." Natasha frowned. "How'd you meet him?"

"He, um, moved into one of the cottages."

"Which one?" I asked. "Nobody's in any of the cottages near me."

"On the other side of the island. I was telling him the place isn't insulated and he said he ran hot and…well." She gave a little tremor of remembered pleasure. "He does."

Hmm. I was a little jealous, actually. Maybe I'd been too cautious with Jack.

Natasha might've been envious, too, because she was still frowning. She said, "That's a little odd, isn't it, that we'd all meet new men in the same week? I mean, besides Marco, are there *any* available guys on the island?"

"I wouldn't even count Marco." I turned to Natasha. "*You* certainly shouldn't."

"I'm serious," Natasha said. "How many new people move to the island in a year? Three? Four? Eve's already taken one of the spots. What if…what if we've all met the *same* guy?"

It felt like the entire restaurant hit a pocket of turbulence, and my stomach suddenly became unsettled. I looked at Natasha, uneasy. "No. No, that can't be."

"What's his name?"

"You say first."

"Johnny."

"Thank God! Mine's Jack."

We both turned to Kim, and her expression was even more closed and internal than usual. Oh, no. What if she'd already slept with Jack, while I was keeping myself pure and remote? What if I'd fucked this up before it even started? I knew I should've slept with him. But no—he wouldn't do this to me. Would he?

"Well?" I said. "What's the primal beast's name?"

"Garrison," Kim said. "His name's Garrison."

After recovering from the waves of relief, I lifted my glass. "To Jack."

"To Johnny."

"To Garrison."

We put our glasses to our lips and drank, and the glass votive in the center of the table cracked. For a moment, we all stared.

"What is it with us and those candles?" Natasha asked.

I started to giggle. "Garrison? Like Garrison Keillor?"

Kim made a face. "Well, that part is not so hot."

Freed from my prison, I once again walked the earth of my island, the forest paths and dry streambeds and cliffside ledges, the meadows crisp with predawn frost. The carpet of fallen pine needles underfoot thrilled me, as did the circling seagulls screaming for food. There was the crunch of deer through the underbrush, and the scent of rotting leaves, of salt water, of wood smoke…and of them.

Apart and alone, each of them was beautiful—but together, they were stunning, ravenous and alive with scent. The perfumes of lust and love, of desire and longing and fear. Waking to the three of them was almost worth my long imprisonment. Almost.

I felt a rumble of amusement—though they were on the mainland and I bound to my island, I was part of them now, they carried me with them everywhere, awake and asleep. And what a capable liar Kim was turning into. Not so unexpected, perhaps, given her forebears, but still amusing. And Natasha, so much closer to realizing her dreams yet still so far from realizing herself. And darling Eve, so luscious. She gave love so easily, she hadn't yet learned that love was a deadly gift.

The three of them were coming into full flower. Rising high and unfurling toward the sun. Toward me.

Soon. Soon they would be ready, soon my power would return. Then the harvest would begin, and I would reclaim what was mine.

✳ 13 ✳

My first graders were fantastic. Having my own class was great, and realizing I really *could* teach was wonderful. This teaching position was going far better than I'd ever have imagined.

You know what made me want to become a teacher? Those ridiculous movies, like *Mr. Holland's Opus* and *Music of the Heart,* and even *School of Rock*. Sadly, I wasn't at all musical, so training for the regional finals of a dramatic and Hollywood-esque music competition was out. But those movies were really about teachers who inspired passion in kids, gave them purpose and a reason to keep learning. That's who I wanted to be.

And so far, despite how well my classes were going, it hadn't worked out that way. I was a good teacher, yes. But not a great one, not a passionate role model, not that *one* teacher who really changed the kids' lives. Maybe I was still held back by the shadow of Mrs. Dale. Maybe I simply didn't have that sort of greatness in me. Or maybe the music was more important than I realized.

But I was damned if I didn't try. So on Friday, when I stood in front of the class, ready to give them their spelling test…I just stopped. I wanted something different, something new. But what?

I laid my spelling test on the desk and said, "Who knows how to spell 'smelt'?"

Connor raised his hand. "S-M-E-L-T."

"Good job! Now use it in a sentence."

"Yesterday," he said, "my dog smelt really bad."

I smiled and we went over the difference between "smelt" and "smelled," then I blurted, "Now, let's make up a play. Do you know what a play is?" The kids all nodded, but I caught a few uncertain expressions, so I continued. "A play is make-believe, like a movie or TV show, but the actors are right there in front of you. Famous plays are performed on stages by trained actors. And today, each of you is going to be an actor."

Anna raised her hand. "What's a famous play?"

"Well, *Romeo and Juliet* is a famous play. And so are, um…" I drew a complete blank of any non-Shakespearean plays. "*Much Ado About Nothing,* and *Hamlet* and—oh! *The Importance of Being Ernest.*"

"Are we gonna do one of them?"

"No, our play will be about…" My eyes fell on my spelling test. "Letters!"

"The kind you mail?" asked Conner.

"Exactly," I said, biting my lip. "Yes. A play about letters you mail…"

They all waited, watching me as my voice trailed off.

Think, Evie, think! What would Jack Black do? Pretend they were all in a Led Zeppelin tribute band. Not helpful.

"Okay. Okay, how about this?"

And the whole thing just flowed out of me, more of a game than a play, but who's counting? In the interest of teaching spelling, I quizzed the kids on words from the test. When they spelled a word right, Conner—our mailman hero—would deliver their "mail," which were flashcards with the letters in their words. Then the student who spelled the word right would contribute to our play by saying who they were—they could be anyone they wanted—and what they were doing in their house before Conner delivered their mail.

The first few kids chose to be themselves, watching TV or playing with a favorite toy when Conner came by for a chat over the mailbox. But as the "play" progressed, the responses got more creative. Elisabeth said she was Sally Sunshine, and she'd been making the furniture grow in her house. One boy chose to be God—he'd been delivering babies, he said, and really needed to get back to it. The best part was that Conner's natural inquisitiveness drew the other kids out when he'd ask them their favorite TV show, meal and toy. We learned that Sally Sunshine's couches were growing well, but her chairs needed mulching, and that God's babies all only had one arm, which was a little unsettling. I saw a conference call with God's mother in my future.

"But you know what?" I told Jack over lunch on Saturday. "It worked. They were totally engaged, helping one another spell words, rooting for more mail—even when it wasn't theirs. Plus, they did so much better on the spelling test than last week. And I got three phone calls from parents telling me how much their kids love me. That never happened to me in New York. It's like something has suddenly clicked." It was Jack. Since meeting him, my life felt so much…easier, like I was more capable or powerful or something.

"So what's the problem?" he asked, around a mouthful of pizza.

We'd taken the ferry into Portland and were having organic pizza topped with homemade sausage and marinated onions and sun-dried tomatoes. And hot maple-sweetened lemonade and cold beer. Tasty, but I know what you're thinking: Why lunch? Why not dinner? Maybe Jack wasn't really that interested, and was playing some kind of standoffish game. But it was me who'd chosen lunch. Not to play any game, because I was afraid dinner would lead to a bottle of wine, which would invariably lead to sex. And this was going far too well to introduce anything new. At least not yet.

"Well, have you heard of 'No Child Left Behind'?" I asked.

"Making teachers train students to pass tests, right?"

"Yeah, but you know what makes me wonder? It's No Child *Left Behind,* like those fundamentalist books, the 'left behind' series, about getting raptured to heaven. I mean, can that be a coincidence?"

"None of that stuff is." He shook his head. "My friends with kids tell me it stinks, too."

"You have friends with kids?"

"Sure, don't you?"

"Actually, no. Is that weird? I hardly even have married friends." Which reminded me, "Hey—how come you're still single?"

"I have the same problem Henry VIII did," he said, unleashing his smile.

"You keep executing wives?"

He nodded. "I save big on alimony."

"Don't you hate those questions? Like, 'You're so terrific, how come you're not dating anyone?'"

"No one's ever asked me that."

Probably because he was always dating someone. "My girlfriend has the best answer," I said. "After years of hemming and hawing, now she says, 'Well, introduce me to someone.' And of course they never can, because there are no good single men."

"None at all?" he asked with a grin.

"Now you're just fishing," I said. "How great is this pizza?"

"Fantastic. We should go to Fore Street for dinner."

"Dinner's six hours away."

"We'll wander around Old Port—you can shop. Have you been to Exchange Street?"

I looked at him for a long moment, then remembered to breathe. "So. So, the problem with doing a play during class is 'No Child Left Behind.' I mean, sure, they learned their vocabulary words—but are the real lessons going to be on the standardized tests in the spring? That's the problem with learning to work together and all the improvisation and creativity—the spelling unit took five times as long as it should've. Did I waste all that time? I don't think so, but I'm not sure my principal would agree."

"Dr. Pepper," Jack said, taking a bite.

"I'm boring you, aren't I?" Why couldn't I be more captivating? No guy wanted to hear about first-graders.

"No," he said. "I love hearing how you spend your days.

I can't imagine doing what you do, wrangling a whole class of kids, and actually teaching them, too. But I don't know enough to give you any advice. Seems to me you just need someone to listen, anyway."

"Yeah." I licked sauce from my finger. "Thing is, I really believe in teaching. It's the best thing—well, one of the best things—about coming to Maine. I've renewed my faith in teaching."

"You make it sound almost like a religion."

"It's not that different. The daily routines and rituals, teaching the Gospel of reading, writing and arithmetic. Some teachers have the gift to inspire, too."

He looked up from his plate. "Are you one of those?"

"I don't know. I never thought so in New York. But here…I'm starting to wonder. I think I'd like to be."

"Then I think you will be. Now, tell me—" he smiled crookedly "—is there a heaven?"

"Of course. It's called summer vacation! There's a God, too." I told him about the boy in school who played "God" in our play. Actually, his mom was one of the parents who called. "Apparently God *does* love me."

"Well, that's reassuring."

"Except they're devout Christians, and they think he's taking the Lord's name in vain—and now he won't listen unless they address him as God. They're talking about home-schooling him, which is a huge mistake. Only I'm not sure how I'm going to convince them of that."

"You'll think of something," Jack said. "After all, God works in mysterious ways."

"He's not the only one," I said.

We finished lunch and wandered through the streets of

Old Port. Ate homemade ice cream from a local candy store, and made it back—at my insistence—on the three-fifteen ferry. The day had been sunny and brisk in Portland, the kind of weather that makes you think there's no better place than New England in the fall. And Broome Isle harbor was idyllic as the ferry churned toward the dock. Boats bobbed in the sparkling swells, ducks paddled in the shallows, and lobstermen called to one another about their catches.

"It's perfect, isn't it?" Jack said.

I smiled in silent agreement, squeezing his hand. For the first time since arriving in my cocktail dress and kitten heels, I felt like I was coming home.

"Be a shame to ruin it," Jack said, a far-off look in his eyes.

"What do you mean?"

"Oh, nothing."

"You mean something, Jack," I said, a bit sternly. Were we about to have our first fight?

"Well, it's looking like a hotel would have a pretty substantial impact on the island."

"Is that what you've been working on? A hotel?"

"Well, that's one thing."

"So wait, who pays you? The state?"

"The hotel chain."

"You work for a developer?"

He nodded. "I was contracted to measure the feasibility of putting up a resort."

"Like a soulless, paved-paradise-type developer?" I asked.

"You ever heard of Windward Hotels?"

"Sure. Upscale resort chain, owned by some Hilton-type family, minus the notoriety."

He eyed me curiously. "How do you know that?"

"Um. I had a housemate who used to subscribe to celebrity magazines?"

"Was her name 'Eve'?"

"Yeah, it was a weird coincidence. Anyway, you'll tell them it's not feasible, right? I mean, a resort would change the whole feel of the island."

He sighed. "I'm not sure."

"You'd better."

"Well, maybe a low-impact—"

"What would happen to the bean suppers? They'd turn into 'local color' instead of being the real thing. And the Smelts Shack? Pretty soon, they wouldn't even be able to tell you the name of the pig you were eating!"

The ferry nudged against the dock, the crew worked their maritime magic, and we de-boated. "Well," Jack said, looking toward the little village. "I won't recommend anything that wouldn't...fit."

A sharp *yip* sounded, and the adolescent black Lab slunk toward us from around a corner. "Oh! There you are, boy," I said as he sniffed my hand, then I turned to Jack. "He was here the other night when I was waiting for the ferry."

"Must belong to one of the lobstermen," Jack said.

The Lab wound his way between Jack's legs, and practically stayed there as we walked up the dock.

"I think he likes you," I said.

"What a clever dog," Jack said, scratching the dog's head.

The Lab followed us into the village, where we stopped to say goodbye. I don't know why I was being so slow and cautious with Jack. Maybe for the same reason I wolfed down Twix bars, but took my own sweet time over tarte tatin. I wanted the good stuff to last.

But we didn't want to say goodbye. We stood on the corner and looked at each other until Jack said, "A couple years ago I was surveying a property in Hawaii that had been a taro farm for a hundred years."

"Is that what they make poi from?"

"You know a little about everything, don't you?" he asked.

"That's the price of teaching first grade."

He chuckled. "Here, we'll walk you home," he said, meaning him and the dog, and we headed through the village. "The thing is, the wetland taro market isn't so strong anymore."

"Well, taro is pretty anti–Atkins, right?" I said as we turned onto the gravel road leading to my seaside cottage. "High in carbs."

"Yeah, you're not going to see any native Hawaiian dieting guide on the bestseller list anytime soon."

I stopped to pick up a stick for the Lab and hurled it into the woods. The dog looked at me like I was crazy. "So you told the hotel people to build?"

"No, the Hawaiian Historical Society opposed the project."

"I can see that," I said. "So they didn't build?"

"Not until they all decided we should keep fields planted with taro, and other local fruits and vegetables, to supply the hotel's restaurants. The hotel agreed that poi would be offered on every menu. It was a lot of land and they built around the farm. And last year the hotel started offering 'Dirty Getaways'—people go to help harvest and take cooking classes."

"Hmm. That's what you're thinking for Broome Isle? People can come help lobster?"

Jack laughed as we stepped onto the front deck of my cottage. "Actually, I was thinking about how you have to prepare kids for the standardized tests, but you're still finding a way to teach that's *your* way." He traced a finger from my shoulder down my arm. "And how much I respect that."

I said, "Oh."

The black Lab snuffled at the side of the road, but I couldn't hear him over the pounding of my heart.

"This is the first time we've been really alone," Jack said, his voice low and rough.

I put my hand on his chest. Maybe I meant to keep him at a distance, but somehow I found myself clinging to his jacket and drawing him close.

Jack smiled as he bent to kiss me. And kiss me. And kiss me. And he was nuzzling my neck and nipping at my ear, and my knees were unsteady and my mind reeled, and I took him inside.

A glow seeped through the veil of fog, like the play of sunlight across white silk. A darker mass rose in the distance, sheer and remote—almost foreboding—while the agitated brushstrokes at the bottom lifted the eye upward. Natasha stepped back from the canvas, her heart thudding in her chest.

She'd done it. She'd finished the painting and could feel the force of it on her skin, the goose bumps on her arms and flush on her cheeks. Ever since the storm, she'd been a woman possessed. Not a misplaced stroke, no second-guessing herself, colors she hadn't known existed miraculously appeared in her pallet. While the experience had been draining, it had also never been easier. She'd finally decided it wasn't *Lost Hope,* but *Last Hope.* Everything she'd hoped for was coming true.

Or *almost* everything, at least.

Natasha turned to pour herself a drink, or…maybe a beer instead. One drink tended to lead to another, whereas one beer seemed to be enough. Last Friday, she'd finished the bottle of Maker's Mark and had bought a six-pack of Allagash she'd been nursing all week. She didn't think she was alcoholic, but it felt good to be in control again. Control of her drinking. Control of her painting.

She grabbed a beer, then opened another for Marco. He deserved her gratitude—even if he was gruff, as befitted a brother—for keeping her fed while she worked. Of course, he wasn't the only one who deserved thanks.

Johnny. She didn't even know his last name, yet she could sketch his face from memory. She hadn't been with a man since Brett, and halfway thought she'd never find someone, but Johnny was quick and kind and handsome and he knew art. And now that she'd finally stepped back from the canvas, she found her thoughts drifting toward him.

Natasha slipped on her barn coat and mud boots and went outside to look for Marco. Since the ice storm the weather had been mild, and she expected to find him in the garden. He wasn't, but a lot of weeds were. Odd. She checked the greenhouse. Deserted, and untidy, too, which wasn't like Marco. Something was going on with him and she planned to find out.

She crossed toward her truck, and stopped when she saw the black Lab gazing adoringly at her from beside one of the Adirondack chairs. Well, maybe she'd have a beer with the dog, first. She threw herself into the chair and patted the dog's head.

"Hey, there, stallion," she said. "You seen Marco?"

The dog cocked his head at her, his eyes bright and in-quisitive. He'd already filled out from the last time she saw him, and his fur was thicker, jet-black and glossy.

"Yeah, he's probably off looking at goats," she said, taking a slug of beer. Marco was dying to buy livestock, but so far hadn't progressed beyond chickens. "You'd like that, wouldn't you? A few goats to chase."

The dog seemed to agree. He was a good listener. So she told him about Amanda Michaels, her dreams for her art. Asked him what he thought of Johnny, and heard a hissing sound from the door of her studio.

She turned and saw Puck through the glass storm door, pacing back and forth, his fur standing on end.

"He doesn't like you," she said to the dog. "He's old-fashioned that way."

The Lab laid his head in her lap, and she sipped her beer, hoping Puck would go back inside so she could enjoy her beer and dog in peace. Instead, Puck yowled, and she was too loyal to ignore him, so she bid goodbye to the Lab and went inside. She tossed her coat aside, settled Puck on her easy chair, and sat on the floor next to him. She rubbed his head until he started purring, enjoying the late afternoon light streaming through the high loft windows, the sound of a contented cat and her ale, which tasted a bit like nutmeg, she thought. Some-thing autumnal, at least.

She held the bottle up to the light and asked Puck, "What color is nutmeg, anyway?"

"Brown, I think," said a voice behind her.

She yelped. "Jesus, Marco! You have to stop doing that."

She turned to glare and it wasn't Marco. "Johnny!" She stood abruptly, startling Puck, who hissed and raced upstairs.

"I don't think he likes me," Johnny said.

"He only likes people who knock."

"Hey, I knocked the other day, and you swore at me."

"I was working then." She ventured a smile. "You're lucky I didn't throw anything."

Johnny returned the smile and gestured toward the front door. "It was open, too. But I should've knocked. I guess I was thinking about—" He glanced at the big canvas, the one that was no longer called *Lost Hope* even in jest. "Whoa. When did this happen?"

She looked down to hide her smile. "I just finished," she mumbled.

He didn't say anything for a long minute, but his eyes shone with admiration—not an expression she'd seen all that often.

"Damn," he said.

"Thanks."

"I mean—*damn.*"

And as he looked back at the painting, she became keenly aware that she was wearing nothing but boxers and a tank top with no bra. Not exactly sexy, but not entirely clothed, either.

"Um. I'll be right back, okay? I'm gonna put on some clothes."

He turned from the painting and glanced at Natasha, clearly surprised. Had he not realized she was basically sitting in her underwear? Okay, men's underwear, but still. I mean, here he was, a good-looking man who loved her art, who seemed to like her, and who clearly thought—she could hardly even admit this to herself—she was talented and everything. And he was like Brett, except not an artist but an art lover, which was even better. And he didn't even notice she was strutting around half naked? Maybe the men's underwear was the problem—she didn't look feminine enough.

Because yeah, this was like looking a gift horse in the mouth and finding a pot of gold, but not only was Johnny possibly her ticket to the New York art scene, he was also possibly her ticket to finally finding someone.

She went upstairs and stared into her closet. God, where was Kim when she needed her? Natasha wished she could summon her like *I Dream of Jeannie*. She'd swiftly appear, blink her eyes, nod her head, and Natasha would be transformed into the kind of woman Johnny couldn't resist.

"I Dream of Kim," she muttered.

"What?" Johnny called from downstairs.

"Nothing."

She'd stripped off her tank top, and now used it to cover her breasts as she leaned over the side of the loft to see what he was doing. He'd removed his jacket to reveal a faded red T-shirt and worn jeans. He squatted on the floor, flipping though a stack of her sketches. She watched him pause at the one of Eve in the bathtub. You couldn't tell the model was Eve, her hair and face were too abstract, but it was enough to inspire Natasha to take a risk with Johnny. What would Eve do? She'd be charming and delightfully bubbly.

Natasha cleared her throat to say something winning, but when Johnny glanced up, she froze. Jesus, she was standing half naked, clutching a shirt to her chest and leaning over the balcony like some wanton Juliet.

Her vivacious sally consisted of "Uh."

Johnny smiled quizzically up at her.

She swallowed and backed away, squeaking, "There's beer in the fridge!"

"You want one?" he called, opening the fridge at the other end of the empty space where the kitchen should be.

Natasha closed her eyes, wishing herself anywhere but here. Why couldn't she even flirt right? "No, thanks." Too late for something sexy, so she chose a black turtleneck sweater and jeans, combed her hair and clomped downstairs.

"Hey," she said, taking a breath to prepare herself. She *did* have one bit of flirtation that never failed. Foolproof flirtation. Men couldn't resist.

Johnny took a pull from his beer, then looked at the label. "Allagash? Is this local?"

"Yeah, from Portland. They make a great Belgian white." She fiddled with her turtleneck. Okay, time to stop talking about beer and start flirting. "Um, but that one's more nutmeggy."

"Ah! I thought you were interested in nutmeg for artistic reasons."

"No, just for the sake of general drunken debauchery."

He chuckled, and didn't even check her out or anything. *Sheesh.* Okay. Gotta just nudge the subject in the right direction...

But before she could figure how, he said, "Cool fridge."

"Yeah, isn't it?"

A glass-faced cooler one of Marco's clients had gotten rid of last month, it didn't have a freezer, but made an awesome fridge. Natasha loved being able to weigh her food options without opening it. Well, in theory. In practice, the fridge was mostly empty.

"It reminds me of college," Natasha lied, struck by a sudden idea. "There was one just like it." And now for the truth. "I used to love the dorm cafeteria—I don't know, everyone else scoffed at the food, but not me. It was open all hours, too."

Johnny nodded, taking another slug of beer. Well, he'd be more interested when she got to the good part.

"At night," she continued, "you could go down for a snack. And one time—I guess I was a little drunk—I kissed a girl."

He scratched his chin. "That's kind of a non sequitur."

Fuck, that *always* worked. He wasn't supposed to be so casual, he was supposed to choke on his beer and press for more details. That's what happened every other time she'd told a guy. It was her one shoe-in, her sure-fire flirt.

"Well, the fridge was there," she mumbled before soldiering on. "But she was really hot. God, we so made out. It was…tingly."

"Kissing girls usually is," Johnny said matter-of-factly. "Actually, in college we had that poster in our lounge. *The Kiss,* I mean."

"Which one?" she asked.

"Klimt. I can't think of another painting called *The Kiss.* Hmm. Munch?"

"You know your art. Yeah, him and Rodin and Hayez and—but I didn't mean a painting, actually, I meant—"

"Oh, the Doisneau photograph?"

She smiled. "And you pronounced his name right, too."

"Mandy's a harsh taskmistress," he said. "But what do you think of *The Kiss?*"

"Eh," Natasha said. "Overrated."

"Which one?" he asked.

"Both."

He considered, then nodded. "I guess. The painting isn't my favorite Klimt, but the photo…"

"It has a certain dorm-room poignancy," Natasha said.

He chuckled, and Natasha started feeling a little more comfortable. He didn't make her feel like an idiot for bringing up the "kissing girl" ploy—and not only did he know Doisneau by name, he knew *The Kiss* wasn't Klimt's best work.

"Sit." She pointed to her easy chair. "Tell me which Klimt is your favorite while I make popcorn."

She plugged in her electric air popper and added popcorn as Johnny finished his beer. "I'm not sure which is my favorite," he said. "I think I prefer his decorative stuff."

"If he were alive today," Natasha said, "he'd be doing Web design."

Johnny laughed. "That's exactly it!"

The popcorn finished and Natasha poured it into an indigo-blue salad bowl, salted it and brought it into the living room. "So who do you like?" she asked.

His brow furrowed, then he said, "Oh, you mean artists?"

"Well, them, too."

But he laughed off this opportunity to express his undying admiration. "I don't know, my taste is pretty ordinary. Gauguin and—well, I tend to like the pretty stuff, much to Mandy's dismay. But I'm starting to get the hang of conceptual art, too. Like this guy who tries to raise the temperature of water by yelling at it—"

"Martin Kersels! I saw his stuff when I was eighteen, and

my mind was absolutely blown. I spent three semesters trying to become a second-rate him, before realizing 'second-rate' wasn't exactly the best goal."

"You're not a second-rate anything."

She felt herself blush. "Sometimes I worry my stuff is too pretty."

"Your stuff is pretty—but it's not too anything. I can't wait for Mandy to see your slides."

Chewing on a mouthful of popcorn, Natasha allowed herself to relax. And fantasize—she was finally going to become recognized as an artist. She cracked two more beers and they talked for hours. The popcorn was long gone when Johnny finally stood to say goodbye. Natasha walked him to the door and he didn't kiss her goodbye.

There was a certain kind of tension, but she didn't think it was sexual. She closed the door behind him and leaned against it. Why was he so utterly uninterested in her? She'd given him all the signals, as clumsily as only she could. And sure, she was a mess, but she knew men usually found her attractive. Well, maybe Johnny was cautious and the romance would slowly blossom.

Maybe.

At the touch of a faint breeze, the red-orange leaves trembled in the spreading tree outside the old farmhouse, and in the distance a dog barked. In the kitchen, steam rose from pots of blueberry jam heating on the stove and bathed Kim's face. She blew her bangs out of her eyes and glanced out the window into the side yard. The black Lab again, of course, trotting around the corner with his pink tongue lolling from his mouth.

She'd asked around, but nobody had claimed him. He must've been wandering the island at night, scavenging in the trash for food, but no one else had even seen him. She mentioned the cats, too, wondering if anyone else had been feeding them. No one had seen them, either, which made her worry. Okay, so she never let them inside and she didn't name them, they were still her cats. Well, they were hearty souls. Right now it seemed more important to nurse the dog back to health. She stirred the jam, then set it on the counter to cool, washed her hands and pulled the cookie jar from the top of the fridge.

She checked the clock. Almost three-thirty. Time for her afternoon shortbread…but she hadn't made any. Instead the jar was filled with homemade dog treats.

She carried the jar to the front door and the black Lab scrambled onto the front porch and pressed himself against her legs. "Hello, my sweet," she said. "Look at you! Can't even see your ribs anymore."

She tossed him a biscuit, and he snatched it from the air and swallowed it without chewing. She laughed and gave him another, then saw an envelope on the front mat. Inside, she found a wad of cash from Garrison with a sticky note attached: *Thanks for everything—delicious.*

She slipped the cash into her pocket, smiling because the other witches would assume it was a double entendre. The Lab barked, and she tossed him another biscuit, then set out a bowl of the kibble she'd just bought yesterday. He was recovering beautifully, his fur an almost silken black, his body bulk returning and his bright, curious eyes sharp and smart.

Back in the kitchen, she poured the warm jam into a pot, and the sweet scent rose around her. She stilled, closing her eyes. *Something was coming—no, it was already here. From the past or…from deep within the ancient heart of the island. Something with a taproot spearing down into the moist earth with barbed leaves and poisoned thorns and hunger. It had a—*

The dog scratched at the door, yelping piteously, and Kim forgot the rush of knowingness and shook her head, seeing the empty bowl. "You cheeky beast," she told him, giving him a refill. "Such a teenager."

Back inside, she closed the door and a man's voice said, "Who are you talking to?"

Instead of startling at the surprise, she felt herself calm at the sound of his voice, felt herself mellow and unfurl, and felt the urge to be nowhere but in his strong hands. "You're here," she said.

"I'm always here," he said, looking around at her kitchen. "Are those cookies?"

"Dog biscuits. That's who I was talking to, that stray Lab who's been wandering around."

"I haven't seen one."

"I'm feeding him, so I guess he'll keep coming back."

He smiled and stuck a spoon in his mouth. "That happens."

She saw he was holding a pot of her jam. "My blueberry jam! I'm selling that at the General Store. I promised them two dozen."

"Sorry."

"You don't look sorry."

"Baby, this is so good." He dug into the jar for another spoonful. "Have you tasted it?"

"Of course I—"

She stopped talking when he brought the spoon to her mouth and put a hand on her waist, his eyes alight. She parted her lips, and he paused, watching her.

"I love you," he said.

Before she could answer, he slid the spoon into her mouth. There was a burst of sweetness, the feel of warm fresh jam on her tongue, along with the husky sincerity in his voice. She reveled in his closeness and warmth. Kim felt her knees buckle and her heart unclench. It was almost too much. She was dizzy with sensation.

He kissed her, his tongue mingling with the honey sweet of the jam, and lifted her, laying her on the kitchen table. He raised her sweater over her head, wrapping her in darkness, as he expertly unclasped her bra and slid her jeans over her hips.

She wriggled to remove the sweater, wanting to see him, wanting to watch him watching her, but he said "No," and pinned her arms over her head, the sweater a blindfold. She heard the *tink* of the spoon against the pot and felt a swirling warmth of jam drizzling on her nipple and then his mouth, his tongue and lips. In the darkness, there was nothing but pleasure.

✳ 14 ✳

So I was driving to the ferry, and *this* happened:

A hundred yards from my cottage, the old, stooped, white-haired crone, with a gnarled hand on a gnarled cane, was walking slowly by the side of the road.

I pulled over and lowered the window. "Hi! You're Kim's great-aunt, aren't you?"

"Schoolteacher," she said.

I beamed. "Yes! I *am* the new schoolteacher. And a friend of Kim's. Do you need a lift anywhere? I was actually just about to meet Kim at the dock, but—"

"The child of darkness is born," she said.

"Oh. That's, um, nice?"

"The child of darkness has slipped his unholy womb. In the dead of the night, he slipped free, and on unsteady legs—"

"Indeed!" I said brightly. "Kim was saying she—"

"His hungry eyes measuring," she continued, her own cataracted eyes wild, "what once was his, hunting for—"

All of a sudden there was a *crack* and a tree on the side of the road fell on the woman. It was just…wham! Her bones crunched and she lay in a growing pool of blood.

Then I blinked, and was driving maybe a hundred yards from my cottage, and the stooped old lady with a cane was walking by the side of the road. I lifted my hand in a wave, my heart pounding. She smiled at me very kindly and returned the wave with a sweep of her cane. And I kept driving.

Weird. It had only been one of my fantasies, yet I'd *never* daydreamed like that before. Such a yucky ending, and without even a starring role for me. I mean, that was the whole point of daydreams, wasn't it? Otherwise, they were just waking nightmares.

I shook my head and kept driving. Must've been something I ate.

An hour later, I turned to Kim and said, "Oh, look! They have *blueberry* iced tea."

"Shut up," she said, smiling. "You're just jealous."

We were standing in line at the Starbucks in Freeport. We'd taken the ferry in with Natasha, but had lost track of her on the highway. Kim was a speed demon, and refused to wait for the law-abiding Natasha, who was carting her paintings in the back of her truck. It's funny, I would've expected them to be the opposite. People were constantly surprising me. Especially Kim.

She'd…well, there was no other word for it, she'd *titillated* us with her tale of steamy, sticky, blueberry-jam sex in her kitchen with Garrison. The story had started in the cabin of the ferry, when Natasha had innocently asked how things were going with Garrison. I don't think Kim meant to reveal all the details, but she did mention the jam, and we started asking questions—and in no time the whole erotic tale was before us.

"You *think?*" I said. "Hell, Jenna Jameson is jealous."

Natasha stepped into line with us. "What are you getting?"

"Well," I told her, "I'm about to score a gallon of blue-berry jam."

Natasha scanned the overhead menu. "No more sex talk. I can't take the envy."

"I'm having a full-fat toffee-nut latte, then." I sighed con-tentedly. "With whipped cream."

"That's what she always gets at the General Store," Kim said.

"I wish. I've been living with Smelts Shack gut-rot in-dustrial brew and nondairy creamer for too long. What about you?"

"Black coffee," Natasha said.

"But they brew it so strong and bitter," I said.

"That's how I like it," she said.

"Like her men," Kim said, and giggled.

We both eyed her, then looked at each other. Natasha shrugged and said, "Two weeks of wild-animal kitchen sex, and she's giggling."

The person in front of us finished paying, and we ordered and paid. The Starbucks was between Banana Republic and the L.L. Bean complex, with Cole Haan across the street. All of Freeport was like an olde-tyme New England town, but instead of olde-tyme New England hardware stores and post offices, there were outlets. Basically, heaven.

We sat in the cluster of gray velour comfy chairs, and Kim asked Natasha about Johnny.

"Well," she said, "there's been no jam involved."

"I'm sorry I ever said anything!"

"I'm not," I said. "I think I learned a few things."

"Yeah," Natasha said. "Like how to get blueberry jam out of your—"

"Stop!" Kim said. "Stop, stop, I'm not listening."

Natasha nodded solemnly. "It's a good thing I like your dining room so much, Kim, because I'm not sure I'll ever eat at your kitchen table again."

"If you keep this up, you'll never be invited back."

"It's not my fault you're always having jelly sex everywhere."

"All right," I said, holding up a hand. "It's gonna be hard, but we'll stop teasing you. But is it more than just sex? I mean, do you see the relationship going anywhere?"

Kim sipped her latte. "I don't know."

"Of course you do."

"Yeah," she reluctantly admitted. "This is it. He's the one. But does he feel the same?"

"Does he?" I asked.

She was silent for a moment, then she said, very softly, "Yes."

"Kim," I said, reverently. "I'm so happy for—"

"But the last time this happened," she said, "I got pregnant. And everything fell apart. And I just—I can't handle that, not again."

We fell silent, and I noticed a strange expression on Natasha's face—bewildered and hurt—and I realized she must be thinking about Marco. I saw Kim notice, too, and decided that an abrupt change of subject was called for.

"And what about Johnny?" I asked Natasha.

Natasha shrugged. "Nothing. He stopped by the other day and we…talked."

"About what?" I asked.

"Art. He's the most informed non-artist I've ever met. We talked for hours."

"Hours? That's almost as long as Kim's jelly sex!"

"Hey," Kim said. "You promised."

I grinned. "No, I didn't promise, I just *said* we'd stop teasing you. Anyway—" I turned to Natasha "—you talked *and…?*"

"No 'and,'" Natasha said. "I even gave him my whole 'kissed a girl in college' speech, and got nothing. Maybe I repel him."

"Sure, you're such a heinous skank," I told her, looking at her classically beautiful features, flame-red hair and ivory skin. "That's the only reason I hang out with you. It makes me look better."

"Well, he's got some reason to be utterly uninterested, because I was prancing around in my underwear and he didn't raise an eyebrow."

"That doesn't mean anything," Kim said.

"What?" Natasha asked. "If either of you did that, a man would be all over you."

"Natasha," I said. "We've both seen your underwear. You mean boxers and a paint-splattered tee?"

"Well… Anyway. What about Jack?"

"What about him?" I asked. "Why are you always questioning me?"

"Yeah, and you mind your own business."

"Jack is okay," I said, trying to curb my enthusiasm. "Do

you guys feel it? It's like all our dreams are coming true. Ever since we made those wishes. Kim and I both met someone, and your art's been recommended to Amanda Mitchells."

"Michaels."

"Whatever. And this is… I don't know. Having my own classroom is fantastic, I love the island and the two of you. Kim's having jelly sex, and I haven't seen you this excited about your art since senior year. Sending slides, and not mocking your own stuff, and delivering paintings to the—"

"Shit!" Natasha said. "I told them I'd be there already. I gotta go."

"Us, too," Kim said. "Burberry's about to open."

Now *that* was a dream come true.

As I dressed for school Monday morning, I wondered if Gregory was already at work, or if he was home in bed with a new girlfriend. I wondered how I was going to get God's parents to let him stay in school. And I wondered about Jack: how could he be both "too good to be true," and true?

By the time I stepped outside, I had a few answers. No, Gregory was not still in bed. He'd always wanted to be seen in the office by six-thirty, so they'd know what a hard worker he was, and I bet he'd be even keener since the nakedness incident. As far as the "God dilemma," a good start would be to call my student by his given name, Caleb, and schedule a parent/teacher conference.

The Jack thing, though… I didn't know. He wasn't what you'd call gorgeous, but I still got warm thinking about him—his voice, his hands, his self-confidence and humor and the way he looked at me. Mostly the way he looked at me.

I stopped at the Smelts Shack for my morning rot-gut

coffee, still a half hour early for school. It was a gorgeous day, unseasonably warm, which was the topic of conversation when I sat at the counter.

"Hi, Eve," Chester said as Marie plopped a cup of coffee in front of me.

"Morning," Eldon said.

"How are you boys?" I asked.

Three of them started talking at once, happily expounding all their digestive and arthritic complaints, with I think particularly delighted expressions at having been called "boys." Once the murmuring about bunions slowed, Chester asked me, "What're you all dressed for?"

"Looking mighty fine," Eldon said.

"Oh, thanks. This is for school."

I was back in my Hester Prynne outfit, somber and puritanical, though this time it really *was* a costume. I was playing Emily Gray, Kim's witchy ancestor. With Halloween approaching, and having introduced the whole notion of playacting as a didactic experience, I thought I'd do a unit on the island's history. I was determined not to include Natasha's story about Ash Street, but it was going to be tough. Maybe if the kids misbehaved...

Marie approached with the pot of coffee-type product for a refill and I covered the top of my cup with my hand, my stomach already burning with her acid brew.

She splashed coffee on the back of my hand.

I screamed.

"Why'd you put your hand there?" she asked. Subtext: *Idiot!*

I flapped my hand. "Generally, that indicates 'no thank you.'"

"In what language?" She pulled ice from the cooler and wrapped it in a dish towel for me.

"Waitress language," I said, witheringly.

"Uh-oh," one of the boys said. "She's getting frisky."

"Five dollars says Marie can take her," Chester said.

Nobody took the bet, but Marie turned her glower to him instead of me, so I said, "Hey, how about I make us all cappuccinos?"

I pulled a bag of fresh-ground Italian roast from my bag and scooted around the counter. I'd bought the coffee for the teachers' lounge, but this was even better.

"What are you doing back here?" Marie said. She might as well have been holding a rolling pin, ready to conk me over the head.

"You take a well-deserved break, Marie." I stepped to the cappuccino machine. "Just sit back and relax."

"I don't know..." she said.

There was no way I was going to get away with this.

"I want to see how that dang machine works," Chester said. "I've been staring at it long enough."

Marie relented.

The machine was similar to Gregory's, and I quickly cleaned it and got it working. The milk was a frothy masterpiece and I poured the first cappuccino for Marie.

She sipped, then narrowed her eyes. "How much could I charge for one of those?"

"I'd start at two-fifty. Once you've got a few regulars hooked, you can go up to three."

She snorted. "Who's gonna pay three bucks for a cup of coffee?"

I shrugged. "Me?"

"Let me try that three-dollar coffee," Eldon called out. "Get a wiggle on, Eve."

I went back to the machine and fixed them all cups. I couldn't stop smiling. There I was, behind the counter of the Smelts Shack, slinging hash. Well, foaming milk—but still. And the old coots loved my cappuccino. Marie demanded I show her how to make them…though she refused to buy fresh-ground coffee, insisting that Folger's was good enough for anyone.

I finished and sat down to a short stack of homemade pancakes, quietly reveling in my newfound acceptance. I listened as they talked about the warm weather and odd microclimates, and worried over the sudden lack of lobsters in people's traps. The season always slowed down in the fall, but lobstermen were complaining about pulling empty traps. Was the warmer weather affecting the temperature of the water or was something else emptying those traps?

"I read a *New Yorker* article once," I told them, "that said lobster traps really aren't that effective. Lobsters treat them like smorgasbords, they go in for a snack and then wander back out. Only like six percent of them actually get trapped. Turns out traps are lobster bait *buffets,* not cages."

I'd finished my coffee by the time the laughter and hoots of the *New Yorker* died down, and stood and told them I had to get to school. They called good-natured teases after me, and I stepped into the morning light, more satisfied with my life than I would've thought possible.

Natasha sat on the floor, under the window, the sun falling across the wide-planked and paint-spattered wooden floor, her sketchbook in her lap. She was absently doodling, her mind far away, her hair falling around her face and reflecting a rosy tinge onto the paper.

The phone roused her from her reverie. She answered for once, before it went to voice mail. "Hello?"

"I'm calling for Natasha Kent," a woman's voice said.

"This is she," Natasha said, which always made her think of her mother, the only other person she knew who answered that way.

"Ah, beautiful art and good grammar? I find myself delighted."

Natasha shoved empty beer bottles to the corner of the table, making room for Puck to jump up. "I'm a great housekeeper, too."

"Can you cook?"

"Not in the kitchen," she said. Meaning, of course, she really *did* cook on canvas.

But maybe the woman misunderstood. She chuckled wickedly. "Oh, my goodness," she said, with a trace of a British accent. "You really are everything he said."

"Okay," Natasha said. "Who is this?"

"Mandy Michaels. I got your slides this morning."

Natasha looked at the phone, then she looked at Puck. She didn't say anything, though, as she couldn't get her mind to connect to her mouth.

"Natasha? Are you still there?"

"Mmm," she said.

"I thought you were expecting my call."

"I didn't know you were English," Natasha said, then silently cursed herself for her stupidity.

"I'm not, or at least I haven't been since I was six. Most people don't pick up the accent."

"Johnny said you'd call, but I—I suppose I didn't really believe him."

"You call him *Johnny?*" Mandy Michaels gave a raspy laugh. "Listen, I want you to come to New York. I love your work, of course, but I've learned never to sign a new artist until we meet in person. There's a—"

The rest of what she said was lost under the sound of trumpets blaring, fireworks exploding and Natasha's heart pounding in excitement. Finally, at a silence on the other end of the line, she said, "What was that again?"

"The whole thing?" Mandy Michaels asked.

"Well, how about you start with the part about loving my work. Be sure to say 'of course' again, though."

Mandy laughed. "So you'll come?"

"To the city? To your gallery?" Natasha realized she was pacing, and collapsed onto the couch. "Yes, I'll come. When? I'm on an island, you know. It's a bit late to leave today, plus I don't have any clean clothes. My brother can feed the cat, though. Today? Tomorrow? Sorry—I'll shut up now."

The throaty laughter continued. "How about Friday?"

"Friday. Yes."

"That'll give you time to do your laundry," Mandy said, her voice light. "I'll put you through to my assistant, she'll arrange everything. We'll talk things over, go to dinner. I'm very much looking forward to meeting you."

Her assistant was enthusiastic and cheerful, and Natasha simply agreed with everything before hanging up. She sat stunned…then started laughing, sending Puck fleeing upstairs. She stood in the middle of the room and twirled until she got dizzy, then collapsed back on the couch and shouted, "Fuck! Yes! Thank you!"

The sound of gravel crunching in the drive cut short her incoherent blurting celebration, and she realized Marco was coming home.

She shoved through the door, found him standing in front of his truck and leapt at him, laughing. "She loves me! She loves me!"

He understood immediately, took her in a hug and spun her around.

"She got my slides and she—she loves my work." She heard herself babbling, but couldn't stop. "Amanda Michaels loves my work. She's *paying* for me to fly to New York! Oh, God. Oh, God, I'm gonna be sick!"

He set her down, and despite his smile his face turned serious. "I'm so absolutely proud of you."

She started weeping. And smiling. And nattering, until she finally caught her breath. "This is it, Marco, this is my one break. Most artists don't get one, and we always think, 'If only I got that one break, people would see how good I am,' but now I'm *getting* that break, and my God, if I fuck this up I'll never forgive myself."

He started to answer when she saw what he'd been doing, standing in front of his truck, inspecting a huge dent in the front fender. More than a dent—a horrible crunch, with radiator fluid dripping from the undercarriage.

"What happened?" she asked. "You hit a tree?"

"No, I got rammed."

"Where?" There was one stoplight in town and a total of maybe a hundred cars on the island. Natasha'd never heard of anyone getting into an accident anywhere but Portland.

"In the village, can you fucking believe it?" He was practically laughing. "A five-car pileup on Broome Isle."

"Are you kidding? Was anyone hurt?"

"Bumps and scrapes, that's all." He shook his head, still grinning.

"Why are you so happy?" Natasha asked.

Marco sobered too abruptly. "No reason."

She eyed him suspiciously. "What have you done?"

"Nothing, it's just funny. When was the last time anyone got into a car accident on the island?"

"Never."

"And today there was a pileup. You know what Jerry said?"

"Jerry at the garage?"

Marco nodded. "This was the third accident this week. One of the Dupree brothers broke his collarbone yesterday, driving off the pier."

"Driving off the pier?"

"His car's still in the water. He says he wasn't even drunk, too, he was blinded by the sun."

"Yesterday was cloudy."

"Well, he's a Dupree all right."

"Three accidents in a week? I don't know, I don't like the sound of that. And it's seriously buzz-killing my news."

"Yeah, a few fender benders, and who cares that you're the next, um…"

"You can't think of a single famous woman artist, can you?"

"Well, there's the one with the eyebrows."

"Frieda Kahlo. She has a name, you know."

He cocked his head. "She was hot, despite that unibrow."

"Jesus, Marco, she was Frieda-fucking-Kahlo, not Salma Hayek. Who cares how she looked? She was talented and—" She stopped. "Oh, shit. What am I gonna wear to New York? I need to call Kim."

"She's not home."

"What? How do you know?"

"I saw her car. At the General Store."

"Did you stop?"

"I didn't even slow down. I'm lucky the truck made it home."

"Well, you really need to talk to her. She's, um…" Natasha looked at the crunched car, not wanting to say it, but knowing she had to. "She's seeing someone."

"Yeah?"

The pool of radiator fluid spread slowly, and Natasha watched it flow, afraid to look away and see Marco's injured expression. "Yeah. She's pretty serious, I think."

"Who is he? She told you she's serious?"

"Just talk to her, okay?"

"We're divorced, Natasha."

"Yeah, and you're not totally in love with her anymore. Sure."

He crouched on the other side of the truck, inspecting the damage, and didn't say anything.

"Marco," she said.

"Don't worry about me, Natasha. I'm glad she's happy and—and that you got your big break. Just focus on this opportunity. You've finally done it. You oughtta be celebrating, not worrying about me."

Something in his tone wasn't right. "Marco, what is going on with you? You're never here anymore, the garden's a mess…"

"Speaking of messes," he said, "are you planning to go to New York looking like that?"

An obvious attempt to distract her—effective, too. She

went inside to call Kim for fashion advice, with Marco's voice floating after her. "Can I borrow your truck while you're gone?"

She ignored him, grabbed the phone and dialed, eyeing her open sketchbook. Odd. From this angle, looking at the doodles upside down, they almost seemed to be a sketch of a car driving off a pier into the ocean.

15

Kim arrived at the General Store wearing her hiking boots and sweatshirt, a case of blueberry jam in her arms. After dropping off the jam, she'd leave her car in the lot and hike across the island. Might as well take advantage of the unseasonable warmth—and she needed to clear her head. She'd cut through the woods behind the store toward the ocean. Her family owned a tract of property that she hadn't visited in a while, and she knew she'd start feeling edgy if she didn't check it out soon. That was the thing about being an island witch—the island was constantly nagging at her.

She nudged the door open with her hip, and Marie met her just inside and asked, "Is that the blueberry jam?"

Kim blushed. "Well, I don't know if it's *the* blueberry jam, but it's—I mean, yes."

Marie peered at her. "Have you been drinking?"

"No. Sorry, my mind was wandering."

"Well, wander your body over here and set that down." Marie turned to the back, where a few of the old fellows were mumbling to themselves, and told them to hush up. "They're all hoppity on cappuccino," she explained. "Eldon's been behind the counter all day, making cup after cup. Gonna be the death of the old farts."

Kim set the jam down. "Cappuccino? Maybe I should start bringing you croissants and scones."

"What you should start bringing is more of those old salves of yours."

"The salves finally sold? Which ones?"

"For rashes. I sold out this morning. Something's going around, looks like the bubonic plague but uglier, and your stuff's all that clears it up. You know little Janice Cooper?"

"Sure." The eldest of a family of eight, at fifteen she was the island beauty—and she knew it.

"She's got it on her face, looks like the Elephant Girl."

"Oh, dear," Kim said. "I'll bring her a mask."

Marie eyed Kim critically. "Bring whatever you're using. You look fresh as tomorrow." She handed Kim the label from a two-liter bottle of Coke. "This is what I need. All your tinctures and soaps and salves."

Kim glanced at the list scribbled on the back of the label. "Tomato chutney?" she asked, confused. "What are people putting that on?"

"Sandwiches."

"Oh. Right, I thought… I don't know."

"All your goop is selling so well, people are grabbing your food, too—brand loyalty. Can you get me all of that?"

Kim smiled. "By this time tomorrow." Everything was

sitting in a cabinet at home, waiting to be tossed in a year or two. But not anymore! "This is great news."

"Ayuh," Marie said. "Nothing like a few rashes to put a smile on your face."

After shelving the blueberry jam, Kim chatted for a few minutes with the old-timers at the back counter. They usually treated her with a combination of reserve and caution—out of exaggerated respect for her family history, she thought—but today they seemed friendlier. Maybe because they were jittery with caffeine overdoses. She pushed through the back door into the crisp and sunny day and cut through the woods. The air was a lot warmer than it should've been, with the leaves already yellow and orange and red, fluttering on mostly bare branches.

She ambled through the woods, ducking under limbs and watching for wild mushrooms. This time of year, she sometimes found cinnabar chanterelles and black trumpets. She walked along, letting her feet choose her path until they found the faint deer trail she'd known ran somewhere nearby. Dead leaves and twigs and pinecones crunched under her hiking boots, and she walked about a mile before she came to a large clearing covered in tall grass. Beyond the meadow, the trail continued another quarter mile to the shore.

She was halfway across the field when she suddenly stopped, delighted. Not twenty feet away, a deer nested in the tall grass, curled restfully, facing the other direction. Deer often slept in fields like this, leaving imprints in high grass in the morning—but they never let her get so close. She stood perfectly still, watching the breeze ruffle the fur along the deer's flank. Other than the breeze, the deer was perfectly motionless, and she crept past, trying not to startle it.

She saw another deer, equally unmoving, just ten feet beyond the first one. A cold, thick dread started in Kim's stomach and moved to her throat as the scent of offal rose in the air, and a faint buzzing grew louder. Flies feeding.

The deer were dead. Hunting season hadn't started yet, and though there were a few guys who might not wait, no hunter on the island would leave a deer to rot. Kim would know. And then everyone would know. And those hunters would find themselves suddenly very alone.

She felt a prickle of fear on the back of her neck, as if she were being watched from the woods. Silly. She wasn't afraid of dead deer. She circled closer to the first one…then stopped, her hand to her mouth in horror.

The deer had been mutilated. Gutted where she lay, and…toyed with. Flies crawled into her empty eye sockets and writhed over her exposed intestines, and the grass was soaked with gore.

Kim backed away and almost lost her footing. She'd stepped on the outflung hoof of another mutilated deer, behind her. Three of them. She gasped and ran across the field. Everywhere she turned, another deer lay bloody and flayed beneath a swarm of insects. She shoved blindly into the woods, and ran straight into someone. A man, in brown, standing there watching and—

She screamed and reeled away, only to have the man grab her.

"What's wrong?" he said. "Kim! Kim!"

She calmed at the sound of her name. The man was Garrison, and she fell into his arms. "Oh, thank God! Oh, no—no. The deer, someone—oh, God."

"What happened? Are you okay?"

"Oh, God, Garrison—" She took a breath. "You have your cell? Call the police. Someone tortured the deer—a whole field of them, maybe a dozen."

His face turned ashen and he opened his phone. "Damn. No signal."

"We'll call from the General Store," she said.

He followed her toward the trail, his face still pale. "What kind of person would do something like that?"

She didn't answer, and they walked together silently for a few minutes, until she said, "What are you doing out here?" She never ran into anyone here. "Not that I'm not grateful, but…"

"Oh, I was just hiking."

She eyed him, hearing the lie in his voice. And she started to worry a little. How well did she know him, really? Could he have anything to do with this? No, his reaction to hearing about the deer hadn't been feigned.

"And, well," he continued, apparently realizing she didn't believe him. "Also doing a little research."

"What kind of research?"

"Not really research—more like fantasizing. Looking at the oceanfront properties around the island. None of the best ones are for sale, but…" He shrugged. "You never know."

"You're thinking of building a summer home?"

"Not really. I guess I—"

Something crashed through the underbrush nearby.

"What the fuck was that?" he said.

"I don't know."

"Jesus. Let's go."

They walked fast back toward the General Store, and a sense of unease gnawed at Kim. Something was wrong. Of course something was wrong, with those mutilated deer, but…something was even more deeply *wrong*.

Garrison kept checking his cell, and when he finally got a signal gave the phone to her. She called Alice Watkins, the closest thing they had to a game warden.

"Alice," she said. "This is Kim Gray. I just found something that—"

"More cats?" Alice said.

"What? No. Deer."

"Shit. Where?"

Kim told her, and asked about the cats, and Alice said they'd found the first last week. "Freaking disgusting," she said. "That's one sick mind at work. I don't know, Kim. This isn't anyone from the island, or we'd've been finding things for years. But there aren't more than a couple dozen tourists still on the island."

Kim looked at Garrison. "Yeah. Yeah, I…yeah."

"Go home, Kim, you sound awful. You don't need to be there."

Kim hung up and she and Garrison walked in silence until they got back to the General Store. She opened her car door and looked at him. He couldn't be involved, but she thought she should tell Alice he'd been wandering around. But really, he couldn't be involved. Impossible. Just look at him.

"Are you gonna be okay at home?" he asked.

She nodded.

"You sure? Maybe you should go to a friend's house or something."

"What about you?" she asked. "Do you, um, need a ride anywhere?"

"No, I'm okay." He gestured to a rental car in the parking lot. "My lawyer's here already."

"Your *lawyer?* What is your lawyer doing here?"

"He likes the sausage. And nobody talks to him, which he also likes."

"No, I mean—you have a lawyer on retainer?"

"Oh. Sure. Yeah."

"What kind of day-hiking oceanfront-property-day-dreaming guy comes with a lawyer on retainer?"

"Always be prepared," Garrison said, moving toward the General Store door. "Well, if you're okay…"

"Fine," she said, sitting in the driver's seat.

You think he could've been a little more open, after all they'd been through together. But hey, if he had to talk to his *lawyer*…

She stuck the key in the ignition and glanced in her rearview mirror. Her great-aunt was standing under the eaves of the General Store, glaring at her with her eerie eyes. And her expression…it was as if she knew about the mutilated deer, and blamed Kim.

She turned the car off and stepped outside to talk to her great-aunt, but now the old lady was nowhere to be seen. She always had been fast with that cane.

✳ 16 ✳

I set my cappuccino on my desk and asked the students to count by tens. Then fives. Then I threw threes out there, just to watch 'em squirm.

"But we don't know our threes!" Conner said.

"Not yet, you don't," I intoned. "But soon the day will come!"

I threatened them with multiplication tables, then we went over the days of the week, and explained when we'd take our field trip to the Portland Art Museum. Then it was story time. I usually used the books as springboards for the rest of the lessons, geography, science, family trees or whatever.

This week, I'd decided to focus on the history of Broome Isle. I'd done a little research at the historical society, and after discovering that Kim had been telling the truth about being descended from a woman hanged as a witch, I'd found my hook. I'd considered a lessons about witches and midwives, the secret history of the witch trials, but that seemed a bit Howard Zinn for first-graders.

It was more fun to make up a story about Kim's witchy ancestry. Hence my once again donning the Hester Prynne costume. I took on the character of Emily Gray as I started my story, explaining how a typical woman spent her days in the seventeenth century on Broome Isle.

My plan was to tie this into Halloween, and explain that Emily wasn't actually a witch, she'd just been mistaken as one. I figured this would lead into great discussions about stereotypes and tolerance. But first-graders will be first-graders, and instead we had a long discussion about what kind of cat Emily Gray had and drew kitty pictures. They liked mine so much, they named her "Piggy."

We got back on track, though, lessons learned and lunches eaten, and all was well until the end of the day. After the kids went outside to the busses, God's parents showed up, clearly apprehensive.

"Please, come in," I told them. "I'm so glad to see you, I wanted to discuss—" For a moment I couldn't recall God's real name "—Caleb's progress with you."

"We came to pull him out of school." Caleb's mother was about my age, a little pudgy with lots of strawberry-blond hair and a timid smile. "We were going to talk to Dr. Epper, but figured we should tell you first."

"Well, thank you," I said. "Are you concerned he's not learning enough here?"

"More concerned he's learning too much," she said.

"Calling himself 'God,'" Caleb's father said. "Taking the Lord's name in vain."

"Yes," I said. "I can see how that might trouble you."

Though not as much as the one-armed babies he'd pretended to be delivering.

"But it's possible we've been a bit hasty," the father continued. "We didn't realize you were a God-fearing woman."

"Oh," I said.

"We don't mean any offense," the mom said, taking my befuddlement for affront. "It's only that we'd…we'd heard otherwise."

"We'd heard you were from New York," the father said.

"Ah," I said, keeping up my end of the conversation.

The mother smiled at me again. "But clearly we got you all wrong, Miss Crenshaw."

"Yes, just look at you," the father said, beaming his approval.

Ah! Aha! My Hester Prynne outfit had struck again. Long black skirt and frumpy beige button-down blouse. In New York, I was mistaken for an Amish woman. But in Maine, to God's parents? I was a Sunday school teacher.

"Oh!" I said. "Yes, that's true."

"And Caleb sure does like you," the mother said.

"I like him," I said. "He's a great kid. He's creative and smart—smart as a whip." I sensed this would be my only opportunity to convince them to let him stay in school. "And he's such a positive influence on the other children. I do hope you let him stay in school. I think he's doing, well, God's work here."

Yup, I was so going to hell for that. But hey, it worked! And it had been easy. Easier than it should've been. As if they couldn't help but believe my every word. Maybe I *was* becoming one of those teachers who inspires.

★ ★ ★

The sun was setting when I got back to the seashell cottage, the light catching in the waves. I almost didn't want to go inside but was surprised when I did. For one thing, the place smelled wonderful, like simmering tomato sauce and garlic bread. Then I saw that the little table over by the window had been set for an intimate dinner for two, with cloth napkins and candles and my mismatched dishes and silverware formally arranged.

Jack stepped from the kitchen in a slim blue linen shirt and dark wash jeans, wiping his hands with a dish towel. He was gorgeous. I don't know how I'd ever found him plain. His quick, welcoming smile turned into a quizzical sort of expression when he saw me, which I found adorable.

"You look surprised to see me," I told him. "You know, I'm the one who lives here. You're the intruder."

"Hey, the door was unlocked. And I'm just surprised to see you wearing *that*," he said, the slow simmering smile returning.

"This isn't what it looks like," I said, smoothing the skirt of my Amish outfit.

"I don't even know what that looks like."

"Hester Prynne?"

"Maybe Hester Prynne as played by a sizzling blond sexpot." He touched my chin, tilted my face toward him and kissed me. "But I guess she *was* sexy, considering all the trouble she got in."

"Oh, blame the victim," I whispered.

Jack pulled the pins from my hair, gently unraveling my bun, wrapping strands around his fingers, lightly brushing my temple and neck. "I always wondered what she wore under those drab dresses…."

His voice faded when I started unbuttoning his shirt, kissing his chest and stomach, down to his jeans, where I popped the top button. I unzipped him and knelt and tugged his jeans over his hips and reached inside his boxers.

He groaned, then said, "Shit! The sauce is burning!"

He half ran, half hopped into the kitchen, laughing and cursing. He banged around for a minute, then came back, looking charmingly abashed.

His expression changed when my Amish dress fell to pool at my feet, and he saw me standing in my matching lavender lace bra and string-bikini pants. I struck a bit of a pose. Although I'd rather be tall and skinny, and able to wear anything, there were compensations to being short and way too curvy. And for a moment, watching the hunger in Jack's eyes, I wouldn't have changed anything.

"You're just…stunning," he said. "I've never seen a—"

"Stop talking," I told him.

He smiled the smile I fell in love with—except this one was hot enough to burn—and came for me. I squealed and slipped into the bedroom, where I flipped onto the bed, waiting for him. He appeared in the doorway, taking his shirt off and throwing it aside. He was more muscular than I'd thought, and his face was suddenly harder in the dim light, his eyes shining with lust and certainty.

He strode across the forecastle of the wave-tossed pirate ship, the sky crashing thunder above, the lashing rain soaking us both as the cannons fired at the pursuing warship, and—

No.

No, I didn't need the fantasy. This was Jack.

He said, "God, do I want you."

"You have me," I told him.

✦ 17 ✦

Natasha woke Tuesday morning burning with the desire to get ready for New York. She did laundry, put the final touches on her portfolio and pored over her old stacks of art newsletters and magazines. Her goal wasn't only to find every mention of Amanda Michaels, but to get back in touch with the art scene.

Then she found a note on the table where the kitchen should be. "I needed your truck, take the bike. M."

She laughed. Marco had never loaned her his motorcycle, a 1972 Triumph Natasha had coveted since she'd secretly taught herself how to ride it in high school. So she spent the rest of the morning and most of the afternoon tearing around the island. Just working off some exhilaration, which was the best preparation for going to New York, anyway.

Back home, she shoved clothes into a duffel bag, put her portfolio in order and tried to tame her windblown and tangled hair. She flipped through the magazines again and threw out the oldest food in the fridge, before cleaning her art supplies. Now all she needed was Kim and Eve to tell her how to dress for her fancy, professional New York dinner. Kim didn't answer the phone, and before she could dial Eve, the phone rang.

"Hi!" Eve said. "It's me."

"I was just about to call you."

"We're at the seashell," Eve said, meaning her cottage. "When're you getting here?"

"What? Did we make plans?"

"Kim said—wait a second." Eve's voice grew fainter as she spoke with Kim, then louder again. "She may be a witch, but she's still a dope. She said you'd want help getting dressed for New York, so we've been here going through our combined closets, but she forgot to tell you to meet us."

"Be there in ten," Natasha said. Then she remembered the bike. "Five."

"No, we're done here. Meet us at the Barnacle for drinks and dessert. We'll send you off in style."

"I want to see what you chose."

"Please," Eve scoffed. "You know you'll wear whatever we tell you."

"Right. The Barnacle, then. Look for the biker chick."

An October evening like this should've been cold on a bike, but the strange heat wave they'd been having kept Natasha comfortable. Portland was ten and twenty degrees colder, but the island was staying in the low sixties—probably something to do with the ocean currents. Whatever the reason, the warm breeze blowing her hair behind her shoulders, the smell of fresh firs and soft ocean air, and the power of the Triumph made her giddy with hope. The meeting with Amanda Michaels tomorrow could change her life.

She rounded a corner, moving fast toward her favorite place on the island: the lone apple tree on the hill. She'd painted and sketched it numerous times. Sat under its summer shade, marveled at its white blossoms, picked the sweet-tart apples and traced her fingers along its bare, crooked branches in the winter. As she came upon it in the fading daylight, it looked…wrong. Natasha had stared at the tree with her artist's eye so many times, she thought she knew what it looked like in every light. Something wasn't right. She squeezed the brakes and parked in front of the tree.

The apple tree was a dull black, as if it had been covered in inky tar. She pulled a shriveled apple from a branch and it fell apart in her hand. Must be some kind of blight, but none like she'd ever seen. She wiped her hand on her jeans and climbed back on the Triumph and drove to the Barnacle. She'd have Marco come look at it tomorrow, but she knew in her heart it couldn't be saved.

She pushed into the restaurant, noticing the marine-blue-and-white decor and captain's chairs for the first time in a long time. Very Maine, very comfortable—and very much *not* New York. She saw a fire blazing in the brick fireplace at the far end of the room, and Eve and Kim sprawled in leather club chairs.

"Isn't it a little warm for this?" she asked, stripping off her denim jacket as she joined them.

"I'm dying for fall," Kim said. "This long summer's all wrong. I told Nelson to light the fire, so we could at least pretend."

"And we ordered hot toddies," Eve said.

They were both dressed in skirts and T-shirts; Kim in black, of course, and Eve in a long-sleeved magenta T and floral skirt that fluttered when she moved. She was barefoot and lying crossways in the chair, her knees hooked over the arm. Natasha always envied her unselfconscious ease.

"God, the two of you," she said, shaking her head. "You look like a couple of overdressed Titian's."

"Is that like being Rubenesque?" Eve asked suspiciously.

"You're the one with the red hair," Kim said.

Natasha laughed at both of them, and noticed the black Lab lying against the hearth, as close as he could get without actually being in the fire. "What's Studly doing here?"

"He followed us," Eve said.

"He's gonna get us kicked out," Natasha said, and turned to Kim. "Remember the fit Nelson pitched when that coon hound started snagging food off the tables?"

Kim grinned. "Yeah, well, this boy's keeping a lower profile."

As if to prove her words, the waitress came with their drinks and didn't lift an eyebrow at the napping dog. She said, "We're not getting a lot of call for hot toddies with this weather," and told them she'd be back with their pie.

"Must've changed their dog policy," Kim said.

Natasha put her mug to her lips to drink when Eve stopped her. "Wait! We have to toast. You always do that."

"Sorry." Natasha felt her cheeks burn. Was she that anxious to get the first sip down? Despite the weather, the blackened tree had left her feeling cold and she craved the warmth of brandy.

Eve lifted her mug. "To Natasha."

"To success," Kim said.

Natasha clinked their mugs. "To art. And to us."

* * *

After half a hot toddy, I broke down and started bragging about Jack. "Maybe it wasn't jelly sex, but wow, spectacular."

"Spectacular seashell sex," Kim said.

"That's all you two think about these days," Natasha teased.

"Only because we're having some," I said.

"Oh, great. You're both off having wild sexual escapades while I remain chaste by discussing Duchamp."

"Who's he again?" I asked.

"In terms you'd understand?" she said. "He's the urinal guy."

"Oh, yeah. I thought maybe he was the beeswax-and-lard guy."

Natasha shot me a disgusted look, and I giggled. She loved the beeswax-and-lard guy.

"But…you're happier that way, aren't you?" Kim asked her.

"Sure," she said. "What woman doesn't love urinals?"

"No," I said. "You really don't like the complications. Remember how you got so fed up with guys in college you starting kissing girls?"

"One girl," Natasha said. "And fat lot of good it did me. Johnny didn't even raise an eyebrow when I told him."

"You know what?" I said. "We should all get together. Jack and Johnny and Jellyson—I mean Garrison. Like a triple date."

"I'm not sure," Natasha said. "We've been doing pretty well so far, keeping the men away from one another."

I nodded. "I know, I've kinda been doing it on purpose. You know how boyfriends get about meeting your friends."

"I know how they get when they meet *you,*" Natasha said.

"One time! One time in college, a boy you weren't even interested in got a crush on me."

She considered, then nodded. "Okay, I'm in if he is. Kim?"

"I don't know," Kim said. "Garrison's a private person."

"You'll have to introduce us eventually."

"I guess, it's just…something creepy happened yesterday."

She told us about discovering some rotting deer that hunters must've shot and left where they fell. Natasha was horrified, but I didn't see why that was so much worse than butchering them into steaks. Still, I kept my city-girl mouth shut, and started to suspect that Kim wasn't telling us everything.

"You think Garrison had something to do with it?" I asked.

"No," she said. "Of course not. He couldn't have."

"Well, was he carrying a rifle or something?"

She shook her head. "Not even a knife."

"A knife?" I asked. "You hunt deer with knives?"

"No, I mean for—" Kim stopped abruptly and drained her mug. "Something's happening on the island. The weather, the deer. People are getting weird rashes… I don't know. Something's wrong."

"I heard nobody's catching any lobster," I said. "You think there's some kind of red tide or oil spill?"

Kim shook her head. "It's more than that."

"My tree is dead," Natasha said. "It's all black and ugly."

"That apple tree?" Kim asked.

"Well, if your tree is dead, then definitely the apocalypse is near," I said. I loved Kim and Natasha, but sometimes they took this island folklore a little too far.

"No, I'm serious," Natasha said. "There was something

really strange about it. And did I tell you Marco got in a car accident?"

"I know," Kim said. "A five-car pileup on Broome Isle."

"There's something else," Natasha said. "Remember that sketch I drew of Gregory?"

"It was just a coincidence," I said. "Gregory was bound to get caught naked in his office sooner or later."

"Well, then I'm probably imagining things, but—"

At the fireplace, the dog suddenly snorted, then let loose a muffled bark and kicked his legs, probably dreaming of chasing squirrels. But one of his paws knocked the table hard, and the flower vase fell and we all lunged to keep our mugs from spilling. We grabbed them before a hot toddy disaster befell us.

When we settled down, I turned to Natasha. "Imagining things?"

She gnawed a fingernail. "All these bad omens. Do you think everything's going to fall apart in New York?"

"No," I said. "No way. New York will be fantastic."

But she wasn't looking at me, she was looking at Kim. For her witchy-knowingness, I guess. "She already likes your art, right?" Kim said.

"So she says."

"Why would she lie? To waste her own time?"

"That's true, she wouldn't," Natasha said, brightening slightly.

"All she wants to know is that you're not a complete freak. That she can work with you."

"Huh. But how much of a freak *am* I?"

"You lived in the city, you know the answer," I said. "You might pass for a freak here, but in New York?"

"Will she like me?" Natasha asked Kim, whose gaze had turned slightly faraway. "I mean, will she want to work with me?"

"I think she will. Yes. You got along on the phone, didn't you?"

"Sorta." Natasha frowned into her empty toddy mug. "Do you think I'm an alcoholic?"

"Are you drunk now?" I teased, jumping at the change of subject.

"No!"

"Then why are you asking?"

"I'm not saying I am, I'm only considering the possibility that—"

"You're not an alcoholic," I said.

"You just drink a lot," Kim said.

"A lot, a lot," I said.

Natasha held up a hand. "All right, I get the idea."

"Speaking of which," I said, looking at Kim. "Tomorrow is the start of Natasha's rise to artistic fame."

"Good point." Kim gestured for the waitress. "We really oughtta send her off with a hangover."

18

On Saturday afternoon, Jack and I finally pried ourselves out of bed and headed to the Smelts Shack for cappuccinos and dinner supplies. We took a shady path through the woods, a shortcut I'd discovered one morning. Jack was wearing dark low-fit jeans and a long-sleeved tee with some obscure band decaled on the front of it. I didn't even know the music he liked.

"Tell me something I don't know about you," I said.

"My mother's name is Eve."

"No way!" I said, then noticed his teasing expression.

He laughed. "Well, how about this? I don't know how to swim."

"You don't?"

"Nope. I can kinda dog-paddle, but that's it."

"Hmm. While unusual, I was hoping for something a bit deeper."

"Like about my evil twin brother?"

"That'd be so cool," I said. "I could really use an evil twin sister. She'd make all the hard calls, you know? Like quitting jobs and breaking up with people."

He stopped and looked at me. "You're not trying to tell me something, are you?"

"What? No! Just thinking about my devilish sister."

"Who you seem to think would do you favors. That's a really cooperative evil twin."

"I have a rich fantasy life." I said. "So? Deep secrets?"

"Well, okay. Promise you won't freak out."

"Um, the very fact that you asked? That freaks me out."

He smiled his smile. "I was married, very young. We've been divorced for five years, almost six, I guess."

"What happened?"

"Teenagers in love." He shrugged. "I guess we grew apart."

"Oh, okay," I said. "Now try explaining again, without the cliché." And give me her name so I can Google her when I get home.

"You're taking this better than I expected."

"What's there to take?" I said, wondering who the fuck she was and why she would leave him.

"Okay. Turned out she's gay."

"Wow. That must've been a shocker."

"Oh, yeah." He smiled, fondly, as if remembering. "The only person more surprised than me was her." He shrugged. "She's a lot happier now."

"You don't hate her?"

"We didn't speak for a few years. Then we ran into each other, and we're friends now. Pretty good friends, actually."

I walked in silence for a minute, trying to figure that out.

Could I be jealous of a gay ex-wife? Apparently, yes. But only because she was still his friend. "I don't know, Jack," I said. "Good friends with your ex?"

"That's bad?"

"Well, I don't wanna be one of those couples who have a—" And I stopped, hearing what I'd just said.

He'd apparently heard, too. "So we're a couple?"

"Well. Well—by couple, I mean, what I meant was, a couple of, um, a couple of people, in a—"

"Eve, I know we've—"

"Had a lot of sex in the past few days? A lot, a lot." Maybe even more than Natasha drinks.

"Well, but that—"

"Doesn't make a relationship!" I finished, not wanting to hear him say it. I knew I was babbling, because I couldn't bear the speech. The "I like you, but…" speech, or the "Let's be fuck buddies" speech, or even worse, the "I've got a girl-friend back home" speech.

"Eve, would you shut up?" he said. "I'm trying to tell you—"

"You have a girlfriend," I said.

He hesitated. "Well, I hope I do."

"You *hope?* What? Wait, are you—"

And I realized what he was saying, and the warm fall day grew perceptibly warmer, and I found myself blushing. I'd never been asked to go steady, or even to be anyone's girl-friend before. I just kinda fell into relationships. So this, making things official, and not just with some jerk I didn't care about, but with *Jack*…

So we didn't make it to the Smelts Shack. Instead, we fondled each other all the way back to my place and made love on the front porch, listening to the pounding surf. I was starting to get sore, and not just from the pine planks—but on the plus side, I was going to get skinny with all this sex and no food. Kim and Natasha would tease me for—

"Oh, no!" I said, disentangling myself. "I've gotta pick my friend up at the airport. What time is it?"

Jack pulled his BlackBerry from the pile of clothing. "Almost five."

"I'm late. Oh, I'm so dead." I finger-combed my hair and got my purse and keys from inside the cottage. Jack was getting dressed when I came back out. "Come with me. My friends want to meet you."

But he was still looking at his BlackBerry. "I can't. I've got a meeting."

"On Saturday?"

"Yeah, Simon's a workaholic. I'm sorry, Eve."

"That's okay. You can meet them next week." I eyed him shyly. "And, um, do you want to come back here after your meeting?"

He sighed. "Well, it's in Portland, so a whole ferry ride back—"

"It's okay, I—"

"—will give me enough time to think about what I'm going to do to you when I get here."

"Oh." I felt myself flush. "Good."

We kissed goodbye and I got into the old Volvo and said a little prayer of thanksgiving when it started. I headed for the ferry, almost forgetting to swing by to get Kim. I pulled an awkward U-turn and raced to her house. I expected her to be sitting on her front porch, tapping at her watch, but there was no sign of her when I pulled into the drive. Her car was there, though, so I ran to the door. No answer. Could Kim have forgotten we needed to pick up Natasha today? Oh, God, I hoped she wasn't occupied with Garrison. What's next—tomato sex?

"Kim?" I called tentatively.

There was no sound. No bedsprings squeaking, no whipped cream squirting from a can. Though, Kim would probably use homemade. I called out again and loudly clomped upstairs. "Kim?" I called in the hallway. "Are you here?"

"Wha…?" From the bedroom. "Eve?"

I did discover Kim in bed, but she was alone, and looking like she'd woken from a bad dream.

"Sorry," I said. "We're late to pick up Natasha."

She wiped sleep from her eyes. "Ugh. I fell asleep."

"Are you sick?" I asked, because she was clearly having a hard time waking up. "Want me to go without you?"

But she didn't look sick as she climbed out of bed, in black jeans and an asymmetrically-cut black sweater, sexy with her mussed hair and perfect body. In fact, she might've put on a few pounds recently, which made her look even better.

"No," she said. "Gimme a second." She stumbled into the bathroom for a moment, then returned with her face washed and hair straightened. "Maybe I am sick, I'm so tired. You ready?"

We were almost an hour late when we finally pulled into the Jetport. Kim and I had barely spoken on the trip. She was still half asleep, and I was basking in the afterglow of perfect love that was me and Jack. We were so late that I didn't park, instead I drove past the curbside, hoping to spot Natasha among the throngs.

"There she is," Kim said.

"Uh-oh," I said, spotting her sitting on a bench, waiting for the bus.

"Yeah," Kim said. "She doesn't look happy."

"Natasha!" I called, honking as I pulled over. "Sorry we're late!"

"Yeah," she said, stowing her bag in the trunk.

I glanced at Kim, who shrugged back at me, looking as worried as I felt. I soldiered on. "So?" I said, driving out of the airport. "How was it? How was she?"

Natasha grunted.

"Was the hotel nice?"

"Uh-huh."

"Did you get a cupcake at Magnolia?" I turned to Kim. "That was our regular pilgrimage on Thursday afternoons." Objectively, the now-famous cupcakes weren't that special, but it'd been fun to dawdle on Bleecker Street, pretending we could afford to shop at Marc Jacobs and waiting in the cramped bakery for a warm vanilla cupcake with chocolate icing.

"Nope," Natasha said.

"Oh."

That was it for me, my last attempt to draw her out, but Kim was less scared of Natasha and said, "She didn't want to represent you?"

I very carefully watched the traffic.

Natasha grunted again, but Kim was undeterred. "Tell us what happened."

No answer. We proceeded in silence until we were seated three in a row on the long ferry bench. Kim finally spoke again about the trip. "Natasha, it doesn't help to keep it buried inside. Get it out so we can comfort you."

More growling from Natasha.

"I know it's gonna happen," Kim said. "It doesn't matter what one agent thinks, your art is beautiful and—"

Natasha said, "I'm so sick of your 'I know things' bullshit."

"Well, I'm just saying—"

"Don't you get it? Nobody gets chances like this. Nobody. Not once—and never twice. I screwed my one shot. One shot, and I blew it."

"She didn't like your work?"

"Oh, she likes my art, she loves my fucking art. But you know what? I fucked everything up, anyway."

"What happened?"

"I humiliated myself, that's what. Does it look like I want to talk about it?" She glared at Kim…and her eyes sharpened. "Why do you look like that?"

"Like what?" Kim asked. "Sorry for my best friend?"

"You're glowing," Natasha said.

"I'm maybe a little feverish. I'm sick and tired and—"

"Sick? You're pregnant, Little Miss Know-It-All."

Kim sat preternaturally still, staring across the sea toward Broome Isle, her hands lying flat against her womb. Even her short hair defied the wind, staying evenly in place. After a moment, she said, "I *am* pregnant."

"You know that just by sitting eerily still with your hands on your belly?" I said.

"No, I can tell because I didn't get my period last Tuesday. I'm never late, I've just been so distracted with…" She bit her lip. "Oh, God, what am I going to tell him?"

"Garrison?" I said. "You really think you're pregnant?"

"Of course she is." Natasha nestled close to Kim, her

anger apparently gone in the aftermath of her revelation. "Her coloring's different and her body's starting to soften."

"Oh, thanks," Kim said. "I'm squashy."

"Just like you wished for," I said. "I mean, that night we found that liquor."

"What *are* you gonna tell him?" Natasha asked.

"I guess I have to tell him something," Kim said. "Eventually."

"Is he the… I mean, is he the daddy type?" I asked.

"Oh, fuck," Natasha said. "What am I gonna tell *Marco?*"

"Don't say a word about this," Kim said, suddenly fierce. "Not a single word, either of you, do you hear?"

We were so taken aback by her intensity that we abashedly vowed silence. I thought we'd moved past the whole Natasha-lost-her-one-chance thing, so I ventured another question about the trip. She growled at me, so I guess I was wrong. And Kim sat, subdued and silent, and more thoughtful than joyous. And we finally arrived, lost in our own individual clouds. Not even the black Lab greeting us at the dock, now bulky and glossy, his tail merrily wagging, really raised anyone's spirits. I guess he didn't get the memo about the soon-to-be single mom and the failing artist. And me—whatever I was.

Natasha sat in her chair, staring at *Lost Hope*. It was named for good now—she'd definitely lost it. She absently stroked Puck, who was purring in her lap. He'd given her the cold shoulder when she'd come home and found him lying on Marco's porch, but then he'd coyly trailed Natasha to her own front door. She'd scrambled an egg to split with him, and they'd fallen into the chair together afterward, Puck grooming himself and Natasha sipping her bourbon and amaretto.

She tried to push the humiliation of New York from her mind, and decided to worry about Kim's pregnancy instead. It wasn't that she wasn't happy for Kim. She was. She couldn't remember a time when Kim hadn't wanted to be a mom, but…well, she worried about Marco. They never discussed it, but Natasha knew he was still in love with Kim. How was he going to take the news? She jiggled her ice cubes, wishing they could all go back in time to when Kim was pregnant with Marco's baby, they were happily married and Natasha still had a chance to break out as an artist.

She sucked an ice cube, trying to decide whether she should make herself another drink. Was there a good reason *not* to drink more? Well, it'd bother Puck if she got up. She'd wait for him to move, then consider whether she really wanted another….

She thought about Johnny. He said he'd call when she got back from New York, but of course he'd speak with Mandy first and then *never* call. Great. No career, no romance. Her best friends were getting all they ever wanted—Kim pregnant and Eve lovestruck—while Natasha was stuck feeling…well, stuck. She squirmed, restless and claustrophobic and Puck leapt from her lap.

She made herself another drink.

Kim fixed a tomato-chutney-and-cheese sandwich, then downed a pint of vanilla ice cream with honey and frozen strawberries swirled into it. Still hungry, she foraged in the cabinet, hoping to find potato chips. She found an old box of whole-wheat crackers that the mice had been in. This was nothing new—you lived in a two-hundred-year-old farm-house and you shared everything with mice. But Kim gagging and retching into the sink? That was new.

She brushed her teeth for a five full minutes, undressed and stood in front of the full-length mirror on the inside of her closet door. She turned sideways, imagining her belly and breasts growing bigger, wondering if she'd make it past four months this time. What would it feel like, carrying a fully formed infant in your body?

She switched off the light and climbed into her honey-moon bed. She cuddled under her quilt and traced circles across her belly. She'd wanted to drive to the General Store for a pregnancy test, but then the whole island would know. *He'd* know, before she told him. What would he say? Would the pregnancy ruin everything, like last time? She was struck by a sudden rush of anxiety: what if everything fell apart, all over again? Then she stilled her hand, willing the little nub to stay healthy. That was all she cared about.

"Eve," Jack's voice said on my machine. "I can't make it back tonight. I'm still in Portland and I'm going to stay in a hotel here. Sorry. I miss you. Call you tomorrow."

The wind shook the cottage as I sat on the couch, listen-ing to Jack's message for the third time. What kind of meeting takes place on a Saturday night? Simon was a work-aholic, sure, but what if there was another woman? Jack wanted me to be his girlfriend, but what if I was just the con-venient island girlfriend? With winter coming, he'd always have the "bad weather" alibi for not seeing me, and if he got stuck here, he'd have a warm bed and a willing woman. Hmm. Where was he going to live this winter, anyway? He had an apartment in New York and traveled all the time. How was I supposed to be his girlfriend if he traveled all the time?

And why was I determined to see the worst in him? Maybe it was because of Gregory. He'd always made me feel so lacking as a girlfriend. No matter how much I'd practiced feeling full of inner poise and beauty and repeating the mantra *I am good enough* while riding the subway to work, he'd still made me feel like shit. And then he'd speakerphone dumped me.

Maybe it was because I hardly even knew Jack. We had chemistry. We had more chemistry than a Bunsen burner. But he was always so interested in me, he hardly talked about himself. Was he shy, or hiding something? I knew he wasn't lying to me about how he felt—I just *knew*. But why was he so unforthcoming about his life? I mean, sure, he'd answer anything I asked, but he never really seemed to just lay everything out there.

Of course, nobody was as good at that as me. I was the *Woman of No Mystery,* as enigmatic as a jackhammer.

I went to the bathroom to brush my teeth. Now Kim and Natasha, they were both mysterious. Natasha never had been before, but now…what had happened in the city? Could she really have screwed her whole career with one bad meeting? And Kim, pregnant by her mystery lover. Had she never heard of birth control?

Well, maybe I wasn't a Mona Lisa–type woman, fine. But at least I wasn't too shy or timid to speak my mind, and the next time I saw Jack, I'd simply demand that he tell me *everything*. I needed to know exactly who I was falling in love with. I changed into my pj's, an old pair of boxer briefs from an ex-boyfriend and a white men's ribbed undershirt and bolted the front door—Jack made me promise not to leave it unlocked. But just as I was stumbling back to the bedroom in the dark, someone knocked.

I unbolted and opened the door and Jack stood on my doorstep. He smiled, but I wasn't going to just melt into his arms. Not this time. This time I had some serious questions to ask him. Like, um…well. Hmm.

I couldn't quite remember, so I said, "How did you get here? The ferry stopped running an hour ago."

"Water taxi." He grinned. "A hotel is cold comfort when there's a warm *you* waiting for me."

"Hey," I said. "No charming me."

He ran his finger along the line of my T-shirt from the strap at my shoulder, across the front, down between my breasts. "Why not?"

"I have very important questions to ask you," I said.

"Such as?"

"Like…why are we still here, and not in the bedroom?" I led him to the bedroom. "And, um, why haven't you told me everything about yourself?"

I wasn't sure if he'd heard, because he was busy stripping off my T-shirt and cupping my breasts in his hands. Frankly, I wasn't sure if I'd heard, either.

He paused at my boxer briefs. "Where'd these come from?"

"They're comfy. Do you think I sleep in a sheer baby-doll nightie?"

He slipped the boxer briefs off me, his fingers exploring what they'd concealed. "They're from an old boyfriend, aren't they?"

"Huh?" I bit my lower lip. "Who?"

His hand stopped moving. "The boxers. They belonged to a boyfriend?"

"Maybe. Yeah, I guess."

"Never wear them again."

"What?"

I pulled away and stood, hand on hip, staring him in the eye. I might be his convenient island girlfriend, but that didn't mean he could dictate what I could and couldn't wear. Still, he didn't look like he was taking me seriously. Maybe it was because I was naked. The whole hand-on-hip thing generally works better when clothed.

"I'm jealous," he said, sitting on the bed and pulling me close. "That's something about me."

"Jealous of boxers?" I asked, lying down next to him.

"Jealous of this." He put a hand between my legs again, speaking so close to my ear that his warm breath raised gooseflesh on my arm. "And jealous of these…"

He licked my breast, and the fabric of his shirt and pants were rough against my naked skin. He could turn me on like a switch, I don't know how, but I'd never responded to anyone like this. I was about to come and he hadn't even taken his clothes off yet.

"Never wear these again," he murmured, making the words sound like sweet nothings, his voice thick with lust. "Only mine, always mine."

I teased him a little further. "Wear what?"

He stopped touching, stopped licking. I mewled in protest.

"Always?" he whispered into my ear.

"Always."

✳ 19 ✳

I spent the weekend trying to convince Natasha and Kim to agree to a Wednesday Night Witches outing. Well, actually, I spent the weekend in bed with Jack, and learned a few things about him. For example, he had a fondness for grilled-cheese sandwiches that bordered on the obsessive. Also, he was heading back to New York in two weeks.

So instead of learning *everything*, we'd had our first fight, surrounded by the scent of grilled bread and gruyere. Why hadn't he told me? Why wasn't he ever going to call me again? Had all of this meant nothing to him? And so forth. Then we'd had make-up sex, which almost made me want to pick another fight.

I'd considered calling in sick for two weeks straight, just so I could spend every minute with Jack until he left, but rationality triumphed. Also, he promised to return for weekends, and I wasn't the type of girl who dumps her best friends the minute she lands a boyfriend. So I was determined not to let the Wednesday Night Witches fade away just because, well, all our wishes had come true. Except for Natasha's. Which meant she was going to be a grumbling nightmare, but she was my best friend and needed a couple of shoulders to cry on, which made me even *more* determined to get together.

I tried to persuade them to go to into Portland. The island remained an unseasonable sixty-five degrees, but I was starting to worry that once the weather turned, I'd become a character from a Stephen King novel. The strange happenings on the island—dead deer, disappearing lobsters, unexplained rashes and inexplicable car accidents—were already painting a horrifying tale of Maine island life. I was just waiting for one of the lobstermen to decide he'd set his empty traps for young single women. Plus, I was already missing Jack, and he wasn't even gone yet. I'd go crazy with loneliness this winter without a regular date with Kim and Natasha—the trips to Portland would reaffirm how close I was to civilization.

But Kim and Natasha had no such worries, and the most I could persuade them to agree upon was coming to my house for a meal I was incapable of cooking. They knew I couldn't cook, but I lured Natasha with the promise of whiskey and Kim with cottage cheese and wheat germ. An odd craving, but there's no arguing with a pregnant witch.

The witchery ran in their blood, all three of them—strongest with Kim, whose roots grew deep in my land, but the other two also brushed the unseen world. Weak apart, together they were more than thrice as powerful.

They'd summoned me back from my prison, ending the banish-

ment Kim's foremothers had forced upon me. And as they healed themselves, they'd healed me. As they came into their power, so I came into mine.

The road was neither smooth nor easy. None of them felt the hunger keenly enough to be of perfect use to me; they loved one another too well for that. I'd given them their fondest desires…and there was no more powerful curse than that.

Eve stumbled into love with a man who held her fragile heart in the palm of his hand. She should have been driven by fear, but trusted him too much. She trusted herself, as well, and was too strong to let the fear rule her.

Natasha had been given a glimpse of the future she so desired, only to have it torn from her grasp for reasons she didn't truly under-stand. Her anger and self-doubt should've ripped her in half. Instead, she mourned…and knew her friends would help her through.

And the seed I'd allowed Kim to have had made her bright and invincible, instead of fearful and sick.

They were stronger than I'd expected. But still not half as strong as I. All it required was a spark. Of anger, betrayal, hatred. One spark, and I would begin to cull the mindless herd that infested my island, taking everything the witches loved, growing stronger with each death.

Wednesday night, Natasha tore down the gravel road leading to Eve's cottage, riding the motorcycle toward the setting sun. Just in time. Any later and she would've had to start drinking at home. A bad sign, feeling the *need* to have a cocktail every day at five. She'd dragged her feet and given Eve all sorts of grief about tonight, but in truth she was looking forward to being together. At least she wouldn't be drinking alone.

And now, sitting on the Triumph beside the cottage,

looking out at the water, she almost smiled. Sometimes she forgot how beautiful the island was—even if her own life was crap, at least she was surrounded by beauty.

She went inside and found Eve in the middle of the living room, wearing a completely spotless apron and looking bubbly and exited. "My first dinner party here!" she said.

Natasha sniffed the air. "And you forgot to make dinner, didn't you?"

Eve laughed and showed her the bottles of Jack Daniel's and Amaretto on the table. "I didn't forget the drinks!"

Natasha grunted, touched that Eve had bought her favorites, and tinkled ice into two glasses. "What about for Kim? Did you get wine or something?"

"I don't think she's supposed to have *any* alcohol."

"Yeah, that's why I said wine."

"Natasha, wine *is*…oh, shut up."

Natasha laughed. "You're so easy. Oh, speaking of which…how's that man of yours?"

Eve's face started glowing brighter and she babbled Jack's praises for two minutes.

"God, you're so *happy*," Natasha said.

"You think I only need a boyfriend to be happy, don't you?"

Natasha handed one of the drinks to Eve. "It's always been important to you. More than to me."

They clinked glasses, not toasting to anything except being together.

"Oh, sure, all I want is a man to marry so I can settle down and have kids."

Pathetic. First Kim, now Eve. Natasha shrugged. "If that's what you want—"

LEE NICHOLS

"Hey!" Eve said. "I was *joking.*"

Oh, shit. "Ha, ha! Got you again."

Eve gazed at her suspiciously. "I can't believe you think that about me."

"Hey, I can tease you all night—I'm the miserable one, remember? You have Jack, Kim has the Jellyman, and all I have is broken dreams and crushed hopes."

"And your optimistic nature," Kim said from the doorway.

"And a drink," Eve said.

Natasha raised her glass. "And the two of you."

Kim closed the door behind her and sniffed. "Nothing's cooking."

"Not yet," Eve said.

"Well, that's not such a bad thing. I've got dog nose."

"Right," Natasha said. "What?"

"Dog nose. I read about it the first time I got pregnant, but never had it before. Odors are magnified like two hundred percent—except for the really horrible ones, which are magnified a thousand percent. Your Amaretto is disgusting."

Natasha lifted her glass to her nose. "I think it smells good."

"How are you feeling?" Eve asked. "Are you having morning sickness?"

"More like 'all day' sickness."

"I got you pomegranate juice," Eve said, pouring what looked like punch into a glass. "It's full of antioxidants. And the woman at the health food store told me to get flaxseed meal instead of wheat germ. More omega threes to help the baby's brain develop."

"Oh." Kim was touched. "Thanks. I didn't know that."

"And I got cottage cheese, too," Eve said proudly.

Natasha looked toward the kitchen. "And that's what we're having for dinner, isn't it?"

"Oh, honey, I could've brought something," Kim told Eve. "I froze a ton of stuff this summer."

"You'll need that when the baby comes. And I *am* going to cook. Well, actually I'm going to assist. Jack's cooking!"

"Jack is coming," Natasha said flatly.

"It'll be fun, I promise," Eve said.

"Yech. Now I'm gonna have to be *nice,*" Natasha said, and Kim kind of felt the same.

"You don't," Eve said. "I told him all about you. He's expecting a total bitch."

"What?"

"Ha! I'm not the only gullible one. No, I haven't told him anything about either of you—you're my only secret, my mysterious friends." She bit her lip. "Except now he's gonna see how boringly ordinary you are."

"What's he cooking?" If it was something good, maybe the evening was saved.

"He makes really good grilled-cheese sandwiches. I know it should just be us witches on Wednesday night, but I wanted you to meet him."

"Sure, it's okay." Though Kim really just wanted to hang out with the girls. If a guy came, the whole evening would change. He'd be the center of attention and they couldn't just be themselves.

"I *do* want to meet him," Natasha said, even less enthusiastically than Kim.

"What if I get him to make us dinner," Eve said, "and meet you two, then tell him to disappear?"

Natasha perked up. "Would he?"

"It's not that we don't want to meet him," Kim said.

"We *do*," Natasha said. "It's just—"

"I know." Eve smiled. "Besides, he'll come back after you two go home. He'll understand. But what about you, Natasha? What's going on with your, um, with Johnny?"

Kim dug a spoon into the cottage cheese, smiling. A nice save. Far safer to ask Natasha about her man than her art.

"Nothing." Natasha crunched an ice cube. "I haven't heard from him since I got back."

"Did you call him?"

"No."

"And he hasn't called you?"

"No."

"Do you think he left the island?"

"I don't know."

"Do you think that gallery person told him what happened in New York?"

"Yeah."

"What *did* happen in New York?"

"We had dinner." Natasha turned to Kim. "What I want to know is, did you tell Garrison you're pregnant?"

Kim sprinkled more flax meal on the cottage cheese. "Well…"

"You haven't told him," Natasha said.

"You really have to tell him," Eve said.

"It's complex," Kim said. "I've been keeping a secret."

"No!" Eve said. *"Not you!"*

"What? I don't keep many secrets."

"You're an enigma in eye shadow."

Natasha shot Eve a look. "First, what the hell are you talking about? Second, let Kim confess her sins, already."

"Okay," Kim said. "I've been—I just wanted to be private, but I guess this has spun a bit out of control. It'll be a relief to get it out in the open. Thing is—"

"Would you spill already?"

"Well, the man I've been seeing? He's—"

A knock sounded at the door.

It was Jack. He stepped inside, carrying a sack of groceries. "Hey," he said, then stopped.

Kim turned. "Garrison?"

"Johnny?" Natasha said, at the same time. "What're you doing here?"

I suddenly found it a little hard to breathe. "No, no. That's Jack."

The three of us stared at him, and for a moment I was reminded of a painting I'd once seen of the Three Furies. The dark one, the light one and the fiery one—each angry and frightening. Though not as angry as I was at the revelation that Jack was not only Jack, but Johnny *and* Garrison.

Maybe he'd seen the same painting, because he dropped his bag of groceries out of what looked like fear, before facing me. "These are your friends?" he asked. "Looks like I already know them."

"Under three fucking names," Natasha said. *"Johnny."*

"Okay, I guess that was a mistake. Let me explain," he said. "Actually, it's kinda funny."

"I'm not laughing," I said.

"Funny-strange, I guess," Natasha said.

"No, no, funny-funny, not funny-strange. Although, maybe it's a little strange, too—I mean, what're the chances that I'd meet all three of you and—"

"Give us each different names," I said.

"Yeah, that. Well. This is what happened. My father's name—" He stepped toward me, but Kim and Natasha stepped in front of me, like human shields.

"What's your name?" Natasha said.

"Well, um—" He swallowed. "This whole thing is just a few misplaced names, nothing important. I'm a junior, so—"

"Nothing important?" I said, flaring up. "What about Kim?"

"What about Kim?"

He glanced at her, and so did I. There was an edge of worry in her face, but she remained silent.

"She doesn't have anything to do with this," Jack said. "I paid her for—"

"You slept with her!" Natasha said.

"Well, yeah. What? No—no, no."

"So yeah, but no?" I said.

"With *you*. I thought she meant with you. I've never touched Kim." He turned to her. "Tell them!"

Kim shook her head. I wasn't sure if she was defending Jack or ashamed that she'd slept with my boyfriend. Or had I slept with hers? I tried to remember which one of us saw him first.

"The day I met you, Eve," Jack said. "When you fell under your car and I pulled you out—I don't know, I felt like I was seeing a woman for the first time."

Well, I guess Jack thought *I* was the girlfriend. "We're not talking about me, we're talking about Kim. And your three identities." Although, even if he could explain giving us three different names, I wasn't sure I could get over him sleeping with Kim.

"Okay. Simon calls me Johnny," he said. "He's the only one, but Natasha overheard and she started calling me that, too. I used 'Garrison' with Kim—that's my middle name—because, um, I paid cash so she wouldn't have my name on a check because, um…"

Oh, God, was he actually *paying* her for sex? "Get out," I said.

"Evie," he said. "Please, just—"

I screamed: "Get *out!*"

"Eve," Kim said, her voice soft, "you know that thing I was about to admit?"

"You knew!" I said, glaring at her. "You *knew!* Get out, both of you, go have jellysex and—go!"

"It's not what you think," Kim said.

"You're standing there, pregnant with his baby, shoving cottage cheese into your mouth," Natasha said. "What else could she think?"

"My baby?" Jack said.

"You stay out of it," Kim told Natasha.

"Oh, like I stayed out of your relationship with Marco? Who's gonna tell him you're pregnant with some other guy's baby?"

"Whose baby?" Jack said. "It's not my baby."

"Yes, it is," Natasha said.

"Maybe you *should* stay out of it," Jack told her.

"Like you stayed out of my life? Setting me up with Mandy?"

"You!" Kim spat at Natasha. "You act like my divorce from Marco hurt *you* more than me. Always the artist, it's always all about *you*."

"I'm not the one fucking Eve's boyfriend. I'm not the one *pregnant* by Eve's boyfriend."

For a moment, an eerie sort of silence fell, and as one they all turned to me. I could see the shock in their faces. Cute, cuddly, sexy, bubbly Eve—that's how they thought of me. Until now. The light from the little lamp in the room grew brighter behind me, as if I'd put a spotlight in it, instead of a seventy-five-watt bulb. And I was controlling it. I could feel it glowing, increasing in strength. Well, maybe I wasn't controlling it, but I was causing it. My regret and sadness and anger. The silence shattered as I started yelling. At Jack, at Kim, at the world. I'm not even sure what I said, I could hardly hear my own words above the pure rage.

The light got brighter and brighter behind me, and I watched as Kim grew perfectly still and silent. Not a passive kind of stillness or silence: she was like a cobra, poised to strike. I could almost see the coiled tension in the air around her. She said nothing, absorbing my anger and giving nothing back but her uncanny stillness. And Natasha, never subtle, never still, paced furiously, radiating red sheets of anger, her voice louder and sharper to match my own.

Until suddenly, all three us turned to Jack.

I knew in my heart that Jack was no coward. But have you ever dunked your head into a tank of water filled with piranhas? Well, that's what a blast from three angry women— *these* three angry women—must've felt like. He fled, and from across the room, I slammed the door closed behind him.

Finally, the spark. Outside the cottage I could feel the anger erupting skyward, buffeting the island, and settling like ash into every hedge and lichen-covered stone. It coated the bare-limbed trees, the rooftops and leaf-piles and birds' nests. And seeped into my blood, my sinews and teeth and claws, wakening the strength I'd long forgotten.

I felt my power return…and the hunger redouble.

I slipped the leash of my weakness and prowled my land, hunting for the next sacrifice. What was precious to the Witches? What would they miss? I'd take everything they loved, one at a time, and grow stronger with each feast.

✳ 20 ✳

The hair stood up on the back of Kim's neck, anger humming in the air like electricity. She felt something writhing between her and the others, she felt something *wrong* walking on her island, and she knew she had to stop this. She didn't know how, but she suspected the first step was telling Eve and Natasha the truth.

She waited for a momentary silence and said, "The baby is Marco's."

"—and you think—" Natasha continued, then stopped. "What?"

"The baby. I never slept with Garrison—Johnny—*Jack!* Marco showed up that morning after we drank the liquor from the old cellar. And he…we've been together ever since. We didn't say anything because we're going slow and…and want to keep this fragile thing alive and—"

"You never slept with Jack?" Eve said.

"I only met him like three times. I just needed to give you the name of some random man, to cover for Marco, and he sprung to mind. I didn't know *you* knew him."

"He told you his name was Garrison," Natasha said.

"Yeah, that can't be a good thing."

"Well, given his real name is probably Ted Bundy, I—" Natasha stopped, clearly remembering something she wanted to talk about more. "Wait a minute. Marco? You and Marco, this whole time?"

"He wanted to tell you," Kim said. "But I wasn't sure. After last time…"

"You were afraid," Eve said.

"I've always loved him, Natasha. I can't remember a time when I didn't love him, not since that day at the Barnacle."

"That's what you wanted to tell us tonight?" Natasha said.

Kim nodded. "I'm sorry, I should've told you before."

"Well, I'm gonna have to kill Marco, of course. God, I was so worried about him learning you're pregnant that I—wait. He still doesn't know, does he?"

"Not yet. But soon." Kim touched her stomach. "No more secrets. We've had too many of those already, and I'm afraid we… I don't know. Something's wrong. That wasn't just three best friends pissed because a guy duped them. Did you *feel* that?"

"What is going on?" Eve asked. She looked shaken. "It was me. I made the lights do that. And I slammed the door on him from across the room. How could I do that?"

"I don't know," Kim said. "The anger caused us to tap into something. Something powerful. Something evil."

"Lies are evil," Natasha said.

"So tell us the truth," Kim said. "What happened in New York?"

★ ★ ★

I looked to Natasha, and for a moment she didn't answer. Then she grabbed her drink and swirled the liquor. "The first day, when I arrived at her gallery, we got along great. Mandy sent a car to meet me and everything. And she loved my stuff—at least she said she did."

"And then?"

"We went to dinner. There was—I don't know. I can't explain it."

"Sashimi?" I asked, to break the tension. "I can't explain that, either."

They gave me a pity-laugh, then Natasha said, "There was sexual tension."

"She was hitting on you?" I asked.

"Yeah. I think. Yes. Definitely."

"Wow. Didn't see that coming."

"It's like I was flown in special to sleep with her, like the art version of a casting couch or something. Like Johnny— Jack, whatever—found some rube from the hick farm and shipped her to New York to show his best friend a good time."

"Wait," I said. "She said they're best friends? She and Jack?"

"Yeah, they used to be close."

"And she's gay?" Everything came together at once. "Ohmigod, Mandy Michaels is Jack's ex-wife."

"He's pimping for his ex-wife?" Natasha asked.

"I'm gonna be sick," I said. "How could I have fallen for such a jerk, *again?*"

"He's the one I found with the dead deer," Kim said, her eyes troubled. "And they weren't just dead. They were…

messed up. Something's wrong on the island. I don't know what, I've never felt this before. But…that morning after we drank the liquor from the old cellar, what happened?"

"Don't look at me," Natasha said. "I blacked out. That's when I started worrying about my drinking."

"You're not the only one," Kim said. "That whole night's gone."

"Me, too," I said. "And when I woke, I was unbelievably—"

"Thirsty," Natasha finished.

"Me, too." Kim nodded slowly. "Okay. That's weird enough. And the next day, I got pregnant with Marco. You met Jack. And Natasha was told about Mandy Michaels. And now, with the dead deer and my cats gone—"

"And the car accidents," Natasha said. "And you know, I never told you, but I sketched one of the car accidents before I knew it'd happened. Which was fucking weird, after sketching naked Gregory in his office."

"C'mon, this is like Ash Street again," I said. "You're just trying to creep me out. You really don't believe in this witch stuff, do you?"

"How do explain what just happened with the lights and the door?"

"I don't know, a power surge, the wind…except…"

"You felt it," Kim said. "Just like we did."

I nodded—then lightning flashed, and a clap of thunder shook the cottage. I shrieked, then laughed, feeling as if we were on a camping trip, telling ghost stories. Yes, I'd felt "something," but what was I suppose to think—that it was magic?

Kim crossed to the window, and when the lightning

flashed again, she said, "Why is my great-aunt Hazel coming down the road?"

"Maybe she got caught in the storm," Natasha said.

"Huh," I said. "Did I tell you I had this daydream about her?"

The house shook with thunder, and we filed silently onto the porch and stared. The night sky was filled with billowy storm clouds, edged with burnt orange, and an awful reek oozed from somewhere.

"Must be fish rotting on the beach," I said, wrinkling my nose.

"Ooh," Natasha said, looking at the sky. "Weather."

I knew she loved bad weather, but this was something other than a storm. Those clouds were catching the faint dying rays of the sun long after sunset. And of course, there was also Kim's great-aunt marching toward the cottage, her white hair glowing and her gnarled cane swinging.

She stopped when she saw us and shouted, "The child of darkness is born! He's slipped his prison, and hunts for sacrifice to feed his hunger...."

I shook my head, willing the image from my mind. "This is just like my daydream."

"Banished generations ago," the old lady intoned, "by the daughters of Broome Isle. You must again banish him into exile, else he will—"

Kim touched my shoulder, her eyes urgent. "How did it end? Your daydream?"

"What? Oh. A tree fell on your aunt and—"

"Aunt Hazel!" Kim shouted at her great-aunt. "Run!"

And there was another clap of thunder, and a *crack,* and a

tree fell on the old lady. Simply toppled over from the side of the road, and…*wham!* She crumpled and lay in a spreading pool of blood.

She wasn't yet dead when Natasha knelt beside her, the wet earth cold on her knees, eyes burning and heart clenched.

Natasha felt herself weeping, kneeling beside Kim as the sky caught fire overhead, like the aurora borealis except the clouds themselves were shimmering. She'd never said ten words to Kim's great-aunt, but the old lady was a fixture on the island, like her lone apple tree or one of the pebbled beaches.

"Aunt Hazel," Kim said. "Please. What's happened? What do we do?"

The old lady whispered, "It took three to unleash him this time. He's getting stronger."

"He…you mean—"

Kim's great-aunt turned, her colorless eyes boring into Natasha. "Your barn. Your easel. Go, child. Go." She turned back to Kim. "We used needles to break his skin. It was all we had." She exhaled one last time and died.

"She's gone," Kim said, after gulping air. "We have to go."

"We have to call the police," Eve said.

"Get your cell," Kim told her. "We'll call on the way."

"Where?"

"You heard her," Kim said. "Natasha's house. The barn."

"But why?"

"I don't know—I just *know.*"

And suddenly, so did Natasha. And, judging from her expression, so did Eve. The sketches, the daydreams—the old lady, dead at their feet. Kim's eerie connection to the island…everything clicked. Something was very wrong. Something was a danger to them. Not just them. A danger to the things they loved. At her barn…

Oh, God. *Marco.*

"Don't say his name," Kim hissed at her. "Don't even *think* it."

The stench grew stronger as they ran for the car, Eve talking desperately on her cell and Natasha revving the Volvo furiously. She thought she'd been fast on the motorcycle, but that was nothing compared to this. They roared along the oceanside road, Eve still on the phone, Kim sitting in silence, and Natasha driving dangerously fast. When they skidded to a halt outside the barn, Marco's car was gone. They burst into the house, and he was nowhere. Ran into the barn, and all stopped short.

Nothing was out of place…except for *Lost Hope.* The large canvas was shredded, hanging from the frame by a few frayed threads. Her best work, destroyed—and she was relieved, because at least it wasn't Marco.

"What do we do now?" Eve said. "This can't be happening."

"Have you had any other daydreams?" Kim asked her.

"No. Not like that."

Kim turned to Natasha. "How about sketches that felt… odd?"

"I don't know. No, I don't think so." She looked at the ruined canvas. "Just this. What about you, Kim—you're the real witch?"

The room grew suddenly darker as the clouds thickened outside, and Kim closed her eyes. "My mother, my great-aunt—they told me bedtime stories about…" She stopped, then started again. "I was raised to feel the island the way I feel my own body. And something's wrong, like a fever or a broken bone. They said something rotten was festering on the island before anyone ever stepped foot here, that's what Emily Gray dispelled and then my grandmother and Hazel years later. I always believed in the island magic, the part of me that knows when a storm is coming, or when flowers will bloom, or the leaves will turn, but I never really believed... I don't know what to do."

They fell silent. This whole thing was so outrageous, yet somehow Natasha didn't question that Kim was telling the truth.

"Those aren't clouds," Eve said, standing at the window.

Natasha looked outside. The orange tinge was from a fire, the billowing clouds were smoke. Something on the island was burning.

Kim got that faraway look in her eyes. "No. It's the General Store," she said. "Burning to the ground."

✳ 21 ✳

The wind moaned through the pine trees, and the scent of burnt plastic and charred wood swirled around me. And though Kim spoke softly, I heard her with perfect clarity, reciting a tale passed down for generations: "Between the old stone fences wandering into the dark heart of the island and the tangled coves guarding the beaches, a pebbled stream rambled through the rich earth, then forked into two. One branch, the larger, grew wider and straight and filled with water, to feed the thirsty roots and fill stone wells. The smaller, long ago setting out upon a fruitless path, became shallower and dryer until disappearing into the undergrowth. And long ago, the spirit of the island divided in much the same way. The larger section grew hearty, feeding and comforting the pines and lupine, the foxes and bobolinks and settlers. The smaller, however, hungered and ached. One severed fragment of the island's heart burned, longing to shed blood, to hunt, to kill. And this wasn't the first time, either. This hunger had been roused before, and had been stopped before by human hands. Yet nothing that still hungers can truly be laid to rest."

We stood together at the edge of the smoldering ruins of the General Store, heads bowed. The building had been reduced to mounds of collapsed timber, a jutting brick chimney I'd never noticed before, blackened humps where the stove and counter had been, and ash—ash everywhere.

I lifted my head to look at Kim. "I don't understand any of that."

"I'm not sure I do, either," she said.

"Who cares what we understand?" Natasha said. "What do we *do?*"

Nobody answered. A spark popped in the wreckage, and a bunch of half-melted plastic bottles clattered from a charred shelf. I couldn't believe this was happening—whatever it was. I couldn't believe the General Store, aka the Smelts Shack was gone. I prayed Marie and Chester and Eldon and the rest were okay. This place had been the hub of the island, with the scribbled notices on the wall and the acidic coffee and the gossip and laughter. Everyone on Broome Isle was connected to everyone else through the General Store, and now it was gone. Despite that I was standing there with Natasha and Kim, the island felt suddenly lonely.

I guess they felt the same, because Kim moved off a ways to stare into the woods and Natasha squatted near the wreckage, stirring the ashes with a stick.

"That was your best painting," I told her, finally breaking the silence. "The one with the cottage falling down the cliff."

"It wasn't falling," she said absently. "And it wasn't a cottage. It's abstract."

"Oh. I thought it was one of Kim's."

"It looks exactly like the one I rent to Garrison," Kim said, wandering over. "I mean Jack."

"You own that one overlooking the cove?" Natasha asked. Kim nodded.

"Weird." Natasha poked at the ashes with her stick. "That's been my inspiration for months, and I had no idea you owned it."

"Jack's living there?" I asked. "In some cliffside cottage?"

"You didn't know?"

I shook my head. "I always call his cell phone, and I saw him at the bed-and-breakfast in the village. I thought he was staying there."

"No," Natasha said. "That's where his lawyer's staying. Simon. They use the parlor as a conference room."

We fell silent again. Felt like the eye of the storm, like hurricane winds had paused to gather strength before returning—and we just stood there, baffled and useless. I finally said, "So, um…do I have to say this out loud?"

"Yeah," Natasha said.

Kim nodded. "I think someone has to."

"You should be the one, Kim, you're the witchy-est." But somehow I knew this was my job. I guess, because I was the most dubious. I didn't grow up with any island folklore. "Okay. Well. When we opened that bottle or drank from it…well, we freed something."

Natasha whacked the ashes with her stick. "The demon. It was bound in Kim's cellar. I *knew* it wasn't us who screamed first."

"'It took three to release it.' That's what my aunt Hazel said. 'One the first time, two the second and the three of us the third.'" Kim turned to me. "It had been waiting for you, Eve."

"The demon. Sure. That makes sense. And it's taking things that are precious to us. Your great-aunt, Natasha's painting, the General Store. And we're all afraid that next comes—"

"Don't think it!" Kim said.

Too late. All the things I loved about the island sprang to mind. My classroom. My kids—Conner and God and the rest. The old coots, the shaded paths, the little village, the birds and squirrels. Kim and Natasha. Jack and Dr. Pepper and Marie. Everything came rushing to mind in a sudden torrent of images and emotions, and I gasped…and saw that Kim and Natasha looked how I felt. Horrified.

"You didn't just—" I started.

"I couldn't stop," Natasha said, looking up. "It's like something…tore the memories from me."

We turned to Kim, and she was standing with one hand on her stomach, her skin pure white. Fierce and cold, like marble, and protective of the first thing that must've sprung into her mind. Her baby.

A great crashing sounded in the woods, and a shape, darker than black, composed of shadows and hunger and gleaming teeth, slipped through the trees. We went motionless and quiet, like prey always does, but the…*thing* prowled closer, and I felt its malevolent attention on me like a razor blade at my throat. In my terror, I could hear nothing but the rush of blood in my ears and see nothing but the encroaching blackness—I'd lost Natasha and Kim, I'd lost myself, I'd lost everything. And I was standing on a bed of burning coals, shrouded in a sulfuric stench, my flesh withering from my bones as a chill shadow reached into my chest to squeeze the life from my heart and I heard a voice—not a voice, a poisoned whisper, a triumphant killing thought. *You freed me with your wishes, because the power was yours, yet you refused to claim and wield your own birthright, you—*

I gasped, and stumbled in the wreckage of the Smelts Shack, and was back watching Kim, who stood fierce and white and still.

She turned suddenly to me. "What?"

"I had a daydream. A…a bad one." I told her everything.

"With our wishes?" she repeated. "Because we refused to claim our own power?"

"Well, I never claimed my daydreams made *sense*. Usually there's just a pirate captain or the vampire Duke of Weathersby and I'm—" I stopped, noticing what Natasha had done with her stick in the ashes. "What's that?"

"Hmm? Oh, nothing."

"That's a sketch," Kim said, narrowing her eyes at the lines Natasha had drawn in the ashes. "That's…the three of us."

"God, I even look fat in sketches," I said. "Ash sketches really do add ten pounds."

Kim ignored me. "What are we doing?"

"Nothing," Natasha said. "It's just a doodle."

"Look from over here."

Natasha moved, and a look of cartoonish surprise crossed her face. "That *is* us! And look, that's the…and what're we holding?"

"Daggers?" I asked hopefully.

"Hat pins," Kim said.

"We're pricking a demon with hat pins? Talk about taking knives to a gunfight."

"My aunt said they used needles. It was all they had. Looks like we've got hat pins. We have to find them," Kim explained as we rummaged through the still-smoldering ruins. "In the wreckage somewhere. Natasha, keep drawing."

And, sure enough, we found a little tin of hat pins. We started a fire—not hard—after tossing a bunch of fallen leaves into an already-scorched trash can.

"What if the volunteer fire department comes back?" I asked, looking around anxiously.

"They know Kim," Natasha said, as if that was all the explanation they'd need. Which, given Broome Isle, was probably true.

"I can't believe we're doing this," I said as we approached the flames with our pins. "I don't understand how—"

"We freed this thing," Kim said, "because we gave it power that we already had. We wished to be granted things that we could've just made happen on our own. That's what your daydream meant. And Natasha's sketch—well, that shows *how* to take back our power."

"Seems like kind of a long shot," I said.

A slow, determined smile spread on Kim's face. "You and Natasha aren't the only ones who see things," she said. "This is right. This is the way. I'm certain."

We looked at one another, and I nodded, feeling my resolve grow. Whatever happened, we were all in this together. We held our hat pins to the fire watched the tips glow cherry red, and reclaimed our hearts' desires.

"I'll be an artist on my own damn terms," Natasha said.

"I'll get my stuff out there myself, I'll never stop trying—and I'll finish *at least* one great painting."

My fingers were starting to burn from the heat of the pin, but I took my time. "You know, turns out I *am* a great teacher, and I'm blessed with great friends and…well, I don't need to *wish* to fall crazy in love, I *deserve* love."

The wind stilled and Kim raised her voice, challenging and unafraid. "Marco is mine, this baby is mine, these friends are mine. Nothing on this island belongs to you—*you* belong to *us*."

The wind whipped through the treetops, the clouds shifted overhead, castings moonlit shadows on the ground. The fire burned suddenly brighter and hotter, rising into a fiery pillar, and for a moment I saw the three of us anew. Standing in smoldering wreckage around a bonfire, the flames lighting our faces and our windswept hair. We looked like three witches on a blasted heath stirring a simmering cauldron.

Well, at least we weren't chanting.

"Now what?" Natasha asked.

"Now we find him," Kim said. "Or he finds us."

"Um," I said. "Well, I guess I'll drive."

"You know where he is?" Natasha asked.

"I figured we'd try his house, first."

"You know where he *lives?*"

I looked at her, then Kim. Did they really not know? Or were they just waiting for me to admit it?

"It's Jack," I said. "Jack is the demon."

✴ 22 ✴

The cottage stood at the end of a long winding drive, and had an even better view than mine. From the top of the cliff, where I parked, the ocean unfolded forever, twinkling with moonlight. The surf crashed far below and the perfume of the autumn meadow combined with the tang of sea air. I turned off the car and sat, feeling Kim and Natasha watching me.

How did I know Jack was the demon? Because who else appeared on the island the day after we unleashed the demonic monster? Who refused to talk about his past? Who lied to all three of us about who he was?

And yet, I still loved him. Granted, I didn't see any way for us to work this out, what with me being human and he the spawn of hellfire and all. But I didn't *want* to banish him to the fiery depths—really, I just wanted to cuddle. And for him to stop stalking the island and killing deer and dropping trees on old ladies. I loved him—yet realized that demonic evil is probably not the best basis for a relationship. Though it possibly explained why the sex was so good.

"Ready?" Kim whispered.

We nodded and crept from the car. The cottage itself was quaint and homey, despite being perched precariously close to the cliff. The parking was on the other side, behind a little stand of trees, and we were going to check if he was home—our theory being, I suppose, that a demon couldn't go anywhere without his rental car—but then we noticed a huge, misshapen shadow fall across one of the curtains. Yeah, Jack was home, all right.

"You let him rent this from you?" Natasha asked Kim, eyeing the cliffs. "You're lucky you didn't get sued."

"He's a demon, Natasha. I'm lucky I didn't get killed."

I shushed them, and pointed to the full red moon hanging over the water. That was, Kim had determined, the sign. We started forward, and I felt a hand on my elbow. "You lure him out," she said.

"What?" I looked beseechingly at Natasha. "I have to go in there alone?"

"We can't kill him in his lair," Kim said.

Natasha shrugged. "Kim knows."

They each kissed and hugged me, before shoving me toward the cottage. I squared my shoulders, strode womanfully to the porch and…hesitated a moment, gathering my strength. I finger-combed my hair, licked my lips and pinched my cheeks for color—not sure if that actually works, as I'd only read about it in historical romances, but I needed all the help I could get.

I considered kicking down the door, or something equally dramatic, but decided instead to knock.

And Jack opened the door, easy as that, looking…natural,

even as he smiled his devilish smile. "I hate fighting with you," he said, "but I guess—if we're together, if two people are really together, they'll fight sometimes, and that's okay. I love you, Eve."

My initial impulse, to fall ecstatically into his arms, was checked by the fresh red stains on his shirt. I pointed. "What's that?"

"Oh." He looked slightly abashed as he let me inside. "Bloodstains, actually."

"Ha, ha," I said, my stomach dropping. I wasn't sure how to get him outside and somehow found myself following him in. I gave a vague look in Natasha and Kim's direction as Jack closed the door behind me. I couldn't say we were here to dispel him, so I asked about the blood. "You're cooking really rare meat?"

"Nah, it's human blood," he said, clearly serious, and with a glint I couldn't read in his eyes. "Listen, I have a confession to make."

"I know all about that."

"You *do?*"

"Yup. I'm here to send you back to the depths from which you came." I took his face in my hands and gave him one last lingering kiss, until my knees almost buckled. When I came up for breath, I said, "I'm sorry."

He laughed as I reached into my pocket. "C'mon, New York's not *that* bad," he said.

Heart pounding and palms sweaty—I couldn't wait for Kim and Natasha—I'd have to weaken him, then drag him outside so they could finish him off.

"Ow!" He leapt back, clasping his arm where I'd stabbed him. "Fuck! Eve! That hurt!"

He didn't vanish in a puff of brimstone, so I swung again. Maybe I'd only scratched him. I got him pretty good this time, and he yelped and scurried into the kitchen, grabbing a frying pan out of the sink.

I followed him with the pin. "Why isn't this working?"

"What are you *doing?*" He brandished the frying pan in self-defense. "Is this payback for giving your friends the wrong name?"

"No, this is sending you back to hell. Or Kim's basement. Wherever you came from."

Jack eyed me suspiciously, looking less demonic than I'd have expected. "Okay," he said, "but before I go, can I finish with my confession?"

"Like a bad movie?" I said. "When the villain admits to all his crimes? Sure, just give me your hand first."

"No way."

I grabbed for him, but he was pretty quick with that skillet. And a fast talker, too, as he gently shepherded me back into the living room. "I'm a property scout for Windward Hotels, and I did come looking for an unspoiled location to—"

"Spoil," I said.

"To build a luxury resort. But you're right, Broome Isle is too… I don't know, it's too 'itself' for a—"

"Back to the confession, demonspawn," I said, raising my pin.

"Okay, okay! I'm not just a property scout, I'm also part of the family. My legal name's John Garrison Pierce."

"Oh," I said.

But inside, my mind was whirling. My boyfriend wasn't just a demon—he was a demon who'd possessed a wealthy celebrity socialite, currently ranked somewhere between forty and fifty on *People*'s most eligible bachelors list.

"That's why I didn't give Kim my full name and paid in cash. I didn't want to attract any attention—or competing bids."

The Pierces owned the Windward hotel chain. "Huh," I said.

"Yeah," he said. "Now, what's with the pin? I need a Band-Aid."

I had the sense I was being lulled away from the point, but I rallied. "Wait a second. What's with the human blood? Oh! And did you sleep with Natasha or Kim?" Because, c'mon, demon or not, I couldn't help asking.

"I'd hardly sleep with Natasha," he said. "And I barely know Kim. Besides, her ex-husband would kill me. That's where the blood came from—"

The front door slammed open and Kim and Natasha burst into the cottage. "He's still here!"

"I stuck him!" I showed them the pin, as if that was proof. "Twice!"

"You're all crazy," he said.

"And look at him," I said. "Look closely."

They did, and grew visibly abashed. "He's not the one," Kim said.

"Is that *blood* on your shirt?" Natasha asked him.

"Yeah, your brother's. He's in the other room—hey!" He lifted the skillet to ward them off. "He's fine, it's just a bloody nose."

And sure enough, Marco stepped in from the hallway. "Kim?"

Kim blushed. "Marco."

"He thought I got Kim pregnant," Jack told me. "He came to beat me into a pulp." He turned to Marco. "But like I was about to tell Eve, I'd hardly sleep with your sister, and I never so much as touched Kim, and—"

"The baby's yours," Kim told Marco. "And this time we're not going to let anything—"

Marco scooped her into his arms and kissed her with such thoroughness that the rest of us started getting a little embarrassed.

"Wait a second," Natasha said, glaring at Jack. "What the hell does *that* mean?"

"Um, which part?"

"You'd 'hardly' sleep with me. What the hell is *that?*"

Jack looked confused. "Um, because you're gay?" There was a short silence that he didn't seem to notice. "That's why I set you up with Mandy, I mean, I knew she'd love your stuff, but also you two are perfect for each other. Hell, she's been calling all week, asking why you freaked. She really likes you. Still wants to rep you, too."

"Don't be ridiculous," Kim said, looking up from Marco's embrace. "Natasha's not gay."

"She just kissed a girl in college, that's all," I explained.

"She likes me?" Natasha asked.

"She *really* likes you," Jack told her.

"She likes me," Natasha said again, with hope in her voice and a smile on her face. "Wow. *And* she likes my work?"

"You're *gay,*" I said, laughing in pleasure. For some reason, that made so much sense for Natasha. *This* was the missing factor in her life. Not anything with her art, or her self-esteem, or her drinking. "You *are* gay."

"Oh, thank God," she said, clearly relieved. "I think I am."

And that's when the cottage slipped toward the edge of the cliff.

Someone shrieked—probably me—and the mirror in the bedroom exploded, and the cottage tilted, and from the kitchen came the sound of pots and pans smashing to the floor. The pretty little chandelier over the dining room table swung wildly, the knickknacks swept off the mantel, the floor buckled underfoot, the clapboards groaned, and the roof started sagging, about to collapse.

I grabbed the edge of the couch, panicked, and Jack grabbed my arm, as if he wanted to shield me but didn't know how, didn't know from what.

Maybe he couldn't see what was happening, maybe his nerves weren't screaming with the awareness of what was outside, maybe he couldn't smell the thing's fetid breath. I could. Natasha and Kim could. Something huge and pitch-black growled outside, teeth bared and hackles raised. *Shoving* us toward the cliff.

Marco rammed the front door with his shoulder. It was jammed shut. Jack let go of me and tried the windows, and each one burst into a shower of glass as he got to it. As the cottage ripped itself apart around us, Kim stood in the center of the collapsing room, and I found myself standing to her right, with Natasha to her left—all of us looking toward the back door.

That's where it was, a dark shadow flickering through the frayed and flapping curtains. As Jack and Marco raced through the debris, looking for a way out, Kim took my hand and Natasha's, and said, "He can't move us. It's our island. Help me."

The cottage creaked toward the side of the cliff, and the porch tore away and fell into the sea as a roof strut snapped with a gunshot *crack*. But the cottage slowed as Kim somehow rooted us to the ground, her characteristic stillness now invested with the weight of a boulder or an ancient tree.

"You did it," I said, almost breathless. "We're stopped."

"But he's not going anywhere," Natasha said. "He'll wait forever."

"He can't enter uninvited," Kim said.

And something yelped outside, a plaintive terrified yip. Then a long pained whine.

"Your dog," Natasha said. "He's out there."

I ran for the back door, my fear rising as I saw the inky shadow oozing through the cracks. A demon. This time it was real. This was no daydream. I wasn't just bracing Jack in his cottage, this was something horrible and deadly and evil.

I felt a terrible dread well up inside me, a sickening fear, and I froze.

For a moment, all I could hear was my breathing. Behind me, I knew Jack and Marco were hammering at the front door, and Kim was screaming "Don't open that! No! Eve!" I knew what she was yelling, but I couldn't hear the words. Just my breath. All I could hear was my deep, panting breath.

Reaching for the doorknob, the whines of the stray dog louder and more pitiful, I knew what I had to do. These were my best friends, these were the people I loved—and our dreams were finally within our grasps. We could make them happen ourselves. Natasha would find success and happiness, finally knowing who she really was. Kim and Marco had taken a risk and given themselves a second chance, and this time nothing would come between them. And Jack. I wanted him. I deserved him. And I wasn't going to settle for less.

I turned the doorknob and the sound suddenly kicked back in. The crash of the bookshelf falling as the cottage shifted again, the *pop* of lightbulbs exploding, Natasha yelling, "Eve! Don't! That's not—"

And I opened the door.

The dog's glossy black fur shimmered with an unearthly translucence, like oil in a puddle, and the dead eyes glowed yellow. The thing had grown as tall as me, and broader than the doorway, with fangs the size of my hands and claws that sliced into the earth as it lunged forward.

The door frame shattered when the demon sprang into the cottage and slammed me against the wall. A low, guttural moan of lust and hunger escaped from the thing's muscled throat when it caught sight of Kim, standing slight and defiant.

Ignoring me, of course. Even ravening demons always went for the tall, skinny girls first. Well, plus I knew that she was the one it hated most, the one it saw as the biggest threat.

It prowled toward Kim, more like a hunting cat than a dog, and I gripped my hat pin tight and stabbed deep into one glossy flank. And slashed again as the thing writhed and snapped, howling and bellowing in rage. Kim and Natasha sprang at him with their pins, again and again, until there was dead silence and we were alone.

The cloudless sky was blue-black, and the moon shone pure white. The three witches stood together at the stand of trees, as Marco and Jack crept around the cliffside, amazed at the freak mudslide that pulled the cottage from its foundation and dashed it into splinters on the rocky beach below.

The witches stood in silence for a long while, amazed to have their lives back. Their dreams back. Feeling powerful in each other's company.

Then Natasha said, "From now on, we stick to beer."

✴ epilogue ✴

In January, I returned to New York.

After helping Dr. Pepper hire a new teacher, I'd called my old principal and told her I was coming back. Back with Mrs. Dale, who after I set her straight about *Buddies,* spent most of her time decorating bulletin boards, supervising potty time and managing snacks. Once you've faced a real demon, an overbearing teacher is nothing.

I'd cried when I said goodbye to Conner and God and the rest—but also promised I'd be back every summer. Jack had bought the property over the cove from Kim, and was building his company's first eco-resort, with her blessing. Well, and her input. He scoffed about feminine intuition, but made sure he cleared all the big decisions with her first. Wise man.

And daring, too. We'd moved in together, and after school I went home to the apartment we shared. I didn't buzz the intercom downstairs, the bathroom was warm and welcoming, and I had all the closet space I wanted. More than I needed, in fact. The place was huge. Actually, the money thing still made me a little nervous, but he never acted like John Garrison Pierce. He was just Jack—my familiar.

I found him on the couch, and after we kissed hello he asked about my day and I asked about his, like the old happily married couple we would one day become. How did I know? I just knew.

He told me Natasha had stopped by with good news. Her show at the Amanda Michaels Gallery got a glowing review, and she'd dropped off a gift for me. Three photographs of new paintings.

The first showed Kim standing in Marco's garden, in full bloom. I mean, *she* was in full bloom—serene and glowing and extremely pregnant—but the garden was, too. Vines and flowers and herbs blossoming around Kim as if she was some sort of, well, Earth Mama.

The next was a self-portrait. Natasha had portrayed herself in a merciless light. She looked almost stark, with a challenging, difficult glint in her eyes. But still, somehow, she was the picture of contentment, a woman entirely comfortable with herself. A graceful hand rested on her shoulder, someone standing behind her—I looked closer and smiled, recognizing the carnelian ring Mandy always wore.

The last was me, of course. I held the photo to the light, and Jack whistled his approval. The picture showed me rising from the sea, naked and pink and standing on a big shell—like Venus, I supposed, except this was the coast of Broome Isle. My hair fell in tendrils around me, and the whole painting had a sort of dewy, dreamy feeling. Yet this wasn't the picture of a blushing nymph surprised while bathing, but of a woman being born into her full strength.

I laid the photos side by side on the coffee table and snuggled back into Jack's arms. "Figures I'd be the only one naked."

"There's something about the three of you together," he said, looking over the pictures. "Some spark or... I don't know *what* it is."

"It's magic," I told him, and brought him to bed.